JORDAN SONNENBLICK

CORNELSEN
SENIOR
ENGLISH
LIBRARY

Notes from the
Midnight Driver

W0172326

Cornelsen

Jordan Sonnenblick **Notes from the Midnight Driver**

Herausgegeben von:
Anne Herlyn

Verlagsredaktion:
Ralph Williams

Umschlaggestaltung:
Cornelsen Verlag Design

Umschlagfoto:
© Dan Burn-Fort / Photographer's Choice / Getty Images

Typografie:
Annika Preyhs für Buchgestaltung+

Technische Umsetzung:
Britta Dieterle, Buch und Gestaltung

Copyright © Jordan Sonnenblick, 2006
All rights reserved.

www.cornelsen.de

1. Auflage, 6. Druck 2020

Alle Drucke dieser Auflage sind inhaltlich unverändert
und können im Unterricht nebeneinander verwendet werden.

© 2014 Cornelsen Schulverlage GmbH, Berlin
© 2017 Cornelsen Verlag GmbH, Berlin

Druck: AZ Druck und Datentechnik GmbH, Kempten

ISBN 978-3-06-033472-8

PEFC zertifiziert
Dieses Produkt stammt aus nachhaltig
bewirtschafteten Wäldern und kontrollierten
Quellen.

PEFC
PEFC/04-31-2260

www.pefc.de

CONTENTS

To my grandfather,
Solomon Feldman,
who inspired this book,
and to the memory of my father, Dr. Harvey Sonnenblick,
who loved it

Abbreviations and Annotations

adj	adjective	**fml**	formal
adv	adverb	**infml**	informal
AE	American English	**Lat.**	Latin
ca.	circa; about	**n**	noun
derog.	derogatory	**sb.**	somebody
e.g.	exempli gratia; for example	**sl**	slang
esp.	especially	**sth.**	something
etc.	et cetera; and so on	**usu.**	usually
fig.	figurative	**v**	verb

The annotations are arranged chronologically; the first time a word is used is where you will find it explained.

MAY

BOOP. BOOP. BOOP.

I'm sitting next to the old man's bed, watching the bright green line spike and jiggle across the screen of his heart monitor. Just a couple of days ago, those little mountains on the monitor were floating from left to right in perfect order, but now they're jangling and jerking like maddened hand puppets.

I know that sometime soon, the boops will become one long beep, the mountains will crumble into a flat line, and I will be finished with my work here.

I will be free.

---

2 **spike**: (v) rise quickly   jiggle: make small, quick movements up and down
heart monitor: machine which measures and shows a person's heart activity
3 **float**: (here) move calmly and steadily   4 **jangle**: (here) make irregular
movements   **jerk**: make sudden, quick movements

LAST SEPTEMBER

GNOME RUN

It seemed like a good idea at the time. Yes, I know everybody says that – but I'm serious. As insane as it looks in retrospect, I was fully convinced on that particular Friday evening last September that stealing my mom's car and storming my dad's house was a brilliant plan. And not brilliant, as in, "That was a brilliant answer you gave 5 in Spanish today." I mean brilliant, as in, "Wow, Einstein, when you came up with that relativity thing, and it revolutionized our entire concept of space and time while also leading all of humankind into the nuclear age, that was brilliant!"

The plan had a certain elegant simplicity, too. I would drink one 10 more pint of Dad's old vodka, grab Mom's spare car keys, jump into the Dodge, and fire that sucker up. Then I would speed through the deserted, moonlit streets, straight and true as a homing missile, or at least straight and true as a sober person who actually knew how to drive. When I skidded triumphantly into Dad's driveway, I would 15 leap nimbly from the car, race to the front door, ring the bell with a fury rarely encountered by any bell, anywhere – and catch my father

---

gnome [nəʊm]: fairytale figure of a small, old man with a pointed hat; made of pottery or plastic, gnomes are often used in gardens as decoration (garden gnome) 2 **insane**: crazy   **in retrospect**: looking back at past events, often with a changed opinion   8 **humankind**: all people   11 **pint** [paɪnt]: measurement for liquids; ca. half a liter   12 **Dodge**: American brand of car   **fire sth. up** (sl.): start sth.   **sucker** (AE, sl): (here) thing   13 **deserted**: empty; with no people   **homing missile**: weapon that flies and finds its target by itself   14 **sober**: not drunk   15 **skid**: slide in an uncontrolled way   16 **leap** [liːp]: jump   **nimbly**: fast and without difficulty 17 **fury**: very strong anger   **encounter sth.** [ɪnˈkaʊntə] (v): experience sth. unexpected with the no-good home-wrecking wench who was once, in a forgotten life we used to have, my third-grade teacher.

Okay, perhaps these plans would theoretically work better if the planner were not already completely intoxicated. But I'd never 5 gotten drunk before – so how was I supposed to know I'd get so smashed so quickly? And hey, if my mom had really wanted to keep me from driving drunk without a license at age sixteen, would she have gone out on a date and left me home with a car, a liquor cabinet, and some keys?

10 I rest my case.

So I downed some more booze straight from the bottle and lunged for the key ring, grabbing it by the wooden number 1 I had made for my "Number One Mom" in Cub Scouts. I threw on my Yankees jacket, slammed my way out of the house, got into the car, 15 and started it. Then I believe there was some drama with the gear stick and the parking brake, and probably a bit of fun with the gas pedal.

The next thing I knew, I was hanging out the passenger door, puking up vodka and Ring Dings. When I got my eyes sort of 20 focused, I could see that the car was up on a lawn. When I got them even more focused, I could see that my last salvo of vomit had completely splattered two shiny black objects – the well-polished shoes of one angry police officer. He yanked me out of the car, largely by the hair, and stood me up. I remember him saying, "Look at that! 25 Look what you did." I also remember trying to follow his pointing

---

1 **home-wreck** [həʊm'rekə] (v): break up a family   **wench** (sl.): young woman
4 **intoxicated** (fml): drunk or under the influence of drugs   6 **smashed** (sl.): drunk
7 **license** ['laɪsns]: (here) driver's license; document allowing you to drive a car
8 **liquor** ['lɪkə]: drink with high alcohol content   10 **I rest my case.**: said by
lawyers when they have finished their speech   11 **down sth.**: drink all of sth.
booze (infml): alcohol   12 **lunge** [lʌndʒ]: move forward suddenly   13 **Cub
Scouts**: scout group for boys between 8 and 11   14 **Yankees**: (here) New York City
baseball team   15–16 **gear stick**: stick you use to change gears (= Gänge) in a car
16 **parking brake** (AE): handle that you pull to stop the car moving when parked
19 **puke** (v, infml): erbrechen   **Ring Dings**: small round chocolate cakes
21 **salvo**: firing of canons; (here) load   **vomit** (n): Erbrochenes   23 **yank sth.**
(infml): pull sth. hard and quickly

finger. And when I finally zoomed in on what was lying in front of
the car, I couldn't believe it. There was a detached head about ten
feet in front of the bumper!

The cop sort of puppet-marched me up to the horrific scene and
forced *my* head down close to the carnage. This head was seriously 5
injured, to be sure. It was upside down, smushed up against a tree
stump. There was no body in sight. I whirled around so fast that the
cop almost lost hold of me, and crouched to look under Mom's car.
Sure enough, an arm and a leg were sticking out from underneath
the left front wheel. 10

"Officer, sir, did I – is he – is – ummm …"

I could feel the tears welling up. My eyes burned, and the next
wave of acid was coming up my throat in a hurry.

"Yes, son. You ruined my brand-new shoes, smashed up your car,
and decapitated Mrs. Wilson's French lawn gnome. You're in some 15
serious …"

"Lawn gnome? LAWN GNOME?"

Now that I looked a bit more closely, I noticed that the head
wasn't bleeding, and that the ear had cracked off with inhuman
neatness. I began to laugh like an idiot, but my relief came too late to 20
halt my barf, which came out mostly through my nose – and landed
on the officer's left side, all over his walkietalkie.

This was even more of a crack-up. I started mumbling, "Walkie-
talkie-barfie, walkie-talkie-barfie," which amused me almost all the
way to the police station. You would think I'd have been pretty 25
scared by this point, but because I had drunk so much vodka so fast,
I was still getting drunker by the second. Even with my hands cuffed

---

2 **detach**: cut off   3 **bumper**: part at the front and back of a car that protects it
4 **cop** (infml): police officer   **puppet-march sb.**: walk with sb., holding them like a
doll   5 **carnage** ['kɑːnɪdʒ]: (here) very violent killing   6 **smush**: combination of
smash (break sth. into pieces) and mush (turn sth. into liquid)   7 **whirl**: turn
quickly   8 **crouch**: bend your legs   13 **acid** ['æsɪd]: sour, chemical substance;
(here) sour liquid in your stomach   15 **decapitate sb.** (fml): cut sb.'s head off
21 **barf** (sl): vomit   22 **walkietalkie**: (here) hand-held police communications
radio   23 **crack-up** (infml): funny thing   **mumble**: speak unclearly   27 **cuff sb.'s
hands**: bind sb.'s hands together with handcuffs (= *Handfesseln*)

behind my back – and the cuffs were REALLY tight, because the officer hadn't been enjoying me much so far – I was like a little one-man house party in the back seat of the cruiser. The last thing I remember was getting bored of the dispatch radio, and shouting,
5   "Change the station! Get me some ROCK!" Then the car turned a sharp corner, and the window was tilting and rushing toward my face.

You know what must really be a highlight of being a desk cop? Processing the arrests of drunk people. After several of my new pals
10   in blue dragged me semiconscious (I mean, I was semiconscious; they were pretty alert) into the station, they left me cuffed to a scuffed-up old wooden seat across from some old guy with a badge. I decided his name was Sarge. He had that fingerprinting pad thing and a bunch of questions for me, and didn't waste any time easing
15   into things.

"Right thumb."

I stared at the weaving, bobbing blurs that had replaced my hands, trying to figure out which was which. "I can't find the right one; they're too bloody." Sure enough, they were, because I had a cut
20   over my left eye, which must have been hidden from view beneath my adorable mop of hair. Sarge apparently saw the blood, but not the source, because he sighed one of those big annoyed sighs that public servants make when they are forced to do actual work, reached into his desk, and pulled out a pack of wet wipes. "Geez,
25   you must'a really banged your nose. Get your hands cleaned up, kid.

---

3 **cruiser** (sl): police car   4 **dispatch radio**: radio used for communication by the police   6 **tilt sth.**: move sth. into a crooked position   9 **pal** (infml): friend
10 **semiconscious** ['semikɒnʃəs]: hardly awake   11 **alert**: able to think quickly
12 **scuffed-up**: old and used   **badge**: (here) small piece of metal on a uniform that shows the wearer is a police officer   13 **Sarge**: short for Sergeant, rank in the US police   **fingerprinting pad**: piece of material soaked in ink used for taking a person's fingerprints at a police station   14 **bunch of sth.** (infml): large amount of sth.   14–15 **ease into sth.**: start sth. slowly and carefully   17 **weave**: move quickly back and forth   **bob** (v): move quickly up and down   **blur** (n): unclear image
21 **adorable**: beautiful; easy to love   **mop**: large, messy amount of hair   23 **public servant**: person who works for the government   24 **wet wipe**: piece of wet paper used to clean skin   25 **Geez** [dʒiːz]: exclamation showing surprise

I'll be back in a minute. By the way, genius, your right hand is the one that ain't chained to the desk."

He walked away to get a cup of coffee or whatever. I got my hands clean, then reached my free hand up to wipe the hair out of my eyes. Which got it all gory again. I repeated this at least three 5 times, creating an impressive pile of crumbled, deep-pink-stained wipes. Then I got the marvy idea that maybe I could just wipe the blood off my head first. I pushed my hair all the way up off my forehead, the alcohol-soaked wipe touched my wound, and I sobered up REAL fast, just as Sarge was putting his cup of steaming 10 liquid on the desk blotter.

"Ooooowwwww!" I screamed. Up I jumped. Up jumped my arm. Up jumped the handcuff. Up jumped the desk. Up flew the coffee.

"Ooooowwwww!" screamed Sarge. Sarge was wet!

Eventually the sodden mass of paper, blood, wipes, and coffee 15 was disposed of by a guy in rubber gloves. Sarge found a new pair of pants, and came back. He took a really long look at my forehead, the mixture of blood, snot, and tears that was flowing freely across my facial features, and the moist abstract painting that had been his desk blotter, and decided to use a trick which always works for my 20 dad: He would make me Somebody Else's Problem.

Sarge shouted across the room, "Call me an ambulance!"

I couldn't stop myself. "Okay, you're an ambulance!"

And so it went, until the paramedics accidentally banged my head against the doorway of the emergency room, and I passed out 25 for good.

---

5 **gory** (infml): bloody   7 **marvy**: (short for marvellous) very good   15 **sodden**: very wet   16 **dispose of sth.** (fml): get rid of sth.   19 **facial features**: parts of the face   20 **desk blotter**: large piece of paper kept on a desk, used for drying wet ink   24 **paramedic** [ˌpærəˈmedɪk]: person trained to help in an emergency (not a doctor or a nurse)   25 **pass out**: lose consciousness

THE WAKE-UP

The next morning, I had two new experiences, and they both hurt. I had never woken up with a hangover or a concussion before, but – WHOA! – I guess there's a first time for everything.

Before I opened my gummy, grainy eyes, a shadow crossed over
5 me. I begged it for help. "Sarge, Sarge, can I please have some water? Water, please? Oh, God, WATER!"

It replied so sweetly that I knew who it was without looking. "Good morning, Alex. Congratulations. You got arrested and ruined everybody's night. The car is in bad shape, too. And who the hell is
10 Sarge?"

"Hi, Mom," I croaked.

As I finally pried my eyelids open, the glare of the sun through the hospital room window almost made me faint. But before I could even lose consciousness in peace, Mom grabbed me in a rib-
15 pulverizing body hug. "Oh, Alex. Oh, my baby!"

"Mom, I'm okay. Really," I gasped like a dying salmon.

She looked me dead in the eyes then, and wiped tears from the corners of hers. "You're not okay," she snapped. "You're an idiot!" Then she whacked me on the arm really hard, just as my father
20 stampeded in.

While I was gingerly checking my bicep area for spurting arteries, Dad burst into high-volume mode. "Oh, good, Janet, why don't you just beat the boy to death while we're here? It will be convenient, with the morgue right downstairs and all."

2 **hangover**: sick feeling after having drunk too much alcohol   **concussion**: confusion or loss of consciousness following a head injury   4 **gummy**: sticky **grainy**: (here) unfocused   11 **croak**: speak with a rough voice   12 **pry sth. open**: open sth. with force   15 **pulverize sth.** (fig.): crush sth. into powder or liquid 16 **gasp**: breathe in quickly (esp. when in pain)   **salmon**: fish with pink flesh 17 **dead** (adv, infml): straight on   20 **stampede** (v): (here) move suddenly and forcefully   21 **gingerly**: carefully   **spurting arteries**: major blood vessels from which blood flows with force   24 **morgue**: place where dead bodies are kept until burial

"Don't 'Good, Janet' me, Simon. It's your fault the boy is lying here all … all … all …"

"Smacked?" I chimed in.

"Shut up!" they exclaimed in unison. See, divorced people CAN cooperate where the children are concerned.   5

"And how is this my fault? You leave him at your house, drunk, *with the car keys*, while you're gallivanting around town with some …"

"*I* leave him drunk?"

"Yes, *you* leave him drunk."   10

"*Whose* liquor is still at the house?"

"What do you mean, *still* at the house? It was *your* lawyer who said I couldn't remove any *common property* from the – "

I couldn't tolerate this Battle of the Italics any longer. I looked away and started picking at an itch on my left arm. My fingers   15
encountered something alarming there – I was hooked up to an IV! What was THAT about? I needed to know, pronto, so I reached out for the button on the side of my bed, and desperately buzzed for help. A nurse came in, threaded her way between my still-raging parents, and stopped by my bedside with an expectant look and a   20
question. "Hi, I'm Miss Anderson. I'll be your nurse today. What can I do for you?"

"Um, hi. My name is Alex and, uh, do you know why I have a needle in my arm? Am I, um, critically injured or anything? I mean, because I'd want to know that."   25

She sighed. "No, you're not critically injured, Alex. But from what your mother told me before you woke up, you're very lucky not to be."

I glanced over at my parents – they were both still going bonkers on each other, to the point where a casual bystander might have   30
started looking for something to hide under in case they reached the

---

7 **gallivant** (infml): have fun going from place to place   14 **Italics**: *Kursivschrift*
16 **IV (short for intravenous line)**: medical instrument for putting liquids directly
into your blood   17 **pronto**: (Italian) immediately   19 **thread your way** [θred] (v):
move carefully between things in your way   24 **critically injured**: seriously injured
29 **bonkers** (infml): crazy   30 **casual bystander**: person who sees an event but is
not involved

"throwing-objects" stage. This wasn't my idea of a very lucky scenario, but whatever. "Yes, ma'am. I just want to know what's wrong with me."

My mom paused in her vicious attack on my father's parenting
5 and general life skills to throw a jab my way: "Yes, Nurse. We'd love to know what's wrong with him, too."

Miss Anderson looked like an innocent Roman who had somehow walked onto the floor of the Coliseum right into the middle of a "Throwing-Christians-to-the-Lions" marathon. She was saved from
10 answering, though, by the entrance of Dr. Friedman, or at least some guy wearing Dr. Friedman's badge. "Ah, Mr. Alexander Gregory, the famous midnight driver. I overheard your request, and I will be glad to tell you what's going on. I'd imagine you're feeling pretty rocky right now – is that correct?"

15 I nodded and tried to look pathetic, which came naturally at that moment.

"Well, there are several valid reasons for that. One, you came to us with a fairly significant case of alcohol poisoning. That's why your mouth and eyes are probably very dry: Alcohol poisoning causes
20 dehydration. That's also why you have an intravenous line in your arm. Two, you sustained at least one strong blow to the head last night, possibly when your head hit the steering wheel of your mother's car. This caused your soft brain to bounce off of the hard inside of your cranium. So you have a concussion, which means that
25 even if the drinking hadn't given you a pounding headache, dizziness, and nausea, you'd certainly have them now anyway. Three, you split your forehead open. It wasn't a deep gash, but it was fairly jagged, so we had to suture it up. A plastic surgeon will be by

---

4 **vicious** [ˈvɪʃəs]: mean; brutal   5 **jab**: (here) hurtful remark   13 **rocky**: unstable; unbalanced   20 **dehydration** [ˌdiːhaɪˈdreɪʃn]: state of not having enough water in your body   21 **sustain** [səˈsteɪn]: (here) suffer   24 **cranium**: bones in your head around your brain   25 **pound** (v): (of pain) get stronger and weaker in a fast rhythm   26 **dizziness**: feeling as if everything is spinning around you   **nausea** [ˈnɔːziə]: ill feeling in the stomach   27 **gash**: cut   28 **jagged** [ˈdʒægɪd]: with uneven edges   **suture sth.** (v) [ˈsuːtʃə]: sew up sth. (e.g. a wound)   **plastic surgeon** [ˈsɜːdʒən]: doctor who does operations that make people look better

later today to check on the stitching job, and you can ask him how bad he thinks the scar might be."

Scar? Holy moley. That was cause for panic. But I didn't have time to think about it for long, because the doctor was still talking: "By the way, does your right shoulder ache?"

I hadn't singled out that one particular strand of discomfort in the thick rope of agony that was twisting around my brain, but, "Yes, it does. Why?"

"Tetanus shot. Do you have any specific questions I haven't covered?"

"Uh, can I get some kind of medicine for my head? It really hurts. Please?"

"We'll see what your next blood toxicology report shows, but right now I don't want to give your liver any additional work to do. You gave it quite a workout last night."

Great. Head trauma without painkillers. Now there's a recipe for wholesome fun.

After the doctor left, my mom announced that she needed some air, and stomped out with one last glare at my dad. Dad ambled over to the side of the bed and sort of punched my shoulder in a fatherly way – which would have been just peachy if he hadn't hit the exact spot my mother had already pulverized. Then, completely ignoring my gasp and wince; he gave me a whole big speech about responsibility while I closed my eyes and tried very hard not to picture him cheating on my mom with my third-grade teacher.

Eventually, I turned my head to the wall and pretended to be asleep – which he noticed after maybe seven or eight minutes. I swear, I almost let out a fake snore just to speed up the process, but was afraid it might make him shake me back to consciousness. It felt

3 **Holy moley**: exclamation to express surprise or displeasure   5 **ache** [eɪk]: hurt
6 **single sth. out**: notice one specific thing out of a larger number   **strand**: (here)
one of a number of things that are closely connected   **discomfort**: feeling of being
not quite well   7 **agony**: great pain   9 **shot**: (here) medication given to you using a
syringe (= *Spritze*)   13 **toxicology report**: results of an examination of poisons in
your blood   14 **liver**: *Leber*   17 **wholesome**: good for you   19 **stomp**: walk
loudly and angrily   **amble**: walk slowly   21 **peachy** (infml): fine, very nice
23 **wince**: expression in your face to show pain

as though getting shaken might very well have made my head fall off, so I wasn't willing to take the risk.

I don't remember Dad leaving, so I must have fallen asleep for real at some point. Next thing I knew, Mom was sitting on the edge of the bed, holding my hand, and crying again. I gave an encore performance of my "slumbering boy" routine, only this time I was doing it for a different reason – I didn't want my mother to see that *my* eyes were welling up, too.

5 **encore** [ˈɒŋkɔː]: repetition of a part of a performance   6 **slumber**: sleep

DAY OF THE DORK-WIT

I spent that whole day in the hospital, and went home on Sunday –
right after a nice lady from Social Services came by to "release me
into the custody of my parents." Before we left, my mom had to sign
a whole bunch of police papers. She also had to promise to get me a
lawyer and deliver me to court in thirty days for a hearing on my   5
drunk-driving case. You didn't have to be a genius to realize this was
going to be a long month.

Mom wasn't particularly speaking to me for most of the morning
at home, but I was too sore to go out and do anything, so I spent
hours in the basement noodling around on my electric guitar. It's the 10
best thing I own, a real American Fender Telecaster with a beautiful
sunburst finish that my dad bought me in a moment of guilt right
after he moved out sophomore year. At the time I spent about twelve
millionths of a second contemplating whether I should refuse to
accept such a transparent bribe gift, but gimme a break – it was a   15
Tele, and my old acoustic guitar from middle school was a cheap-o
imported job. So I just told myself that living well is the best revenge,
plugged the Tele in, and played for about a month nonstop.

Anyway, I took lessons until a couple of months after my parents
separated, so I picked up a lot of the basics from my teacher. Then I 20
quit the lessons because I figured *somebody* had to attempt to
conserve my college fund in the face of my parents' rising legal bills.
After that, I worked hard on figuring out the exercises from books

---

dork-wit (infml, derog.): made up of 'dork' and 'half-wit', both referring to a very
stupid person   3 **in the custody of sb.**: state of being sb.'s responsibility   5 **court**
[kɔːt]: place where legal meetings are held   **hearing** (n): meeting at court where
facts of a case are presented and decisions are made   10 **noodle** (infml): play
11 **American Fender Telecaster**: popular type of electric guitar, produced in the
USA since 1950   12 **sunburst finish**: type of colouring for string instruments; usu.
lighter yellow in the middle, gradually turning darker at the edges   13 **sophomore
year** (AE): second year of High School (= 10th grade in Germany)   14 **contemplate
sth.**: think deeply about sth.   15 **bribe**: *Bestechung*   **gimme** (infml): give me
22 **fund**: sum of money saved for a specific purpose

and magazines, and kept playing in the high school jazz band. I
wasn't a great jazz guitar player, because jazz is the hardest guitar
music on the planet, but I could ROCK. So there I was, raging along
with a pile of CDs with my little amp cranked, until I got really
5   woozy. Then I turned the amp way down, turned the CD player off,
and did some finger exercises and scales until the nausea and
boredom became too overwhelming. I knew I couldn't stay down in
the basement until my mom forgot all about my little automotive
adventure, so I trudged up for lunch.

10   There she was at the table, dipping a biscotti into a cup of coffee
over and over without taking a bite. She looked up and pointed the
soggy baked good at my chest, dripping brown semiliquid goo
everywhere. "Alex, I've been sitting here for hours, listening to you
play, and trying to understand something. Do you know what I can't
15   figure out?"

She waited so long I started to worry that maybe the question
wasn't rhetorical.

"I can't figure out WHY you got drunk and took my car. Where
were you trying to go, besides Mrs. Wilson's azalea bush? You're a
20   smart boy, but this is just … stupid and pointless."

I suppose that I could have told her about my boffo plan to bum-
rush her ex's house, but the whole separation thing wasn't something
that got discussed much at our table. "I dunno, Mom. I just wanted
to DO something. You were out having fun, I was stuck here alone,
25   the computer wasn't working, and you TOOK my phone away last
month, if you recall, so what was I supposed to do? Study precalc on
a Friday night? Invite over some other loveless, unpopular dork to
play Nintendo? Organize the bathroom cabinet?"

"Well, you could have …"

---

4 **amp** (infml): (short for amplifier) electrical device that makes the sound, e.g.
of an electric instrument, louder   **crank sth.** (infml): (here) make sth. louder
5 **woozy** [wuːzi] (infml): dizzy   9 **trudge** [trʌdʒ]: walk slowly and with difficulty
10 **biscotti**: Italian biscuit   12 **baked good**: (here) biscuit   **semiliquid**: half liquid;
mushy   **goo** (infml): soft and sticky substance   21 **boffo** (sl): clever   21–22 **bum-
rush sth.** (sl): enter sth. forcefully   26 **precalc** (infml) [priːˈkælk]: pre-calculus;
preparation course for calculus, a difficult part of mathematics

Aha, she was on the defensive. As soon as you get your mom out of attack mode, you're home free. "Could have what?"

"I don't know, Alex – but almost anything would have been better than what you actually DID. What if you had KILLED someone?"

Okay, maybe she wasn't quite ready to lay down her guns.   5

"Mom, I didn't kill anyone. I didn't even hurt anyone. I broke a stupid garden-elf thing. I should probably be getting a reward for making the neighborhood more tasteful, for God's sake. And I wasn't even trying to do anything bad. I just wanted to go to Dad's house and yell at him for leaving *you*!" So much for avoiding the separation   10
topic.

"You were trying to go to Dad's? *That's* what you were trying to do? But you didn't even make it to the end of the block!"

"Mistakes were made, Mom. Is that what you want me to say? Mistakes were made."   15

"Yes, mistakes were made, Alex. Like me trusting you, that was a biggie. Now let me tell you how things are going to be for the next month until your court date. You will be driven to school by ME, you will be picked up at school by ME, you will do your homework the instant you get home in front of ME, and then you will engage in   20
quiet activities IN THE HOUSE until bedtime at ten p.m."

Ten p.m.?

"Mom, how are you going to drop me off, pick me up, get to work on time, and sleep?" Mom is a night-shift nurse at an old people's home, so she usually slept while I was at school.   25

"I don't know, Alex. I will have to work something out, because I am going to be on you like a bad rash for the next thirty days. And if you don't like it, maybe you should have thought about that BEFORE you got arrested."

Just then, I tried to brush back the hair that was falling over my   30
eyes as I slumped down at the table. A searing pain slashed along the stitches in my forehead and my head jerked forward. Instantly tears sprang to my eyes.

"Oh, Alex, did that hurt?" I sniffled. "Yeah, Mom." "GOOD!"

---

27 **rash**: red spots on the skin caused by illness or an allergy   31 **slump down**: sit down heavily   **searing**: (of pain) extreme; like burning

Obviously, home was somewhat tense. So I thought school on Monday would actually be a relief for once. Which might have been true, if every single kid in the building hadn't somehow turned into a fanatical newshound over the weekend. In the hallway that first
5 day, most people just looked at me quickly, sideways, and then looked away to avoid staring at my bruised face and zigzag of black stitches. But there's always some weasel that just can't let things go, right? When I got to homeroom, my weasel struck.

"Whoa, look, it's Harry Potter! That scar is a great look for you,
10 Gregory. Really. Who does your makeup, and can you get me an appointment for – oh, I don't know – never?" It was Bryan Gilson, the most obnoxious guy in the junior class. It used to be, back in middle school, that we were all constantly busting on each other. But somehow, Bryan hadn't quite noticed when everybody else grew
15 out of it. Plus, his dad was a police officer, so it figured that he would have the whole lowdown on my situation. I tried to walk past him to my seat without saying anything.

"Hey, don't worry, it could be worse. Sure you look bad, but you should see the other guy. Or GNOME, I should say."
20 I took a deep breath. Two. Three. Sat down in my seat. Bryan walked over and stood next to me. Everyone was staring now, naturally, waiting to see whether I would jump up and try to slug Bryan. Who weighed about three hundred pounds more than me and played football, just in case my concussion, head wound, and
25 crippling soreness weren't enough of an advantage for him. Just as the standoff was becoming unbearable, just when I would have had to say or do something, my best friend, Laurie Flynn, came streaking

---

1 **tense**: not relaxed   4 **fanatical**: very enthusiastic   **newshound**: person who finds interesting information for the news   6 **bruised**: covered in blue, green or brown marks that are the result of having been hit   7 **weasel** ['wiːzl]: (here) treacherous (*verräterisch*) person   8 **homeroom** (AE): classroom where students in a specific class meet at the beginning of each school day   12 **obnoxious** [əb'nɒkʃəs]: unpleasant   **junior class** (AE): year before the final year of High School or college
13 **bust on sb.** (infml): be rude to sb.   16 **have the lowdown on sth.** (infml): know important facts about sth.   22 **slug sb.** (infml): hit sb. hard with your fist
26 **standoff**: tense situation where no agreement is reached   **unbearable**: too unpleasant to deal with   27 **streak**: move very fast

into the classroom. She ran over and pushed Gilson out of the way like he was a toddler. Yay! Laurie was here to deliver me from evil, to smite my enemies, to …

"Move it, siddown, and shut up, Bryan. Just because you're a hulking water buffalo doesn't mean I can't waste you with one hand tied behind my back like I did in third grade. And close your mouth before you drool on my shoes, you cretin!"

Then she actually TURNED HER BACK on Bryan, knowing he would slink away from her wrath. Of course, that meant all ninety-three pounds of her was suddenly focused on me. Before I could attempt to calm her down with a "thank-you," she leaned over with her forearms on my desk and let me have it.

Geez, where are homeroom teachers when you need 'em?

"Alex Peter Gregory, you are a moron." She slammed her palms down on my desk and stomped her foot.

I get a lot of that.

"You are a bonehead. You are a complete goober. You're worse than a goober. You're like … an assistant goober! You're a dork, a half-wit. You're a … a … a dork-wit!"

I gave her a cheesy little puppy-dog face, but nothing was going to slow this steamroller down. "Please don't yell at me, Laurie. I'm in pain here, and you're not helping. Plus, everyone's staring at us. And, uh, you're standing on my foot."

She gave me the same demonic grin that she'd once used to make a substitute teacher quit in the middle of sixth-grade music class, and said, "I know."

"Well, do you think you could get off my toes for a minute and let me explain?"

"Oh, your mom explained everything, buddy boy. Didn't she tell you I called on Saturday, four times? And then again yesterday, twice? She must have gotten tired of telling me you 'just couldn't

---

2 **toddler**: young child who has just learned to walk   3 **smite sb.** (old use):
kill sb.   5 **hulking**: large, slow and heavy   7 **drool**: *geifern*   **cretin** (infml, derog.):
very stupid person   14 **moron** (infml, derog.): very stupid person   17 **goober**
(infml, derog.): extremely stupid person   20 **cheesy**: exaggerated   21 **steamroller**:
Dampfwalze

come to the phone,' because she finally gave in and told me the whole ugly, pathetic story while you were downstairs goofing around on your guitar."

A brief bit of explanation, here: Laurie is only five feet tall, and looks exactly like Tinker Bell from Peter Pan. She has perfect blond hair, a little upturned button nose, sparkly blue eyes, a sweet little angel mouth, and even slightly pointy little elf ears – plus a perfect gymnast body that the other girls are always giving her dirty looks over. All of which she hates. So she takes karate three nights a week, including a special class in Chinese hand-weapon combat, wears nothing but baggy black clothes, and has three rings in her left eyebrow.

She still looks like a pixie – but she looks like a terrifying Goth pixie.

One other key fact about Laurie: Ever since she moved here from New York City when we were six, she has been pretty much my only friend. Oh, yeah, and my mom loves her. She's like the daughter Mom never had, but would have liked very much if God hadn't given her a dorky, uncoordinated nerdball of a son instead.

"I wasn't goofing around, I was practicing. What was I supposed to do, sit in the kitchen and let my mom beat me with a wooden spoon all day?"

"And why didn't you call me on Friday night if you were planning to do something so half-witted?"

"Laurie, I wasn't planning to do something half-witted."

"I suppose with your fantastic natural gift for it, who needs planning?"

"Ha-ha. Look, you weren't home on Friday night, remember? You were working at the Gap."

"Oh, that's right – stores don't have phones. And you've only known my cell number for half a decade, so you couldn't possibly get in touch with me that way."

"Okay, maybe I didn't *want* to call you, Miss Understanding Friend of the Year. I didn't want to get lectured, I wanted to get

---

2 **goof around** (infml): waste time doing silly things   7 **pointy**: *spitzig*   10 **combat**: fighting   12 **pixie** (AE): small fantasy with magical powers   33 **lecture sb.**: tell sb. how to behave

drunk. And face my dad. Instead of just sitting there all worried about …"

"About what? Whether the police might be getting bored without an idiot to arrest?"

"About my mom's first date, okay?"   5

Laurie actually stopped and thought about this for a moment. And the bell rang for first period.

1 **face sb.**: confront sb. about their bad behaviour

MY DAY IN COURT

Thirty days is a long time. I mean, it's not a long time if you're sitting
and watching a glacier move, or if you're waiting for a chunk of
radioactive uranium to become a safe material for jewelry-making.
But it's an eternity if you're doing nothing but going to school,
5 cranking out homework, and pacing around the house bickering
with your mom. I was avoiding pretty much all human contact, with
a special focus on ignoring my dad's attempts to communicate with
me. He called daily, but I let the machine pick up, and then erased
the increasingly pathetic messages. He e-mailed TWICE a day, but I
10 never opened the files, and then I blocked him with my spam filter.
Too bad my life didn't come with one of those; I would have been
able to screen out his very existence. My parents didn't have a whole
official custody thing worked out, partly because I was already
sixteen, and partly because, like I said before, their divorce lawyers
15 were too busy milking them for my college money to get the legal
stuff finalized. But unofficially, my dad was supposed to be able to
see me whenever he wanted.

Of course, he was also supposed to have stayed with my mom
until death did them part, but we all know how that turned out. So
20 if he could dump us, I could delete him like one of those suspicious
e-mails from Africa where they ask for your bank account number.

I was more mixed up about why I was ducking Laurie at every
turn. She could have listened, and maybe even given me some
advice, or helped me figure out why I had basically nuked my life on
25 a random Friday evening. Plus, her parents had been divorced since
her sixth birthday party, when her mom hadn't showed, and her dad
had stood up and announced that Daddy's "special present" for his

---

2 **glacier** ['glæsiə]: large amount of ice that moves very slowly   5 **crank sth. out**
(infml): produce large amounts of sth. very quickly   **pace** (v): walk back and forth,
esp. when you are upset or worried   **bicker**: argue over unimportant things
9 **pathetic**: weak and unsuccessful   20 **dump sb.** (infml): (here) leave sb.
22 **duck sb.**: avoid sb.   24 **nuke sth.** (infml): (here) destroy sth. completely

little princess was going to be a real, live suburban dream home for two. So she knew the ropes, for sure.

But I kept remembering this time when we were nine. I can see it now: I was wearing my pin-striped Yankees bathing suit. I had set up a skateboard ramp on the roof of my back porch, and a trampoline 5 on the patio next to the pool. It seemed totally realistic to me that I could climb up onto the roof with my hot-green board, zip off the ramp, kick the board away in midair, bounce off the trampoline, and finish the stunt with a perfectly executed swan dive into the pool. I called her up and told her to rush over RIGHT NOW with her suit 10 and her dad's video camera – this would be a moment that should be preserved for posterity, I figured.

So Laurie got there a few minutes later, took one look at my spectacular and well-planned-out setup, and immediately started trying to talk me out of the entire escapade. I can still hear her little 15 pipsqueak voice echoing off the bricks of the patio: "Alex, this is dumb. A billion thousand things could go wrong."

"Duh, that's not even a real number. Plus, this is totally safe. I planned it SCIENTIFICALLY (my big word that summer, like when I had SCIENTIFICALLY spilled honey on a bees' nest to see whether 20 they would die of happiness. The emergency-room doctors were getting lots of overtime thanks to my selfless devotion to SCIENCE). What could possibly happen?"

"Well, you could fall off the board on the roof, tumble off the roof, and die. Or you could make the jump, land on your board on 25 the trampoline, and die. If you're better at this than I think you are, you might make the trampoline jump, then miss the pool, and die. Or make it into the pool, but hit your head on the edge, and die."

---

1 **suburban**: outside the center of a city or town   2 **know the ropes** (infml): understand how things work   5 **porch** (AE): veranda on the front or back of the house, with a roof   6 **patio** ['pætiəʊ]: garden area with hard flooring   9 **stunt**: dangerous action, usu. in a film   **execute sth.** (fml): (here) perform sth.
12 **posterity** (fml): people who will live in the future   15 **escapade** [,eskə'peɪd]: exciting but risky activity   16 **pipsqueak** (old-fashioned, infml): small or young person who is not taken seriously   22 **devotion**: spending a lot of energy on sth. important to you   24 **tumble**: fall

I admit, that last one was a pretty good guess. The following
September, the video became a truly legendary show-and-tell, but
Laurie has never been one for looking on the bright side where my
adventures are concerned. Which, again, is why I wasn't in a rush to
5 consult with her on this latest escapade.

Anyway, between school, mom-time, and the big excitement of
meeting with my lawyer (who is also my uncle Larry; his only
comment was, "You really SAID and DID all this?"), the month
passed. And I got my day in court.

* * *

10 You wake up in the morning on your court date, and it's Showtime.
You shower and shave the nine faint peach-fuzz follicles that may or
may not yet exist on your face even though you tell your friends you
have 'em. You brush, floss, brush again, gargle mouthwash, and still
worry that you might get sent to jail due to bad breath. Your mom
15 supervises you as you garb yourself for the battle in your only suit.
Then you have to lean all the way forward as you eat your cornflakes
so that no milk gets on your lovely babyblue silk tie. Last spring's
band-concert shoes go on; the blisters start. Your head buzzes with
nervousness. Your palms are ice-cold and sweaty at the same time,
20 which seems to defy all of the laws of nature, but whatever. Somehow,
Mom shuffles you into the car, with its shiny new front bumper. The
drive downtown is so quiet that you you can leave the radio off and
just hear the sound waves directly through the frames of your
sunglasses.

25 Mom parks three blocks from the courthouse, just so your
blistering feet can really get some grind time in. The walk brings out
more icy sweat, only this time it's all over your entire body. At the
bottom of the marble courthouse steps, Mom gives you a quick hug,

---

2 **show-and-tell**: activity in which children bring an object to school and tell the
class about it   5 **consult with sb. on sth.**: ask sb.'s advice before making a decision
about sth.   11 **follicle**: (here) hair   15 **garb yourself** (fml): put on clothes
18 **blister**: painful spot on the skin caused by rubbing or burning   19 **palm**: inside
of your hand   20 **defy sth.**: not follow sth.'s law or order   26 **grind**: (here) rub
hard   28 **marble**: expensive, polished stone used for building

yanks off your sunglasses ("You don't want to look like a *criminal!*"),
ruffles your hair like you're still five, and then tries to ruffle it back
into neatness, even though you fully realize that if any aspect of your
hygiene is going to get you sent to the slammer, it will still probably
be the breath and not the comb & curl.   5
    You wait in line, go through the metal detectors, meet your lawyer
at the door of the courtroom, and walk in.

                              *   *   *

I was shocked when I first saw this particular courtroom, by the way.
I had been expecting a big marble gallery-type room, with vaulted
ceilings, dark wood everywhere, and maybe gargoyles of justice on   10
top of Greek columns. But this place was just a tiny, plain box, with
folding tables, which were for the defense and prosecutors, facing a
metal desk. A smooth-looking old guy with greased-back hair and a
suit so dark that it seemed to suck in the sickly fluorescent light was
sitting sort of sideways in the prosecution chair, chatting with the   15
judge and drinking coffee out of a paper Manhattan Bagel cup. He
and my lawyer/uncle greeted each other like they worked together
every day, which I guess they basically did. This was discouraging,
though; I wanted my lawyer and the prosecutor to bare their teeth
and snarl at each other, like gladiators entering the ring, not wave   20
and nod like old college buddies.
    If they were pals, who was on MY side?
    The judge smiled at my mom. She was motherly looking, with
dark hair tied in an old-fashioned bun, tiny black-framed glasses,
and a regular gray business suit. Again, this was weird: Where was   25
her robe? Where was her wooden hammer thing? And why was she

9–10 **vaulted ceiling** [vɔːltɪd 'siːlɪŋ]: rounded ceiling, higher at the centre than the
sides   10 **gargoyle**: ugly, stone figure on an old building   12 **defense** (AE): (here)
lawyer who claims their client is not guilty or work for a milder punishment
prosecutor: lawyer at court who claims that a person is guilty   18 **discouraging**
[dɪs'kʌrɪdʒɪŋ]: making you lose hope   19 **bare your teeth**: show your teeth in
order to threaten others   20 **snarl**: make an angry, threatening sound   24 **bun**:
long hair tied into a round knot and worn on top of the head   26 **robe**: official
clothing that is long and loose

saying, "Hello, Janet. I haven't seen you for a while. Still working at the home?"

Was this a court session, or a class reunion?

Before my mom could answer, the door swung open behind me, 5 and things got a lot less chummy in a hurry. I was afraid to look anyone here in the eye, but I peeked sideways to see whose entry had clammed everybody up. Four guys in uniforms walked in. Two were paramedics, and two were familiar-looking police officers.

Oh, crud. These guys were my squad-car amigo and a guy who 10 looked just like Sarge, only less blurry than I remembered him. Wow, this was enough to get me thinkin' about something my grandma had always said: *Be careful how you treat people, because you never know when you'll need their help later on.* And I hadn't exactly sown the seeds of love with these gents with all the spilling, laughing, and 15 ralphing I'd done at our first encounter. Oh, and the underage drunk driving. Guess we shouldn't forget the underage drunk driving.

We all sat down at the flimsy collapsible tables, and the judge started my big hearing, the most serious moment of my life to date. "Good morning, everybody. I've looked over the papers here, and in 20 the case of New Jersey versus Alexander Gregory, the whole probable-cause schtick seems like a waste of time."

A waste of time? Was she just going to dismiss this whole thing, since everyone was in cahoots with each other anyway?

"Honestly, Mr. Sharpe (that would be Uncle Larry), this looks like 25 a slam dunk."

Whoa, hold on a minute – SLAM DUNK? Shouldn't Uncle Larry be leaping up and shouting, "Objection?" The two officers were

---

5 **chummy** (infml): very friendly   7 **clam sb. up** (infml): make sb. stop speaking
9 **crud** (infml): unpleasant substance; (here) swear word   **squad-car**: police car
used by a group of police officers who work together   14 **gent** (old-fashioned): man
15 **ralph** (v, sl): *erbrechen*   **underage** (adj): done by a person who isn't legally old
enough   17 **flimsy**: badly made   **collapsible**: able to be folded and made
smaller   20 **versus**: against   21 **schtick** (Yiddish): piece of comedy   23 **be in
cahoots with sb.** (infml): working with sb. secretly in order to do illegal or
dishonest things   25 **slam dunk** (AE, fig.): (here) act that is certain to be successful
27 **objection**: said in court when one lawyer thinks another lawyer did sth. wrong

smirking, and the smoothie prosecutor was practically packing his briefcase already.

Uncle Larry leaped heroically to my defense, right after taking a big sip of coffee and flipping through his notes for ten seconds or so. "You're right, Judge. I know it's irregular, but since my client is a first offender, why don't we save everybody the time and expense of a trial and see what kind of plea we can figure out?"

Whoa, Unc. Way to stick up for the family honor.

The judge said, "Sounds good to me. Gentlemen?" She scanned the faces of the assorted 9-1-1 guys and prosecutor, all of whom now HAD started to get their things together. They were all mumbling and nodding, and suddenly the judge had the wood hammer dealie in her hand. "All righty, then. All rise." All rose. "In the case of New Jersey versus Alexander Gregory, the court accepts the defendant's guilty plea. The State of New Jersey will meet with the defendant for sentencing, right here, immediately following a fifteen-minute break." I couldn't stifle one panicky joke-thought: How were they going to get the whole state in this one little room?

Everyone except Uncle Larry, Mom, and I filed out the back door, making small talk and generally acting relieved that my defense had been a farce, a sham, a ...

"Well, that went well, Janet."

Huh?

---

1 **smirk**: smile unpleasantly   **smoothie** (sl): polite and pleasant in an insincere way
3 **heroic** [hə'rəʊɪk]: in a courageous way   5–6 **first offender**: person who has committed a crime for the first time   7 **trial**: legal process in which facts of a case are examined to find out whether a person is guilty   **plea**: formal statement by a person accused of a crime   8 **way to do sth.** (AE, infml): expressing you are pleased with how sb. does sth.; (here) used ironically   10 **assorted**: mix of different types   **9-1-1**: telephone number you call in the USA in an emergency   12 **dealie** (infml): thing   14 **defendant**: person in court accused of a crime   16 **sentence** (v): (done by judges) say officially which punishment a guilty person will get   17 **stifle sth.** [staɪfl]: try not to do sth.   21 **farce**: ridiculous situation   **sham**: situation that is not as good or important as it seems

"Just like I told you when you first called me about this, nobody wants to deal with a trial for such a small-potatoes case when the defendant is so blatantly guilty."

"Umm, Uncle Larry, what's the 'went well' part, exactly?"

5 "The 'went well' part is that now the judge will have a couple of free hours to catch up on paperwork this morning, so she'll be in a good mood for your sentencing."

"But what's my sentence going to be?"

"I told your mom this – didn't she fill you in? You've got no
10 priors, you're a decent student, you play in the school jazz band, for Chrissakes. I think we're looking at a slap on the wrist for the criminal charges."

"And what about my license?"

"You'll probably get it a year or two late."

15 He clearly thought this was no big deal, and was kind of staring off distractedly over my shoulder at this point.

"A year or two late? All of my friends are going to have their licenses this year. I can't believe this.

Am I supposed to get a ride to the prom from my mother? How
20 am I going to get to a summer job this year? This is so STUPID. I'm not a criminal. I didn't hurt anybody! I broke a lawn gnome. A LAWN GNOME!!! Isn't the judge going to see I'm harmless? Why didn't you fight this?"

A voice hovered over my left ear, and I knew what my uncle had
25 been looking at. "He probably thought you would prefer human-service time to jail time. And he knew how much I HATE drunk driving."

Boy, those judges take short breaks.

---

3 **blatantly** ['bleɪtəntli]: very obviously   10 **priors**: (here) previous crimes
decent: good   10–11 **for Chrissakes** ['kraɪseɪks]: for Christ's sake: exclamation to
express annoyance   11 **slap on the wrist**: (here) very mild form of punishment
12 **criminal charges**: crimes that a person is officially accused of   16 **distracted**:
not concentrating because you are thinking of other things   19 **prom** (AE): formal
dance at high school   25–26 **human-service time**: work in a social institution as a
punishment for a crime

SOLOMON

You know, you walk into a nursing home, and there's a lot to contend with. First of all, you're hit with that smell – like somebody just cooked up a rotting turkey carcass marinated in Lysol. Then there's the color scheme, with its exciting variations that run the full spectrum from white to off-white to beige. And the PEOPLE! There are grumpy-looking charge nurses ordering everyone around, grim-faced orderlies wheeling patients to and fro in wheelchairs and gurneys, the occasional detached doctor striding through on an urgent mission, and of course the patients. Okay, my mom told me to call them "residents" but who's kidding who here? They're sick, right? Therefore, they're patients.

Residents, my butt.

Anyway, all I'm trying to establish is that as I walked into the Egbert P. Johnson Memorial Home for the Aged to start my sentence, I was in no giggling mood, and the atmosphere therein wasn't likely to cheer me up anytime soon. I marched up to the third-floor north nurses' station, where they must have been expecting me. Three women were sitting with their heads sort of gaggled together, and they hushed up with an almost audible snap when I came around the corner from the elevator lounge.

"Hi, my name is Alex Gregory, and I've been assigned to work with Mr... . umm ... Solomon Lewis. Am I in the right place?"

---

1 **nursing home**: place where old people who can't take care of themselves live and are cared for   1–2 **contend with sth.**: have to deal with sth. unpleasant
3 **carcass**: body of a dead animal   **Lysol**: brand name of disinfectant (liquid with which you kill bacteria)   5 **off-white**: white with a bit of yellow or grey in it
6 **charge nurse**: nurse responsible for one part of a hospital   7 **orderly**: person who works in a hospital doing jobs for which you do not need special training
to and fro: back and forth   8 **gurney** (AE) [ɡɜːni]: hospital bed on wheels
detached: not showing emotions   **stride**: walk with long, fast steps   9 **urgent**: very important   10 **kid sb.** (infml): tell sb. untrue things   13 **establish sth.**: (here) make sth. clear   18 **gaggled together**: together in a group   19 **audible** [ˈɔːdəbl]: easy to hear   21 **assign sb. to do sth.**: tell sb. to do sth. (e.g. a particular job)

One of the three, a heavyset middle-aged woman whose name tag read CLAUDELLE GREEN, RN, looked me up and down, chuckled, and said, "Oh, you're in the right place, baby. We got the one and ONLY Solomon Lewis, don't we, girls?"

5 "Mmmmm, hmmmm," added a Miss Juanita Case, LPN, who was much younger, very pretty, and basically snickering in my face. "Your mother sure picked you a good one! Ever since we got our Solomon Lewis the other floors are all envious. Nobody else got anything LIKE a Solomon Lewis. Are you the new volunteer who's 10 going to make Mr. Lewis all happy and cheerful for us?"

The third member of the trio was Leonora McCarthy, Certified Social Worker, a tiny woman who looked practically old enough to just get out of her chair and into a bed in one of the rooms. She said under her breath, "This ought to be a hoot." Then she looked at me 15 and pointed to the first door on my right. "We keep Mr. Lewis in three-forty-four, so he's close to the station here and we can minimize the damage he does, so to speak. You can go in now; he loves getting a new volunteer. In fact, he's had about four different ones since July. Just one piece of advice: Don't be nice to him. He'll eat you up if you 20 let him get an edge."

The other two echoed her with cries of "You got THAT right" and "You think this one will last through supper?"

You can imagine how delighted I was as I stepped into Room 344.

25 The room was standard hospital issue: white walls, off-white floor tiles, turkey/Lysol scent. It had no decorations whatsoever – no cards, no "Get Well Soon" balloons, no family pictures. So the only thing I could possibly look at was the man on the bed. He was sitting, propped up on two pillows, staring at the TV with the sound 30 off as he switched channels at lightning speed. His hair was a metallic gray, and his face was surprisingly red, which served to highlight his

---

2 **RN**: registered nurse; nurse who has passed an examination   5 **LPN**: licensed practical nurse, nurse who follows orders from a more qualified nurse   6 **snicker**: laugh in a mean way   14 **be a hoot** (infml): be very funny   20 **get an edge**: have an advantage   23 **delighted**: very happy   25 **standard sth. issue**: typical for sth. 29 **propped up on sth.**: leaning against sth.

large, hooked peninsula of a nose. We once learned about Charles
Darwin in ninth- grade biology class, and how he found something
like thirteen different species of these birds called finches in the
Galápagos Islands. I remember each species had a radically different
beak shape. One kind used their beaks to make holes in trees. Then   5
they would reach down into the openings at a steep angle and pull
out grubs to eat. Well, Mr. Solomon Lewis would have fit in perfectly
with those particular finches. Behind the beak, shadowed by his
looming single eyebrow, two laser-blue eyes were doing their best to
burn a hole in the TV screen. Beneath the beak was a regular, thin-   10
lipped old-man mouth, drawn into the fiercest grimace I'd ever seen.

The overall effect: Solomon Lewis was an ancient, merciless
gargoyle, armed with a remote control and a trigger-quick thumb.

I stood there in the doorway for a few minutes, semi-scared to
speak. I cleared my throat softly, then more loudly. He had to know   15
I was there, but was clearly dishing out the Silent Treatment. Well,
Leonora McCarthy had warned me not to be nice, and I wasn't
necessarily getting all huggy and teary-eyed watching this hawk-
man ignore me, so I sat down in the big armchair next to his bed and
waited. And waited. And waited. The only sound in the room was   20
the buzz of the overhead lights, and the rattling wheeze of the old
man's breathing. He was a remarkably loud breather.

After a few minutes of staring at his face and hoping he would
give in and look at me, I tried tuning into the TV. Which had its own
frustrations, because at the exact moment I became interested in any   25
given channel, Solomon Lewis hit the clicker. It was uncanny. For
the first but definitely not the last time I almost suspected the old

---

1 **peninsula**: piece of land that sticks out into a body of water   3 **species** ['spi:ʃi:z]:
type of animal or plant   **finch**: *Fink*   5 **beak**: hard outside part of a bird's mouth
6 **angle**: *Winkel*   9 **loom**: appear frightening   11 **fierce**: looking wild and angry
grimace [grɪ'meɪs]: facial expression of anger of pain   12 **ancient** ['eɪnʃənt]: very
old   **merciless**: showing no pity   13 **trigger-quick**: fast, usu. when shooting a gun
16 **Silent Treatment**: not speaking with a person to show you are angry   18 **hawk**:
large bird of prey (*Raubvogel*)   21 **wheeze** [wi:z]: sound made when breathing with
difficulty   26 **clicker**: remote control for the TV   **uncanny**: strange and hard to
explain

man was reading my mind – like he had the superpower of dialing into the annoyance center of my brain.

When I had just about decided to jump up, block the screen, and burst into a few verses of "Getting to Know You," Solomon Lewis
5   spoke.

"Sit up in that chair, you little *pisher*. Didn't anyone ever teach you about posture?"

"Excuse me, sir?"

"What are you, another slow kid? My last volunteer was such a
10   *schmendrick*, he needed Velcro shirts because he couldn't do buttons. I said you should sit up."

All right, I had known I wouldn't be walking into a picnic here. But between this guy's tone and the unfamiliar foreign words he was throwing in, I was too stunned and confused to speak.

15   So he did the slow-talking thing that you might use for, like, a brain-damaged pet monkey. "Ssss-iiii-tttt uuuu-ppppp. Good boy.
•   Maybe soon you can learn to stand up or even chew food. In the meantime, why are you here irritating defenseless old men when you should be in school, learning to hold a pencil or something?"

20   "Umm, Mr. Lewis, my name is Alex Gregory. I'm a high school student, and I'll be spending about ten hours here with you every week until … well, for a while."

"So, Alex, they send me here to be nursed, and you they send here to keep me out of the nurses' hair. Do you know what my
25   grandmother would have said about this *cockamamie* situation?"

"I, uh, don't think so, sir."

"Well, I don't know either. She's dead, and I'm so forgetful that last week I tried to unlock my room door with my toothbrush. But she would have said something. God, that woman could talk! Once,
30   when we were leaving Poland to come to America, I remember she spent so long *kibitzing* with the ticket taker that we almost missed

---

6 **pisher** (Yiddish): unimportant or inexperienced person   7 **posture** [pɒstʃə]: how you hold your body   10 **schmendrick** (Yiddish): stupid person   **Velcro** (AE): brand name for a material used for fastening clothes easily   14 **stunned**: shocked 18 **irritate sb.**: make sb. angry   25 **cockamamie** (AE, sl): silly   31 **kibitz** (Yiddish, infml, v): talk a lot

the ship. Finally my grandfather says to her, 'Sadie, when we get to America, you can't be holding up people's business all the time with your *kibitzing*.' She says, 'Irv, when we get to America I won't say a thing.' He winks at me and says, 'Hallelujah, America really IS a new world!' " 5

I almost laughed out loud, but the moment was lost when another "resident" walked past the doorway behind me. Sol got out of bed, darted over to the door, and said, "Good afternoon, Mrs. Goldfarb." Mrs. Goldfarb looked kind of startled and nervous when she saw who was addressing her. She gave a pinched little smile and 10 murmured, "Hi, Sol. How are you today?"

"Fine, fine. But how many times have I told you that you have to put your TEETH in before you leave your room?"

She clamped her hand over her mouth, wheeled on her heels, and scurried back the way she'd come. "Gotcha!" Sol exclaimed with 15 deep satisfaction. "That's the fourth time this week."

I was a bit slow to process this. "Umm, Mr. Lewis, her teeth WERE in."

"A rocket scientist, you aren't. Of course her teeth were in."

"But why did you –" 20

"Alex, *boychik*, if you're going to last at all in this crazy house, there's one thing you need to understand about the old people in here: They need to be kept on their toes. The minute you let them stop thinking, you might as well just put laughing gas in their oxygen tanks, crank it up, and finish 'em off." 25

I didn't have the slightest clue of how to respond to that, so I sat there shifting my weight from foot to foot, studying the stubborn Ring Ding stains on my sneakers. Solomon Lewis strode past me, chuckling to himself between loud breaths, and sat down on his bed. All of a sudden the chuckles were gone, and he was making this 30 horrible "Hoo-hah-hoo-hah" noise. His hands were on his knees,

---

4 **wink at sb.**: zwinkern   10 **pinched**: looking ill and tired   14 **wheel on your heels**: turn around very quickly   15 **scurry**: walk fast with small steps   **gotcha** ['gɒtʃə] (infml): "I've got you" (when you have tricked sb.)   21 **boychick** (Yiddish): boy; young man   23 **keep sb. on their toes**: surprise sb. regularly to keep them prepared for unexpected events   25 **finish sb. off**: kill sb.   29 **chuckle**: laugh quietly

and his head was hunched to his chest. I asked twice whether he needed help, but he didn't respond. The third time, I jumped up, went over, knelt down right in front of his face, and spoke loudly: "Mr. Lewis, are you okay?"

5   He glanced up with a mixture of anger and fear that I'd never seen on anybody before. "Don't – hoo-hah – worry. This is just what – hoo-hah – happens when I'm dying – hoo-hah – you imbecile!"

October 27

Dear Judge Trent,

10   *I am writing to update you on my progress with the human-service project you assigned me. I think it is great that you gave me a chance to right my wrongs and learn from my mistakes, even though my accident did not hurt anybody but myself. However, I have just completed my first visit to the nursing home, where I worked with a very interesting*
15   *patient resident named Solomon Lewis, and I feel you should change my assignment.*

First of all, while I know the assignment is to serve humans, I am just not qualified to assist Mr. Lewis. Apparently, he has some problems with memory and attention that should be handled by a competent
20   *mental-health professional, rather than a teenager. He is also, frankly, verbally abusive. Within minutes of meeting me, Mr. Lewis called me an imbecile, said I was "not a rocket scientist" and "irritating," and suggested that maybe the other pati residents should be mercy-killed. He also berated me repeatedly in some foreign language, which the*
25   *nurses said must be something called "Yiddish."*

---

1 **hunch** (v): bend   7 **imbecile** ['ɪmbəsiːl] (derog.): idiot   20 **frankly**: honestly
21 **verbally abusive** [əˈbjuːsɪv]: saying rude and disrespectful things   24 **berate sb.** (fml): criticize sb. angrily

Secondly, nobody alerted me to this ahead of time, but Mr. Lewis is afflicted with a serious health problem called "emphysema." He started choking to death right in front of me, and I didn't have the skills to help him. A nurse had to come rushing in with a big mask and give him some kind of emergency breathing treatment. He survived, but it 5 *looked like a close call to me. Then when he finally caught his breath, I asked him whether he was feeling better, and he told me to, "Gay kocken offen yom!" I looked on the Internet when I got home, and apparently Mr. Lewis feels that, rather than assisting him at the nursing home, I should "Go take a dump in the ocean" instead.* 10

In closing, I feel that I have grounds for concern here. I am glad to do human service so that I can learn a valuable life lesson about responsibility and trust. However, I am just not qualified to meet Mr. Lewis's needs. The home should replace me with a psychiatrist/linguist/ paramedic/saint, and the court should find me a new assignment that 15 *will be less traumatic for my sensitive adolescent mind. Sincerely,*

Alex Gregory

---

1 **alert sb. to sth.**: point sth. out to sb.   2–3 **be afflicted with sth.** (fml): suffer from sth. (usu. an illness)   6 **close call**: situation where something bad almost happens   10 **take a dump** (sl): pass solid bodily waste   16 **sensitive**: easy to upset **adolescent** [ˌædəˈlesnt]: between 13 and 18 years old

October 29

Dear Alex,

Contrary to your assertions, Mr. Lewis sounds like the perfect match for you.

5   *As I explained to you when we accepted you into the Full Circle pretrial intervention pilot program, the human- service component is only half of the picture. The point of the program is that by working through the challenges and difficulties of serving others, you will ultimately be serving yourself. I look forward to more letters from you so that I can*
10   *enjoy the unfolding process of your personal growth, and Mr. Lewis's, as well. In the meantime, you are hereby ordered to continue your service with Mr. Lewis.*

Sincerely, Judge J. Trent

P.S. A Yiddish phrase that might come in handy for your use with Mr.
15   *Lewis is "Bluz in toches!" Like Mr. Lewis, I am Jewish, and in the proud language of our people, this means "Blow it out your butt."*

---

3 **assertion**: statement which you strongly believe   5–6 **pretrial intervention program**: program offering people who have committed a crime an alternative to a trial in court   6 **pilot**: (here) newly introduced program serving as a guideline for the future

PLAN B

For my second visit to see Solomon Lewis, I had to pump myself up just to make it through the door. All the way on the bus to the home, my inner drill sergeant was delivering a high-energy sermon to my inner coward – who is remarkably similar to my outer coward, now that I think about it.   5

DRILL SERGEANT: Buck up now, son. There's a job waitin' for you up in that room. Now you're just going to get in there and ... and ... and ... HUMAN SERVE until I tell you to stop ... uh ... human servicin'!

INNER COWARD: But, sir, I'm not trained for this mission.   10

DRILL SERGEANT: First, don't call me "sir." I work for a living. Second, you have all the training you need, boy. Now show some old-fashioned red-blooded American guts and GET IN THERE.

INNER COWARD: Why should I?

DRILL SERGEANT: Why? WHY? There ain't no "why" in this man's   15 army, son. You are just a weapon. The orders come down, and you attack. Does a *gun* ask why? Does a *tank* ask why?

INNER COWARD: No, but what about a smart bomb? Does a smart bomb ask why?

DRILL SERGEANT: Umm ... uhh ... I'm not too sure about that   20 technical stuff. I mean, I suppose you could *program* a smart bomb to ask why. But could it ask WHY it asked why? I guess the

---

1 **pump sb. up**: make sb. feel more confident   3 **drill sergeant** ['sɑːdʒənt]: soldier who teaches new recruits   **sermon**: (here) moral speech   4 **coward** ['kaʊəd]: person with no courage   6 **buck up** (infml): be strong   13 **guts** (infml): courage   15 **there ain't no** (infml): there isn't any   17 **tank**: large, strong vehicle used in wars   18–19 **smart bomb**: bomb controlled by a computer

true question is whether a smart bomb can ever attain true awareness. In the immortal words of Socrates …

INNER COWARD: You're scaring me, sir.

5 **DRILL SERGEANT**: Doesn't matter. We've reached the drop zone. Now go, go, GO. And STOP CALLING ME "SIR"! I don't know why we let snot-nosed punks like you into the military anyway. When John Wayne was alive, you didn't see a bunch of lily-livered, weak-kneed, sniveling, scrawny pantywaists tryin' to make excuses for every …

10 **INNER COWARD**: Thank you, Sergeant. You're an inspiration. Honestly.

I paused before entering Mr. Lewis's room, took a deep breath, and marched myself right in. The old man was sitting up in bed reading a book I had read in school, *Angela's Ashes*, by Frank McCourt. So I
15 cleared my throat and tried to start right in with a discussion.
 "Good morning, Mr. Lewis. I'm Alex, your volunteer. Remember?"
 He just stared at me like I was a walking, talking fungus.
 "Anyway, I read that book last year. Great, isn't it?"
 "Who the hell are you? I've never seen you before in my life.
20 Nurse. NURSE! Help! There's a thief in my room. I think he wants to –"
 This was alarming. "Mr. Lewis, wait! I'm just your … um … I'm Alex."
 "Help! Alex, the Um, is here to get me. NURSE!" Claudelle came
25 pounding through the doorway. "Mr. Lewis, calm down. It's okay." She gestured to me. "This is just …"

---

1 **attain sth.** (fml): achieve sth.   2 **immortal**: living forever   6 **punk** (AE, infml): (here) young man who behaves badly   7–8 **lily-livered** (old-fashioned): not brave   8 **scrawny**: thin and ill-looking   **pantywaist** (derog., infml): person with no courage   17 **fungus**: *Pilz*   25 **pound** (v): (here) walk with heavy, noisy steps

"Alex, the Um." Then Mr. Lewis started laughing so hard I thought he might start choking again. "Gotcha! Alex, the Um! Boy, are you two gullible."

Come to think of it, I kinda *hoped* he'd start choking again.

"So, Mr. Um, you liked *Angela's Ashes*?"   5

Maybe I could show him I wasn't so stupid. "Yes, I enjoyed the way he made his memoir feel like fiction."

"Oh, what a load of *chazzerai* that is. 'Made his memoir feel like fiction.' Ha! Did you like it? Did you cry? This book, do you know where it hit me? Right in the *kishkes*, it hit me. Pow! Those Irish, they   10
know from suffering, let me tell you."

"Well, I *said* I liked it. It was deep."

"Deep, schmeep! Nurse, are you hearing Mr. Um here? For this, you're paying school taxes?"

Claudelle shook her head and clicked her tongue as she walked   15
away, leaving me to sink or swim in this riptide of undeserved criticism.

"Listen, Mr. Lewis, I don't know why you're picking on me. You liked the book, right? I liked the book. You liked it, I liked it – so don't torture me, okay?"   20

Mr. Lewis looked fairly pleased with me all of a sudden. "Call me Sol, Mr. Um. Now that you've raised your voice to me in anger, I figure we're on a first-name basis."

"I'm sorry, Mr. Lewis. I just didn't come here to get …"

"Listen, Mr. Um. First of all, I told you to call me Sol. Second of   25
all, don't apologize for showing some backbone. Especially for a slow kid like you – no offense – you're going to need some of that *chutzpah* to get you through life. Everybody needs a meal ticket, and if you aren't blessed with looks or brains, a big mouth isn't such a bad substitute."   30

---

2 **choke**: not breathe well because you cannot get any air   3 **gullible** ['gʌləbl]: quickly willing to believe what people say   28 **kinda** (infml): kind of   7 **memoir** ['memwɑː]: book in which the author writes about his or her life   8 **chazzerai** (Yiddish): (here) nonsense   10 **kishkes** (Yiddish): intestines   16 **riptide**: fast-flowing, rough water   28 **chutzpah** ['xʊtspə] (Yiddish): courage to speak up against authority   **meal ticket**: (here) quality that helps you succeed in life   29 **big mouth**: (here) ability to say what you think

Wow, that was the most backhanded compliment I ever heard. But at least I've got *chutzpah*, whatever that is.

"Anyway, Mr. Um, what are we going to do today? We've already had our literature lesson for the week, so what do you think? Some
5   chess, maybe? Or for you, checkers? Tic-tac-toe? Go fish? War?"

I don't know what on earth possessed me, but Sol had pressed my buttons again. "Hey, Sol, I've got about three more hours here tonight. How's about a nice friendly game of poker?"

Sol produced a pack of cards from his nightstand, and a bone-
10   chilling grin spread across his face.

November 10

Dear Judge Trent,

As you know, when you stipulated as a condition of my probation that the nursing home assign me a "challenging" resident, my mother delib-
15   *erately selected Mr. Lewis as the perfect match. I also know that, in your last letter, you supported my mother's selection. However, because my mother has a direct personal and financial stake in my case – one might even call it a "grudge" – I must once more implore you to re-assign me.*

20   *Because I am a good and conscientious worker, I showed up for my fourth through sixth hours of service to Mr. Lewis on Thursday, November 9. However, as you will read below, things did not run smoothly. If the terms of successful completion for the Full Circle project are that I: a) teach someone a life lesson, b) learn a life lesson,*
25   *and c) pay back the $500.00 in damages I did to Mrs. Wilson's lawn,*

---

1 **backhanded**: expressing praise and criticism at the same time   5 **checkers** (AE): *Dame (Brettspiel)*   13 **stipulate sth.**: demand officially that sth. is done   **probation**: period of time in which a criminal has to behave well in order to avoid prison 14–15 **deliberate**: on purpose   17 **have a stake in sth.**: be interested in the successful outcome of sth.   18 **grudge** [grʌdʒ]: anger towards a person who has done sth. bad to you   **implore sb.**: ask sb. very urgently   20 **conscientious** [ˌkɒnʃiˈenʃəs]: paying close attention to doing work correctly

accepting as I must her inflated claim that her little elf statuette was worth $374.59, I don't know how my time with Mr. Lewis will ever result in my release.

Number one, I don't know how I am going to teach Mr. Lewis anything. I tried to engage him in an intellectual discussion of literature on 5 *Thursday, but he was markedly unreceptive. He thinks I am stupid and funny-looking, so I don't think he is ready to believe I can offer him any wisdom at all. I told him at one point, "If you would listen to me for a minute, maybe I could teach you something." He replied, "And if my grandmother would grow wheels, maybe she'd be a trolley car."* 10

Number two, Mr. Lewis cannot teach me anything because he is too busy abusing me. I will admit I am picking up some choice Yiddish sayings. For example, I now know that a "schlemiel" is a clumsy man, and a "schlemazzel" is the schlemiel's victim. However, I would hate to believe that Mr. Lewis spilled a large glass of ice water in my lap for 15 *the sole purpose of improving my vocabulary. Also, vocabulary is not a life lesson. I might not be a rocket scientist. I might even be an imbecile or a schlemazzel. But I think I would know it if Mr. Lewis were able to enhance my personal growth, which is clearly not the case.*

Number three, I know I am supposed to earn back the $500 for the 20 *garden sprite at $5.00 per hour. However, Mr. Lewis took advantage of my youth and innocence to swindle me out of $27.25 in a poker game. If I keep earning $15 a visit, and losing $27 and change, I will still be working here when it is time for them to move me into my own retire-ment room. That Mr. Lewis has a lot of chutzpah ripping off a defense-less teenager like that!* 25

---

1 **inflated**: higher than is acceptable   5 **engage sb. in sth.**: get sb. to take part in sth.   6 **markedly**: clearly   **unreceptive**: not willing to listen   12 **choice** (adj): good   19 **enhance sth.**: make sth. better   21 **sprite**: small fantasy creature with magical powers   22 **swindle sb. out of sth.**: cheat so that you can take sth. away from sb.   24–25 **rip sb. off** (infml): cheat sb.

Please let me offer you a final assurance that I am not lazy. I would gladly build houses for Habitat for Humanity, or carry fifty-pound water jugs for the Special Olympics. I'd cheerfully and eagerly paint playgrounds, spackle schools, dig ditches. I will shovel out stables, mow
5   *the grass of every park in town. I'd be thrilled to wash the whole fleet of police cars by hand – which would also be a more fitting punishment for my particular "crime." If you spare me the torment of another ninety-four hours of Solomon Lewis, I will do your bidding for TWO hundred hours ANYWHERE, ANYTIME.*

10 *Just say the word and I will put on my work gloves.*

Sincerely, Alex Gregory

Your Damp and Frozen Schlemazzel

---

1 **assurance** [əˈʃʊərəns]: serious promise   2 **Habitat for Humanity**: charitable project that builds houses for poor people   4 **spackle** (v): put a special substance on a wall before putting on the wallpaper   **ditch**: long, narrow hole   5 **thrilled**: very happy   **fleet of sth.**: group of sth. (usu. vehicles)   12 **damp**: slightly wet

November 14

Dear Alex,

Keep plugging away there. I think you are on the verge of a marvelous breakthrough.

Sincerely, Judge J. Trent   5

P.S. – "Schlemazzel" is not such a horrible insult. If Mr. Lewis starts calling you a "meshuggener," or "crazy man," that's when you will know you are being insulted.

---

3 **plug away** (infml): work hard at sth.   **be on the verge of sth**: be at the point where sth. is going to happen very soon

LAURIE MEETS SOL

"So, Laurie, Princess, is your husband here a *meshuggener*, or what?"

"Mr. Lewis, Alex is not my husband. We're only sixteen years old. Besides, I told you, he's my best friend. He has no romantic interest in me at all."

5   "I know. That's why he's a *meshuggener*!"

*   *   *

There are certain things on earth that just don't mix. Oil and water come to mind. Cobras and mongooses. Lit cigarettes and barrels of dynamite. Alcohol and lawn gnomes.

But if there was ever a combination that filled my heart with
10   terror and dread, that recipe for disaster was Laurie and Sol.

Of course, I was still best friends with Laurie. Ever since my hearing, she had stopped bugging me about the accident. At first she had been trying to show sympathy because of the whole driver's license thing. Now, she was just too busy enjoying my tales of misery.
15   Every Wednesday and Friday in homeroom, she would dash up to me with a barely hidden grin and ask, "How was your visit with Sol last night?"

So I'd tell her the highlights: He suckered me in poker and froze my leg. Or he called me a chimp. Or he hid Mrs. Goldfarb's wig in
20   the planter again.

Laurie's eyes would sparkle with demented pixie dust as she said, "So when can I meet this guy?"

What was a boy to do? For someone who always scolded me about my bad ideas, she sure was blind to her own disaster potential.

---

7 **mongoose** [ˈmɒŋguːs]: *Mungo*   10 **dread** [dred]: great fear   12 **bug sb.** (infml): annoy sb.   18 **sucker sb.** (AE, infml): beat sb.   18–19 **freeze sb.'s leg**: take all sb.'s money in a poker game   19 **chimp** (infml): chimpanzee; large monkey that lives in Africa   **wig**: fake hair that you wear on your head   20 **planter**: pot for plants
21 **demented**: crazy   **pixie dust**: powder that pixies use for magic   23 **scold sb.**: tell sb. off

Can you imagine what he'd say to her? What she'd say to him? What they would do to each other?

I had visions of epic battles with remote controls, wheelchairs, Chinese throwing stars pinging off the old man's oxygen tank. But somehow it never crossed my mind that the irresistible force and the immovable object would become fast friends. 5

So here we were at the historic first meeting. Maybe I should hit the rewind button so you can catch the whole painful encounter.

It was a Friday night, and Laurie stopped by my house. Mom was walking in frantic little circles in the kitchen, getting ready for her second big first date – the original "Mister Right" hadn't wanted to see her again after my little vehicular adventure interrupted their evening. Mom was afraid I'd do something stupid while she was out, and Laurie saw her chance to strike. 10

"Mrs. Gregory, I have the perfect way to keep Alex out of trouble." 15

"So do I, but the child welfare people think it's cruel and unusual to cage him up with the dog again." That mom of mine and her wacky child-abuse humor!

"This might be less satisfying for you, but it's totally legal. Wanna hear it?" 20

"Laurie, sweetheart, could you get my top button in the back there? Okay, what's the plan?"

"I'll take custody of the boy, and bring him on the bus to the nursing home to visit Mr. Lewis."

Ignoring my gasp, my dirty look, and my vicious ankle kick, she continued with her charming-the-parents voice. "We'll kill three birds with one stone: You will be free for the evening and Alex won't have access to a car, Alex will get in some extra hours with Mr. Lewis and impress the probation people, and I won't have to sit home all alone because my loser best friend is grounded." 25

30

---

3 **epic**: very large   4 **Chinese throwing star**: small star-shaped, metal object and that can be thrown as a weapon   **ping off sth.**: make a short, sharp sound when bouncing off of sth.   **oxygen** [ɒksɪdʒən]: part of air that people and animals need to live   5 **irresistible**: very strong or attractive   12 **vehicular** (fml): to do with vehicles   18 **wacky** (infml): crazy   25 **vicious**: violent   30 **be grounded** (infml): not be allowed to leave your house as a punishment

"Hmm … let me think for a minute. Is this necklace too clunky for the dress?"

"No, it's nice. So what do you think of the plan?"

"Sorry, honey, but Alex is staying put."

5 I smiled, and it was Laurie's turn to kick MY ankle. "Mrs. Gregory, why don't you wear the little gold hoop earrings? They really set off your eyes."

"I already said no, dear." My mom picked up her tiny, fancy-looking purse-thingie.

10 "I know. I just think you should be well accessorized for your big night. You have your cell phone, right?"

"Yes, but why? Alex knows where I'll be: at the Pluto Grill, on the river."

Laurie gave me her sweetest and most sinister smile. "Alex knows
15 where you'll be, but the police and ambulance crews don't."

Just then a car horn beeped outside. My mom looked at Laurie. Laurie grinned at my mom. Mom snarled. "Oh, take him, you rotten thing. But you will have him home by the time I get back." Then she realized this had come out sounding a tad harsh, so she gave Laurie
20 a quick hug and muttered, "Take care of him for me, okay?"

Mom dashed out the door before I could mention my own vast, legendary ability to take care of myself. Laurie turned to me and said, "Grab your coat. And don't get too carried away thanking me – you'll make me blush!"

25 I was too mad to say much on the bus ride, but as we got off the bus and started walking into the home, I couldn't let Laurie go in there without a warning. Even the Queen of Manipulation deserved some preparation before she headed into battle. So I gave her all of the tips I'd picked up: Go easy on the eye contact, never show
30 friendliness, don't go out on a limb with personal information, opinions, or observations. She wanted to know what she COULD do. "Run away home, child," was all I could come up with.

---

1 **clunky**: big and awkward   4 **stay put** (infml): remain in one place   6 **hoop**: ring
17 **rotten**: annoying   19 **a tad** (infml): a little bit   23 **get carried away**: not be in
control of what you do because you are very excited   24 **blush** (v): go red in the
face because you are embarrassed   30 **go out on a limb**: (here) be very generous
and risk being hurt

Nurse Claudelle came around the corner as we were emerging from the elevator, overheard the end of my speech, and clucked her tongue at me. "Why are you telling tales on our Mr. Lewis? Don't listen to this one, honey. Solomon Lewis is a fine old gentleman. By the way, Alex, where have you been hiding this sweet little thing? Hi, 5 my name is Claudelle Green. I'm the charge nurse on the unit here. You must be very proud of Alex. We got him all worried about Mr. Lewis before his first visit, but he marched in there like a trooper and things have been going fine ever since. Isn't that right, Alex?"

I spluttered. "He – you – you all said he was – Wait! She's not a 10 sweet little thing. She's my friend Laurie."

Claudelle clucked again. "Miss Laurie, you've got a nice boy here. IF he ever learns some manners and starts telling you that you ARE a sweet little thing."

I stomped into Sol's room, just to get away from the baffling fe- 15 male madness. Sol was reading Hemingway this time, *The Old Man and the Sea*. He held the book up to me for comment, but before I could say anything, he started in: "Ah, Mr. Um. So nice to see you – and on a Friday, no less. Did you come by to give me an extra litera- ture lesson? Some poker advice, maybe?" 20

Then he saw Laurie over my shoulder, and broke into a mammoth grin. It was like a friendly, bodysnatching alien had abducted him and taken his place. I figured those thin little lips would snap under the unaccustomed tension, but they held. "Oh, and you brought a friend. Isn't that what the young men are calling their young ladies 25 these days?"

Laurie beamed right back at him. Hadn't she listened to my advice AT ALL? "Hello, Mr. Lewis. My name is Laurie. I'm so glad to meet you. Alex talks about you all the time."

Good golly. This was turning into some sort of sickening love 30 fest.

---

2 **cluck**: make a noise like a chicken   8 **trooper**: low-ranking soldier   10 **splutter**: talk in short, incomplete sentences because you are angry or embarrassed
15 **baffling**: very confusing   21 **mammoth** (adj): very big   22 **abduct sb.**: kidnap sb.   23 **snap**: break suddenly   24 **unaccustomed**: (here) unusual
hold: (here) survive a difficult situation   30 **good golly** (old-fashioned, infml): expression of surprise

"About *me*, he talks? When he's looking into those pretty eyes of yours, it's not about me your friend should be talking."

On second thought, at any moment Sol was probably going to trigger Laurie's fabled Anti-Sexist Death Stare, and then we'd all be
5 diving for cover.

"Oh, stop it, Mr. Lewis. Alex and I are just best friends."

"With the way he's looking at you, I figure I should start calling him your husband."

"Friend, Mr. Lewis. F-r-i-e-n-d. Fffrrrriiiieeeennnnnndddd."
10 "Husband. Laurie, darling, trust me. Husband."

"Friend, amigo, buddy. You know – like, pal? Friend."

"Husband."

"Friend."

Which is where we came in a few pages ago. I couldn't believe
15 this. Laurie and Sol were bantering, or sparring, or flirting, or something. Not that I cared, aside from the creepiness. Since she and I were just friends, after all. And what did Sol mean, exactly, about the way I looked at her?

Wait. The guy was old, grumpy, and at least half insane. Why was
20 I even thinking about this? I needed to clear my head.

"Sol, since you and my wife are hitting it off so well, I think I'll just go fill out my time forms at the nurses' station, okay?" He didn't even look away from Laurie, but kinda waved his hand at me in dismissal.

25 I walked out, trying to tune out the conspiratorial laughter behind me, and sat down behind the desk at the station. Claudelle was there, drinking coffee. She started talking with me about her kids, her husband's health problems, and her aching feet, and I listened for a good, long while – she was a pretty interesting lady
30 when she wasn't teasing me. Plus, it was easier than trying to handle

---

4 **fabled**: famous   11 **buddy** (infml): friend   15 **banter**: talk in a joking way
spar: argue in a friendly way   16 **creepiness**: causing uneasiness by being very
strange   21 **hit it off**: quickly like each other   23–24 **dismissal**: (here) allowing
sb. to leave   25 **tune sth. out**: not listen to sth.   **conspiratorial**: behaving like
you share a secret   30 **tease sb.**: make jokes to upset sb. or make them feel
embarrassed

the two-headed runaway freight train of Sol and Laurie. But eventually Claudelle let out a huge sigh, and eased herself back onto her sore tootsies. If she was getting back into action, I supposed I should be, too.

Back in the room, the scene was a shocker. Sol was sitting in his chair, and Laurie was fluffing the pillows on his bed. "Laurie, honey pie, you might be prettier than Alex, but when he makes my bed, he does hospital corners. Floppy sheets is not my idea of comfortable. And this water, it's too warm. Alex always gets me ice from the fourth floor."

"But, Mr. Lewis, I don't usually do those …"

Laurie spun and cut me off. "You don't make his bed?"

"No, the nurses' aides do that."

"You don't fluff his pillows?"

"Nope."

"But you do go get him water, right?"

"Nuh-uh."

Laurie looked back and forth from me to Sol, whose facial expression was starting to look familiar. "So I'm guessing you never, um, rub his feet?"

Sol finally broke out with his booming bark: "Gotcha!"

I told her not to be nice to him, but apparently, wives never listen.

---

1 **runaway** (adj): (here) uncontrollable   **freight train**: train for transporting goods
3 **tootsies** (infml): toes   8 **hospital corners**: method of stretching a sheet neatly
around the corners of a mattress, the way nurses do it   13 **aide** [eɪd]: person whose
job is to help others in their work   14 **fluff sth.**: (here) shake sth. to make it softer
21 **bark**: sound that dogs make

SOL GETS INTERESTED

The next week, I got to Sol's late because I had jazz band practice
after school. We'd gotten this new chart called "Jumpin' with
Symphony Sid," and I was struggling with it. The accents were all in
really strange places, so I kept hitting the accented notes at the
5   wrong time. Or I'd get the timing right, but concentrate so hard on
THAT that I'd slip into the wrong key. Then the conductor, Mr.
Watras, would stop the band and try to correct me, which was
embarrassing. I never did get it right at the rehearsal, but Mr. Watras
must have decided to just ignore my spastic rhythm and blatant
10 pitch errors.

So anyhow, that's why I was late. And Sol wasn't in his room. At
the nurses' station, Juanita Case was on duty. She seemed a little
annoyed that she'd missed the big night with Laurie, which had
provided endless hours of laughter for the staff when Sol had told
15 them about it. Still, having missed the original action didn't
disqualify her from picking on me about it.

"So how's the Pillow Fluff Girl? Will she be back soon? Sol's
pillows are looking a mite droopy."

"Oh, please give me a break, Miss Case. I just spent an hour
20 getting publicly humiliated in jazz band at school, and now I have to
see Sol. I'm not sure how much more I can take in one day."

"How did they humiliate you up at that school?"

"Oh, it wasn't the school, it was me. I just couldn't get my parts
right today."

---

2 **chart**: (here) musical notes arranged on pages that you use to play a song
3 **accent**: notes in a piece of music that are stressed   6 **conductor**: person who
stands in front of musicians and gives signals to show how they should play
9 **blatant** ['bleɪtnt]: very obvious   10 **pitch**: how high or low a musical note or a
voice is   16 **pick on sb.**: trat sb. in an unfair way, e.g. by criticising them harshly
18 **a mite**: a bit   **droopy**: hanging down at the edges   19 **give sb. a break**: stop
teasing sb.   20 **humiliate sb.** ['hjuːmɪlieɪt]: make sb. feel bad about themselves

"Well, baby, Sol is at hydrotherapy right now, and he won't be back for a good half hour. Why don't you close yourself up in his room and practice that guitar?"

The instant I started to think, I'd mess up again. My old middle school English teacher, Miss Palma, used to talk to my class about   5
how we should be "Writing Zen Masters" who could "think without thinking." Weird, right? She always said writing was like bike riding, and that if you ever stopped and thought about HOW you were balancing on your bike, you'd fall. Even though I thought Miss Palma might have spent a little too much time on mountaintops, I   10
never forgot the advice. So while I was playing this piece, I concentrated so hard on not concentrating that I didn't hear Sol being wheeled in behind me until he started whistling the melody of the song over the chords I was playing. I stopped and turned to say hi.

"So today you're serenading me, Mr. Um? To what do I owe this   15
privilege? Is it maybe 'Sing to a Fossil Day'? And why is your music paper on my bed? I'm telling you, the service around here is slipping without that lovely Laurie girl here."

I jumped up, almost dropping the Tele in the process, and grabbed up the sheet music with a fast sweep of my hand. "I'm sorry,   20
Sol. I was just early for our visit, so I decided to use the time practicing."

"Wait a minute, Mr. Um. You weren't early, you were late. Just because I can't breathe doesn't mean I can't tell time. And what is that thing in your lap?"   25

"It's a guitar."

"This much, I know. I mean, what is it doing in your lap?"

"Well, I play it. I mean, I play in the school jazz band. I'm not very good, but I ..."

Sol got out of the wheelchair and into bed. "You play fine. I knew   30
what song it was, didn't I? Now, why don't you make yourself useful and play for me?"

---

1 **hydrotherapy** [ˌhaɪdrəʊˈθerəpi]: exercises in water that treat certain illnesses or injuries   14 **chord**: muscial notes played together   15 **serenade sb.**: sing a song or play music for sb., usu. in order to show your love for them   17 **slip**: (here) get worse   25 **lap**: *Schoß*

"Well, I don't know many of this kind of songs. Plus, I don't even have my amplifier with me, so it's not going to be loud enough."

"So play what you know, as loud as you play. It has to be better than hearing your thoughts on Hemingway. I promise I won't criti-
5 cize."

Well, that would be a refreshing change, anyway.

I took out the only other sheet music I had in my case, which was a Miles Davis tune from the 1960s called "All Blues." I carried it around and played it all the time because it was much easier than
10 most of the jazz we played in school. I used to try to get Mr. Watras to call for it at every rehearsal so I could have three minutes of not feeling like a complete half-wit. I also just liked Miles Davis. I once read a book about him for a biography project at school – he was tough and confident, and used to play with his back to the audience
15 sometimes because he didn't care what people thought. So of course they all flipped over him – women used to line up to meet him, and he was like a rock star before there even were rock stars. He was kind of like Laurie with a trumpet, in a lot of ways. Anyhow, I got the music arranged on the nightstand, counted it off to myself (1-2-
20 3, 1-2-3), and started playing. I was nervous, so I started the song at a pretty quick tempo. "Slower," Sol muttered. So I slowed down. I looked up about halfway through the chart, and his eyes were closed. His face looked almost peaceful, and his breathing was the quietest it had ever been in my presence. I figured I was either im-
25 pressing him or putting him in a coma. For the last chorus, I played harder and more rhythmically, and Sol's fingers started rubbing together in the ghost of a snap. So he was dialed into what I was playing, which was both cool and scary.

When I stopped, and the last dominant-seventh chord was still
30 floating in the air like a bell you might have once heard in a sad dream, Sol opened his eyes and looked at me. I couldn't read any-

---

11 **rehearsal** [rɪˈhɜːsl]: practice, (usu. for music or theatre)   16 **flip over sb.**
(infml): be very excited about sb.   19 **count sth. off**: count a few beats before the
music starts to give the players the tempo   27 **dial into sth.**: make a connection
with sth.   29 **dominant-seventh**: musical term (*Septdominante*)

thing in his expression at all. Did he like the song? Did he think I'd played well? Was he really not going to criticize?

"More," he whispered hoarsely. "More."

I couldn't believe it. I had found something I could do that Solomon Lewis liked.   5

And, try as I might, I couldn't see a "Gotcha" angle anywhere.

November 22

Dear Judge Trent,

I am writing today with my first piece of positive news. As you may remember from my hearing, I play the guitar, and am a member of my   10
high school's jazz band. This week, Mr. Lewis asked me to play my guitar for him, and I did. The playing seemed to entertain him. As I was leaving for the day, Mr. Lewis even told me, "If you ever want to practice more for somebody old and defenseless, feel free. I'm stuck here in bed anyway." Which is the kindest thing he has said to me yet.   15

I don't know how this will allow me to learn a lesson or teach one, but at least while I'm playing the guitar, Mr. Lewis is not mocking me, swindling me, or spilling icy beverages on my innocent flesh.

Thank you for your faith in me. Sincerely,

Alex Gregory   20

---

3 **hoarse**: with a rough voice   17 **mock sb.**: make fun of sb.   18 **beverage** (fml): drink

HALF AN ANSWER

In December, there was a serious cold snap. My mom finally un-grounded me so I could go shopping for her Christmas presents, but I spent tons of time in my basement practicing my jazz tunes for Sol. I even bought a tiny amplifier the size of a Walkman so I could play
5 a little louder during my visits, even though the extra $30.00 added six hours to my sentence at the home. And twice a week, I dragged my Tele and the mini-amp onto the bus and up to Sol's room.

One day, I had just walked in when Sol asked me, "Where's your little wife, Laurie?"

10 "We're friends, Sol."

"About this, my grandmother had a saying: '*A halber entfer zogt oiget epes.*' That means, 'Half an answer also says something!'"

"Whatever. Do you want to hear something new I've been working on, just for you?"

15 "Oh, just for me, heh? Not for your tremendous worldwide audience, then?"

"Ha-ha. Do you want to hear it or not?"

"Who says I don't want to hear it? I'm sitting here, aren't I? You're a very sensitive boy, Alex. You have to toughen up, or the world will
20 be a hard place for you."

"I'm not sensitive, Sol. You have no idea how strong I am."

"Oh, and *you* have an idea how strong you are? How do you know, with the easy life you kids are having nowadays? Strong, schmong!"

25 "Anyway, Sol, I'm going to play now." And I played a piece I had dug out of the jazz-band folder at school. I wanted to do something that Sol would know was just for him, so I found the medley from this play called *Fiddler on the Roof*. It's about a Jewish guy in the old country somewhere whose daughter wants to marry a guy who's not

---

1 **cold snap** (infml): period of cold weather   15 **tremendous** [trə'mendəs]: very large and impressive   27 **medley**: piece of music made of a number of songs or parts of songs

Jewish. I figured he would like to hear something a little different, and maybe he could relate to it or something. I had worked really hard on the piece, because the school's music was only for the piano, and it's hard to rewrite piano music for the guitar. Actually, it was probably the most effort I had put into anything since before my dad   5
had moved out.

The medley starts out with this funny song called "Tradition." It's a big "oompah-oompah" kind of thing, and pretty fast. Then it se-gues into "Matchmaker, Matchmaker," which is the easiest part – a fast waltz with a simple melody. Next comes another "oompah" part   10
called "To Life," which is the translation of a Jewish toast, *L'Chaim*. I was pretty proud that I knew that – Sol always said it right before he swallowed his pills. Anyway, the part after that is called "Sunrise, Sunset." It's a song the father sings about how he can't believe his daughter is old enough to move out and get married. It's a bittersweet   15
kind of waltz and was really pretty when I didn't mess up the big finger stretches I had to pull off in order to play through its chord changes. Which was about forty percent of the time, but hey – I was tryin'.

So I started playing. You know how in, like, a Disney movie or   20
something, the princess will start singing and all the birds and bees and deer and stuff will gather around to listen? This was a lot like that, but the birds, bees, and deer had walkers, wigs, and hearing aids. Residents came in. Nurses came in. Mrs. Goldfarb almost came in, but couldn't quite get herself to enter Sol's room, so she was just   25
sort of leaning on the door frame.

"Tradition" flew by under my fingers. "Matchmaker, Matchmaker" might have been a tad slow, but when I looked over at Sol, he was nodding in time like he was conducting me with his fearsome eye-

---

8 **oompah** ['ʊmpɑː] (infml): way of describing the sound of a brass band
8–9 **segue** ['segweɪ]: move from one song to another without interruption
10 **waltz** [wɔːls]: piece of music which you can dance to, with three beats to the bar
(Takt)   11 **toast**: (here) act of lifting up a glass and wishing sb. well before drinking
17 **finger stretch**: part of a guitar piece that requires quick and difficult finger
movements   **pull sth. off** (infml): do sth. successfully   23 **walker** (AE): metal
frame with wheels which help old or sick people walk

brow. "To Life" was great – I had the little Gypsy-sounding rhythm part really snapping along. And then I started to ease my way into "Sunrise, Sunset."

But as soon as I played maybe the fourth note of the first line ("Is 5 this the little girl I carried?"), I chanced to look at Sol again, and what I saw made my fingers trip and crash all into one another, like the Three Stooges had suddenly taken possession of my digits. His head was bowed to his chest, and it looked as though he was crying silently. I stumbled through the rest of the song, and all of the 10 assembled oldsters clapped, but by the end all I wanted was to find out what was wrong with Sol. As soon as the others started walking out, I turned to the bed.

"Sol, are you all right?" No response.

"Sol? Mr. Lewis?"

15 He ignored me just long enough for the clacking of the last cane to fade off down the hallway, and then looked up. His eyes were still brimming and bloodshot. "I'm fine, Alex. What? A man can't be moved by some music once in a while?"

"But I didn't mean to make you upset. This was supposed to be, 20 like, your Hanukkah present."

"Alex, Alex. I'm not upset. You gave me a very nice present. New socks, I don't need. A sweater from the mall, I don't want. Music, I like. And you played all right today."

"I did?"

25 "Don't fish for a compliment, *boychik* – it's not dignified. I'm not saying you should quit your day job and head for Broadway, but you're learning something."

He watched without saying anything as I packed up my guitar, and I wondered why that one song would make him so emotional. I

---

1 **Gypsy** ['dʒɪpsi]: (here) culture of people who travel around and live in caravans (many prefer the term "Roma")   6 **trip**: (here) become unsure   7 **Three Stooges** ['stuːdʒes]: American Comedy trio popular from 1930–1960 who did slapstick, which involves being clumsy (*ungeschickt*)   **digit** ['dɪdʒɪt]: (here) finger   9 **stumble through sth.**: (here) do sth. with difficulty   20 **Hanukkah** ['hænʊkə]: Jewish holiday that lasts eight days in November or December   25 **dignified**: deserving respect

was feeling rather brave, since I had been such a big musical hit with him lately, so I asked. "Sol, was there something about that Sunrise song that bothered you?"

He smiled tightly, without showing a single tooth. "I didn't so much enjoy the part where you lost the time and played all the wrong notes. Other than that, I'm fine." 5

Right before he kicked me out of his room for the day, I told him a saying I'd just heard: "Half an answer also says something!"

HAPPY HOLIDAYS

Christmas break was looking grim. I planned to visit the old man every day of the vacation so I could really pack in the hours, but that wasn't exactly a one-way ticket to Party Land. Plus, Laurie was in New York with her mom until just before New Year's Eve, and my
5 mom was working double shifts at the home so that "other people can enjoy time with their families."

What was I, her dog? Her goldfish, maybe? A really, really under-qualified chauffeur?

Of course, my mom wasn't my whole family. And the missing
10 one-third of our little trio was sitting on Mom's front step one day when I got back from a day at the home.

Dad looked tired and kind of old. I stopped about ten feet in front of him, wondering how long he'd been sitting there in the freezing weather, with nothing but a suit jacket to keep him warm
15 and his expensive wing-tip shoes frosted in the drifting snow. He's some kind of junior vice-president guy at the local bank, and is always dressed super-fancy, even hours after work. But for the first time I could ever remember, his face was completely covered in stubble.

20   "Hi, Alex."

"Uh, hi, Dad."

"It's been a while. You know, I called a few times."

"Yeah, I've been really busy with my community service, and school, and the SATs are coming up. I was going to call you, but –
25 you know …"

"And I sent you some e-mails."

"Yeah, my stupid mail server has been acting up."

---

1 **grim**: unpleasant   15 **wing-tip shoes** (AE): elegant men's shoes with a decorative piece of leather on their tips   19 **stubble**: short, hard hair on a man's face when he has not shaved for a few days   24 **SAT**: Scholastic Aptitude Test; exam American students take before university

"Well, that would explain why you blocked all messages from my address, I suppose. What a relief. I thought you were mad at me." Boy, between Mom's sarcasm, and Dad's, Laurie's, and Sol's, it's a wonder I even stay sane. "Anyway, I just came by to see you before … before … well, I'm going out of town for a while." 5

"What do you mean, out of town?"

"I've accepted a job in Philadelphia. It starts on January fifteenth."

"But that's like an hour and a half away. It's in a whole 'nother state."

"I know. That's why it's considered 'out of town.'" 10

"Are you taking the home-wrecker with you?"

"You mean, Sandy?"

"Uh, yeah, Mrs. Simonsen, my third-grade teacher who made you break up with Mom."

"She didn't make – oh, whatever, Alex. Things aren't as simple as 15 they appear to you. No, she isn't coming with me. We broke up a few weeks ago. That's one of the things I was calling to tell you."

"So why are you moving?"

"I need a change, Alex. I need to get away from all this." He made a sweeping gesture that took in everything around, including his 20 only son.

"Well, thanks for telling me. I guess leaving Mom and me wasn't enough of a change, huh?"

"Look, Alex, I didn't come here to fight, but you're just wrong about this. I didn't 'leave' your mother – she kicked me out. Like I 25 said, things aren't so simple. People are complicated and contrary."

"Mom kicked *you* out? I don't believe it."

"Well, I don't want to say anything bad about your mother, but she did."

"Why?" 30

"That's not important, Alex. What's important is that I'm trying to be your father, and you aren't letting me."

---

4 **sane**: not mad   8 **whole 'nother** (infml): completely different   20 **sweeping gesture** ['dʒestʃə]: movement with your arm that indicates around you
26 **contrary**: behaving in unexpected ways

"You're trying to be my father by moving out of state? Wow, thanks for the show of support."

"It's not like that, Alex. Look – do you remember when Wink died?"

5   Wink was our cat when I was five. He ran out in front of a car because I had left the front door open and he'd gotten out. My parents had hidden the truth from me for weeks. "Yeah, are you trying to tell me he really just moved to Philadelphia?"

Dad nearly smiled, and he suddenly looked a lot like my old dad, my Little League-coaching, arm-wrestling-before-bed, taking-long-walks-to-see-the-turtles-in-the-park dad. "No, I'm saying sometimes parents try to shield their kids from hard facts. Maybe one day, Mom will be willing to tell you why she told me to leave. But that's between you and her."

15   Mom's car turned the corner at the head of our block, and my dad jumped up from the snowy stoop. "Gotta go, kid. Are we friends?"

"I don't know, Dad. I'll call you. Does your phone still work?"

"My cell does."

20   He struggled a bit with his frozen hands and his ice-cold car keys, but still managed to get the door of his fast little midlife-crisis mobile open before Mom could pull up and start arguing. He ruffled my hair, which he hadn't done since maybe sixth grade, hopped in the car, and zoomed off.

25   If he had told me the truth about the divorce, then he wasn't the bad guy. So who was?

Mom walked over to me. "What was that about?"

"Philadelphia, Mom."

"Philadelphia, the city?"

---

10 **Little League** [liːg]: baseball league for children   **arm-wrestle** ['resl]: find out who is stronger by trying to press the other person's hand down onto the table
11 **turtle** (AE): reptile with a hard shell on its body   12 **shield** (v): protect
16 **stoop** (AE): space in front of the door of a house   19 **cell** (AE, infml): (here) mobile phone   21 **midlife-crisis mobile** (sl): expensive car you buy when you get older that makes you feel better about yourself   24 **zoom**: move very fast

"No, Philadelphia, the cream cheese."
Tough family.

*   *   *

The next time I went to Sol's, it was three days after Christmas, and
also the first night of Hanukkah. I hadn't prepared another special
song or anything, so I stopped and bought Sol a book about jazz his-   5
tory. He was sitting in his chair staring at a huge vase of white flowers
on his nightstand. The vase had a blue- and-white bow around it.
Sol had a transparent tube wrapped around his head and stuck right
under his nose. The tube made a constant hissing noise, so he didn't
hear me until I was right in front of him. He looked groggy, and only   10
gave me a little nod. Even that looked like a big effort.

What the heck? I decided he'd explain if he wanted to, and that
I'd pretend everything was normal.

"Sol, how are you? Happy Hanukkah."

He muttered, "Happy Hanukkah. Where's – HOO-hah – your   15
guitar?"

"I didn't bring it today, but I got you a book about jazz. It's called
Monk, and it's about this great, crazy piano player named Thelonious
Monk. Have you ever heard of him?"

The next thing Sol said sounded a lot like, "I knew him."   20

But of course it was hard to make out the exact words, and I
didn't want to make Sol talk more than he had to, so I just nodded.
"Nice flowers. Who brought them?" It had never occurred to me that
Sol might have other visitors.

"I did. Claudelle went ... to the ... store with me. On ... her day   25
off. For my ... daughter ... Judy. HOO-hah! She's a hotshot lawyer.
Very smart. Very ... busy."

"They're beautiful. I'm sure she'll love them."

"Yeah. Heh. She ... always liked ... flowers. Her mother, too –
always with the flowers. HOO-hah.   30

---

8 **tube**: long, hollow pipe through which liquids or gases can flow
18–19 **Thelonious Monk** [ðə'ləʊniəs]: US Jazz musician (1917–1982)
21 **make out**: (here) hear; understand   26 **hotshot** (sl): successful

'Sol, did you get me any flowers? Sol, let's plant … a garden. Sol, those are GORGEOUS! A little past their – HOO-hah – prime, maybe, but – nice.' "

He took a few moments to catch his breath and let go of his
5   memories, and I spoke over his gasps.

"Are you comfortable? Can I get you anything?"

"Does this, to you, look so comfortable? HOO-hah!"

"Well, I mean … what happened?"

"Nothing. I was walking … in the store with … Claudelle. Such a
10   heart, that girl has. Like gold. Anyway … I walked too far. So now
… I need … a little breathing help. That's all."

"Can they do anything to make it better?"

"Well, they're giving me …" He touched the tube around his face.
"Oxygen. And breathing treatments. And some pills, I don't know.
15   HOO-hah."

"Is it working?"

"If I'm not dead, it's working. If I die, you'll – HOO-hah – know
it wasn't maybe working so good."

I had never asked him about his health before, but now seemed
20   like as good a time as any. "They told me when I started here that
you have emphysema. How long have you had it?"

"A million years. I don't know … *boychik*. Too … long."

"How did you get it?"

"It's funny, Alex. You smoke a million, two million – HOO-hah –
25   cigarettes, and they don't … hurt you. But you take one … puff … of
number two million and one – and all of a sudden you're – HOO-
HOO-hah – in the hospital. Do you smoke?"

"No."

"Good. Don't start, or I'll have to get up and give you … a *klop* on
30   the *tuchis*."

He looked up at me, and his eyes were more tired than I'd ever
thought eyes could be. "Lesson over. Class – HOO-hah – dismissed.
Now get out of here and let … an old man … read in peace."

---

2 **past your prime**: no longer young and fresh   29–30 **klop on the tuchis**
(Yiddish): slap on the behind

I stopped at the nurses' station, where Claudelle was talking with Leonora. "She never comes. We buy her them *damn* flowers every year, but she never comes. And now her daddy's all wired up in there."

"I heard the paramedics almost had to intubate him."   5

"Forget that. They almost had to shock him, right in the middle of aisle five of Kmart. It was like he was the Blue Code Special. But he got his flowers for Judy, the Big-Shot Lawyer."

"A shame. He's really almost a sweet man, sometimes."

"You got it a little mixed up, Leo. Sometimes he's sweet and   10 sometimes he's almost a man!"

They both laughed a little, and then their voices subsided as they turned their attention to me. Claudelle spoke. "How are you today, Alex?"

"Is he going to die?"   15

"Not today, child. Not today. He's a tough old thing, don't you worry. You'll get in your hundred hours before this is all over."

This made me mad. "That's NOT why I asked."

"I'm sorry, baby. I know that. Sol will be all right in a day or two, long as he doesn't get the pneumonia again, like Mrs. Johnson last 20 spring."

"Who's Mrs. Johnson? I don't think I've seen her around."

Both women just looked at me blankly, until I realized I wasn't EVER going to see Mrs. Johnson around. I had to get out of there. I mumbled something about having to catch my bus, and headed for 25 the elevator like I was getting off a sinking ship, at least for a couple of days. Not that I had been keeping count, no matter what Claudelle had said, but I still had forty-four hours left with Mr. Lewis.

---

5 **intubate sb.** [ɪntjubeɪt]: make a cut in sb.'s throat and put in a tube to help them breathe   7 **aisle** [aɪl]: space between shelves in a supermarket   **Kmart**: chain of shops in the USA   **Blue Code Special**: special offer at Kmart marked by a blue light   12 **subside**: become weaker or quieter   20 **long as** (infml): as long as **pneumonia** [njuːˈməʊnɪə]: bad infection of the lungs   23 **blank**: (here) without understanding

December 27

Dear Judge Trent,

I am just checking in with my December update. It was a hard month, but I think I may have learned a lesson: You can't just throw somebody
5   *out of your life when they displease you. Mr. Lewis has this daughter somewhere who's a lawyer, and every year he buys her flowers for Hanukkah. He puts them on his nightstand, and then he waits and waits for the daughter to show up and get them. But she never does. Maybe he's so grouchy because his daughter doesn't love him. I'm*
10   *getting used to his grumpiness, though. He threatened today to give me a klop on the tuchis, which I looked up and learned is a smack on the butt. However, he actually said it kind of affectionately.*

I know I am halfway done with my mandated hundred hours of community service, and just a few weeks ago I was counting the days
15   *with glee. However, am I allowed to keep this job past the 100 hours if I wish to do so? It just seems that Mr. Lewis could use the company more than I could use the free time, especially since I can't drive and my family is falling apart anyway.*

Sincerely,

20   *Alex Gregory*

---

3 **check in**: (here) letting people know where you are or what you are doing
9 **grouchy**: in a bad mood   12 **affectionate** [ə'fekʃənət]: kind   13 **mandated**:
ordered by law   15 **glee**: happiness

THE BALL FALLS

On New Year's Eve day, I messed some things up. I don't know why, because I woke up in a fine mood. My plan for the day was to practice guitar for a couple of hours, and then maybe go over to see Sol after lunch. My mom had a date that night (which made two nights in a row), and Laurie was going to come over and have a little   5
loser-geek slumber party with me. When I got to the kitchen, I made a big pot of coffee and got out Mom's favorite mug, which for some reason featured my first-grade Mother's Day drawing of three Ninja Turtles under a tree with a huge machine gun. When I was little, I used to make coffee for both of my parents and serve it to them in   10
bed sometimes. They would sit up and I would climb between them with my own special "coffee" drink, which was really just nuked milk with sugar in it. There were days we sat there snuggled up, playing little tickle games and laughing for hours, or at least it seemed like that to me. And no matter how hot my feet got under   15
the covers with my footie pj's on, I never, ever wanted to be the first one to leave the bed. Interestingly enough, that honor generally fell to my dad.

Okay, enough of my sob stories. The thing was, I had the feeling my mom's date the night before hadn't been so ultra-groovy, because   20
she had marched in at maybe nine p.m. without saying a word to me and stomped off to bed. So I made her the pot of coffee for old times' sake, or to cheer her up, or possibly just because I am just a much more swell son than you may have gathered thus far. When she came down, the obvious depressedmom danger signs were there: 25
the puffy eyes, the ancient terry-cloth bathrobe, even the dreaded

---

1 **mess sth. up** (infml): do sth. very badly   8 **feature sth.**: have sth. as an important part   12–13 **nuke sth.** (infml, AE): (here) warm sth. up in a microwave 13 **snuggle up**: sit comfortably   16 **footie pj's** (infml, AE): children's pajamas with feet   19 **sob story** (infml): sad story you tell about yourself to make people feel sorry for you   20 **groovy** (infml, old-fashioned): very good   26 **terry-cloth**: soft cotton fabric used to make towels

hair curlers. This was a woman who probably needed to skip the caffeine and go right into electroshock therapy.

But since I didn't have the right equipment for home mom-zapping, I filled the mug and held it out to her. She said, "Do I look
5 that bad?"

"No, Mom. I just had the coffee all made anyway, so I figured you could put your feet up, relax, and enjoy a cup. Why would you look bad?"

"Oh, nothing. I'll be fine."
10 Not "I'm fine," I noticed. "I'll BE fine," which is different.

"Do you want to talk?"

She looked at me and snapped, "What, should I be getting my life advice from you, of all people?" Holy crap. That was basically uncalled for.
15 "Ho-kay, Mom. I'm going out now. Have a nice day and a happy new year!"

She may have been shouting, "Wait," and trying to apologize as I left the house, but with my Walkman on and blasting, I just saw a weird scary lady in a bathrobe standing on our porch with her arms
20 waving.

My next stop was the home. I was starving, so I picked up some candy and a pack of cookies from a vending machine in the lobby, and gulped most of it down in the elevator. When I walked into Sol's room, he looked a lot better. His oxygen-tube thing was gone, and
25 he was pacing back and forth. The white flowers were gone, too.

"Good afternoon, Mr. Um," he said almost cheerfully. "How are you today? I liked the book you gave me, even though Monk was a more interesting man in person."

I had to ask. "You met Thelonius Monk?"
30 "Many times. What, you think I was born here? I had a very interesting life in the old days."

"I'm sure you did."

---

4 **zap sb.** (infml): hit sb. hard, especially with an electric shock   13 **Holy crap**
(infml): swear word used to avoid saying the word 'Christ'   15 **Ho-kay** (infml): long
way of saying 'okay'   17 **apologize**: say sorry   21 **starve**: (here) be very hungry
22 **vending machine**: machine which sells sweets, cigarettes, etc.

"Anyway, how were your holidays, Alex?"

At that moment I could have tried to stop Sol from changing the subject, but I just didn't feel like risking an argument. Naturally, I got one anyway. AND I missed some info that could have changed everything.   5

"Fine." We were both big communicators today.

" 'Fine,' he says. What 'fine?' How are things? Did you get nice presents? How are your parents? How is the little wife? I hope you're taking her somewhere special tonight. Hey, maybe you could drop by here with her on your way to do your young people monkey   10
business."

Young people monkey business?

"Sol, we're just staying in tonight, at my house, if you really want to know."

"Without a chaperone? Better you should come here. We'll get   15
some cups and some drinks, and I'll keep the two of you from doing anything you might regret."

"Sol, nothing is going to happen between us. We're just friends. My mom trusts us, so why can't you?"

"Sure she trusts you. She isn't a man. She doesn't know how you   20
think. I remember how it is to be with a beautiful girl … alone … in the moonlight. But do what you think is best."

"Okay, I get the point, Sol. I'm a deranged, hormonal fiend, and no female is safe anywhere near me, even if she's a deadly martial-arts expert AND we're just friends. So, you want us to come here   25
tonight?"

"*Boychik*," he said, reaching over to grab a pack of licorice out of my hand, "I thought you'd never ask!"

Wow, I had spoken to only two people the whole day: one who bit my head off for getting her some coffee, and one who manipulated   30
me into spending my New Year's Eve at the old folks' home. The

---

10–11 **monkey business** (infml): dishonest or bad behaviour   15 **chaperone**
[ʃæpərəʊn]: (in the past) older person who is present when an unmarried couple
meet   23 **deranged**: completely mad   **fiend**: violent and cruel person
24–25 **martial arts** [mɑːʃl]: sport in which you learn to defend yourself, such as
judo or karate   27 **licorice** (AE spelling) ['lɪkərɪʃ]: black sweet with a strong flavor

thought occurred to me that maybe life would be better if I had been
born without a tongue.

Especially now that I had to tell Laurie I'd booked us an extra-
wild party night.

5 I took the bus over to Laurie's house, where she was sitting in her
kitchen, in her bathrobe, with a coffee mug. I almost turned and ran
when I saw the déjà vu scene, but then – unlike my mom – she
looked happy to see me. I had the horrible thought all of a sudden
that she really WAS very pretty. When she hugged me, it was like Sol

10 had put an evil spell on me: The Curse of Noticing Laurie. I somehow
managed to push the thought away as we got ourselves arranged at
the table, and soon I launched into a recap of the week's torments. It
turned out, though, that Laurie hadn't had the peachiest time in
New York.

15 "My dad is nuts."

"No, MY dad is nuts."

"Well, my MOM is nuts."

"So's mine."

"Oh, yeah? I bet YOUR dad isn't fleeing to another state to get

20 away from YOU, Laurie."

"I bet YOUR dad isn't accusing you of treason for wanting to
spend a few days with your mom, Alex."

"Well, that's just because my dad doesn't WANT me."

"Well, my mom doesn't want me, but I just went and spent

25 Christmas with her. And she got me a swell present." Laurie started
to cry, which is pretty rare for her.

"What?"

"She's pregnant."

"Wait, isn't she, like, too old?"

30 "Apparently, some random guy she met online didn't think so."
And the grown-ups don't think WE can be trusted together.

---

7 **déjà vu** (French) [ˌdeɪʒɑː ˈvuː]: feeling that you are once more experiencing sth.
you have experienced before   10 **curse**: (here) bad magic   12 **launch into sth.**:
begin saying sth. that will take a long time   **recap** (infml): summary   **torment**:
strong suffering   13 **peachy** (AE, infml): fine   21 **treason** [triːzn]: (here) not being
loyal to sb. by supporting their enemy

Somehow, Laurie and I wound up hugging each other for a bit too long then, until suddenly we both jumped up and away. Laurie fled to the upstairs bathroom to take a shower, and I went to the couch, watched MTV, and tried not to dwell on the scent of her hair. Holding her had felt so right, and so wrong, that I knew it was going to be a long evening. Which reminded me: I hadn't told Laurie about the groovy new plan for our intergenerational New Year's festivities. Fortunately, when she came back down and I laid the news on her, she took it well. Or at least she only hit me twice and called me "The Nerd King." After a couple of hours shopping for snacks to bring to the oldsters, Laurie and I stopped at my house to drop off her overnight bag. I didn't feel like facing my mom, but it turned out she wasn't home anyway. There was a note on the table:

Hi, Honey. I am sorry to have snapped at you. I was upset, as you may have noticed, but everything will be fine. Also, I meant to tell you that Judge Trent called me. She's so impressed with your progress that she said you don't need to see a probation officer as long as you keep writing letters to her every few weeks. I am proud of you, even if I do not always show it.

Love, Mom

PS – I will be out with my date until at least midnight tonight. If you need me, I will have my cell phone on. I am sure you and Laurie will be fine, though. Behave!

PPS – I bought bagels and Philadelphia cream cheese (ha-ha) for tomorrow morning's breakfast. I look forward to catching up with Laurie.

"See?" Laurie said. "Your mom loves you. Plus she's not trying to pump out a replacement baby."

---

7 **intergenerational**: with a mix of younger and older people   17 **probation officer**: person whose job is to help and watch people who are on probation
28 **replacement**: sth. in place of sth. else

I didn't have a reply for that, so I just kind of patted Laurie on the arm. She dropped her bag on the couch in the living room, and we walked out into the cold setting sun, our arms reloaded with chips, dips, cups, plates, candy, cheese, crackers, and even little noisemakers
5 for Sol and company.

At the home, there were pathetic little decorations up for the occasion, to supplement the lame-o Christmas tree from the week before, which was one of those artificial jobs that they create to give the illusion of a real, yet sickly, one. Why wouldn't they just make a
10 healthy-looking plastic tree? They also had a dorky electric menorah, so the Jewish patients wouldn't feel left out of the overly commercial and transparently manufactured good cheer. And, of course, now they had added the horns and streamers so the fogies could celebrate a new year of captivity.

15 I was in a weird mood, I guess. Laurie has always been one of those people who can just shrug off their sadness at will, though, so she jumped right into the party spirit. While I was gloomily filling cups with bright blue juice at the nurses' station counter, she was getting Sol up out of bed for a hug. It was incredible: Here was this
20 guy who hadn't been able to walk three steps a few days before, and within seconds, she had him hustling from room to room inviting everyone out to the nurses' station. She even gave Claudelle a CD to put into their little boom box. I don't know where she got it, but it was this *Christmas with the Rat Pack* disk, which had nothing but
25 Frank Sinatra and his buddies singing holiday tunes. Sol was almost dancing along, and the other residents were emerging from their rooms with smiles on. Laurie even got Mrs. Goldfarb out of her

---

7 **supplement sth.**: thing added to sth. to improve it   **lame-o** (sl): silly
10 **menorah** [mɪˈnɔːrə]: candlestick with seven candles used in Jewish religious
ceremonies   13 **horn**: (here) small trumpet made of paper and used at parties
streamer: party decoration made from long strips of colored paper   **fogy** (infml):
old person   14 **captivity**: when you are locked in a room or cage and aren't allowed
to leave   16 **shrug sth. off**: (here) push sth. aside (e.g. sad feelings)   17 **gloomy**:
in a sad, hopeless mood   23 **boom box**: large CD player and radio that you can
carry around   24 **Rat Pack**: popular music trio in the USA in the 1960s and 70s,
made up of Sammy Davis Junior, Dean Martin and Frank Sinatra   26 **emerge from
somewhere**: come out of somewhere

room a second time, after Sol had temporarily convinced her that she wasn't wearing pants. Within moments, everyone was munching, drinking, and shuffling feet along with the music. God knows how, but Laurie even convinced Sol and a few others to put on cone-shaped party hats that she had produced from somewhere.   5

Even I had to admit two things:

– Laurie was good at this stuff

and

– This wasn't such a painful way to spend New Year's Eve.

I was almost starting to feel rather cheerful myself, right until   10
Sol's fit.

I was chowing down on these little pretzel morsels with cheese and pepperoni in every bite, and Laurie was saying to me, "You know, when you told me your sentence, a hundred hours seemed like forever. Can you believe you're more than halfway done?"   15

I was about to tell her how I planned to keep on at the home after I finished my mandated time, but a hand on my shoulder stopped me. The hand belonged to an angry Solomon Lewis. "Wait a minute, Alex. You're not a volunteer? I'm your sentence? I'm your PUNISH-MENT?"   20

"Oh, my gosh, Sol. I always assumed you knew. I was assigned to spend a hundred hours here by the juvenile court, with the patient of my mom's choice. She picked you because she said we would be a good match."

"So now I'm a charity case, heh? I never thought I would live to   25
see the day when I would be a burden for the state to put on somebody else's back."

"It's not like that. They thought I could learn from you, so I wouldn't … um, you know … get arrested again."

---

1 **temporary**: only for a short time   4 **cone**: long shape which is round and wide on one end and whose sides come to a point at the other   12 **chow down on sth.** (infml): eat sth.   **pretzel**: hard, salty biscuit in the shape of a long stick or a loose knot   **morsel**: small piece of food   13 **pepperoni**: spicy Italian sausage 22 **juvenile**: to do with young people who are not yet treated as adults   26 **burden**: difficult or unpleasant thing you have to deal with

"What in the world did they arrest a clean-cut boy like you for anyway?"

"Well, it was nothing, really."

"Nothing? Like what kind of nothing? Jaywalking? Skipping
5 school to be with your darling, here?"

"No, I … I got drunk and tried to drive my mom's car to my dad's house. But it was no big deal. Really."

"No big deal? You didn't hit anybody?"

"No, I didn't hit anybody. Well, except a lawn gnome."

10 "A lawn gnome, you hit? So you drove up on somebody's lawn?"

"Well, yeah, but …"

"And this is the 'no big deal'? You're lucky to be alive, Alex. And you're lucky that you DIDN'T kill anyone. 'No big deal,' he says. You're even more *meshuggeh* than I thought."

15 "But …"

"Just get out of here, you little criminal. Old I might be, and sick I might be, but handouts from a crazy outlaw who doesn't even know how stupid he is, I don't need."

I was stunned. I noticed that the music had stopped, and the
20 whole roomful of people had turned to stare at me. Laurie put her hand on my arm, but I shrugged it off and walked out.

The last thing I heard was Laurie saying to Sol, "You know, that wasn't fair. He really isn't as bad as you …"

Then the elevator door closed behind me, and I was headed for
25 the lobby. It occurred to me that I was still holding a little plate of food and a Dixie cup of juice. Leave it to me to get shouted out of a New Year's party, at a nursing home no less, and make my dramatic exit, dateless, with snacks in hand. Oh, well. If you're going to look like the biggest goober on the planet, you might as well wash down
30 the lump in your throat with some nice cheese curls.

When I got home, the light on our machine was blinking with a message from Laurie's cell phone: "Come back, Alex, all is forgiven.

---

1 **clean-cut**: looking clean and tidy and behaving in a socially acceptable way
4 **jaywalking**: crossing a road where you are not allowed to 14 **meshuggeh**
(Yiddish): crazy 17 **handout**: free thing given to poor people 26 **Dixie cup**:
paper cup (brand name) 30 **lump in your throat**: feeling as if you have to cry

Stop being such a drama queen! Sol is even sorry. Aren't you, Sol?"
She must have held the phone out to him, but all I could hear was a
cough, and then a quick, "Get your little car-crashing *tuchis* back
here before I …" At that point, Laurie hung up in a hurry.

There was no way I was going back there. By the time I hiked all   5
the way to the bus, all the way back to the home, and all the way
upstairs, all the fogies would be popping out their teeth, whisking
off their wigs, and settling down for their sponge baths. It was much
better all around if I took a nice shower, changed into raggedy old
sweats, nuked some popcorn, and sat on the sofa for hours watching 10
all the people with lives wishing each other a happy new year on TV.

But after my l-o-n-g shower, the machine light was blinking a
whole bunch of times. I pushed play with that sense of dread you'd
get if you pissed off a karate master who had a key to your house.
Sure enough, the messages got progressively worse. After the third 15
one – "All right, wuss boy, I'm on my way over there, and I'm all
pumped up to jump on you and start working your head like a
speed bag" – I just hit delete eleven or twelve times, and waited for
the invasion.

Which came as soon as I curled up in an old throw blanket and   20
settled in to watch the MTV Beach Party Unplugged Cribs TRL New
Year's Rockin' Eve Bash. There was a rattling of keys, a turning of
tumblers, and a whoosh of cold air. I was afraid to look, but the
deceptively small-sounding footsteps were coming up behind me.
Then Laurie did her famous somersault couch flip, landing just   25
opposite me with her feet up on my legs. She took a long look at me
– the mop of damp, uncontrollable hair, the popcorn bucket held
protectively on my chest, and the tragic little-boy frown that had
saved me from her wrath a thousand times, minimum – and reached
into the bucket. She scrunched up so her face was inches from mine, 30

7–8 **whisk sth. off**: take sth. off quickly   8 **sponge** [spʌndʒ]: *Schwamm*
9 **raggedy** (infml): old and well-worn   15 **progressively**: increasing as time goes by
16 **wuss** (sl): coward   20 **throw blanket**: piece of cloth that you put over a sofa to
make it look better   23 **tumbler**: part of a lock   25 **somersault** [sʌməsɔːlt]:
acrobatic jump in which you flip over in the air   29 **wrath** [rɒθ]: strong anger

blew her bangs out of her eyes, and said, "You're too pathetic to kill. Hand me the remote, will ya? Before I change my mind."

We had a pretty good night being pals, as long as I didn't think about my mom being out on a date when I wasn't, or Sol evicting me
5 from the home, or the warmth of Laurie's legs on mine. We watched the New Year's countdown shows and played Monopoly at the same time, while I ignored the blatant cheating that Laurie always referred to as her "little bank errors." As payback, Laurie lent me money to buy back my properties when they went bankrupt again and again.
10 Just once it would be cool to think that Laurie wasn't nine steps ahead of me at any given moment, but hey – you can't have everything. When there were only ten minutes left until midnight, Laurie finally allowed herself to finish me off in the game, and we went to the kitchen to make egg creams. An egg cream isn't as gross as it
15 sounds. It's a New York thing: First you pour chocolate or vanilla syrup into a tall glass, then you pour in milk, then you spritz in some seltzer really fast and whip a spoon around in there. What you get is essentially chocolate (or vanilla) milk, but with an extra zap of fizzy goodness. Well, whatever you might think of the egg-cream
20 concept, the point is that Laurie and I have been making them as a late-night snack beverage since Bill Clinton was president, and we aren't ready to stop yet.

By the time we were done pouring, pouring, spritzing, stirring, sipping, and cleaning up, it was 11:59. We stood very, very close
25 together in the living room and watched the ball fall over Times Square. At the big "Happy New Year!" moment, we clinked glasses and drank. Then Laurie wiped some chocolate froth off of my lip with one finger, and we stared into each other's eyes through the whole obligatory "Auld Lang Syne" saxophone serenade. At what I
30 thought was the exactly, precisely perfect instant, I leaned toward her, suavely raised one eyebrow, and made my voice low and

---

1 **bangs** (AE): hair cut above the eyebrows   4–5 **evict sb. from sth**: tell sb. to leave sth. (e.g. a place)   27 **froth**: small bubbles on a liquid (e.g. beer)   29 **obligatory**: you have to do it   31 **suave** [swɑːv]: elegant and self-confident

gravelly: "How about a new year's kiss?" She laughed, said, "In your dreams, buddy boy," and punched me in the arm, hard.

This prompted an outbreak of pillow-related violence, which was only quelled when I missed Laurie's head with a mighty overhand clout and accidentally shattered both our egg cream glasses. By the time we tweezed the last glass shard out of the carpet and threw a towel on the floor to sop up most of the brown, gooey stain, we were both feeling tired. So we set up our sleeping bags, did all our toothbrushing-type-stuff, and lay down in the living room between the TV and the chocolate-coated rug disaster area. I was just drifting off to sleep when Laurie reached over and put her arm around me. She murmured, "You know, Sol really likes you a lot, buddy. G'night," and rolled back away from me. She fell asleep like she always does, almost instantaneously. But I was still lying there, half out of it, trying to ignore the loud tick, tick, tick of our kitchen clock and the ghost of Laurie's arm on my shoulder, when the front door opened.

I didn't open my eyes, but I didn't have to. My mom had that loud whisper people use when they're doing a really miserable job of being quiet, and she was only fifteen feet away. "Ssshhhhh!" she said, "They're asleep."

Then a man's voice answered: "I see them. What the hell is that splotch on the rug next to them, though?"

I had a question, too: What was my dad doing here with my mom at two a.m.?

---

1 **gravelly**: deep and rough (usu. of a voice)   4 **quell sth.**: stop sth. by using force
5 **clout**: hitting sth. hard   6 **tweeze sth.**: pick up very small pieces of sth. between
your finger and thumb as if with tweezers (*Pinzette*)   7 **sop sth. up**: clean away sth.
(usu. liquid) with a cloth   14 **instantaneous**: immediately   22 **splotch**: wet mark

HAPPY NEW YEAR!

Okay, I admit it: I employed the "fake sleep" trick, at least until the murmur of my parents' voices eventually blended into the strange language of dreams. The next thing I knew, it was morning, and Laurie was desperately spraying vast quantities of carpet cleaners on
5 the chocolate amoeba that had nearly swallowed the room. "Funny," I remarked. "The stain didn't look so big last night."

"Well, now it looks like one of those giant oil spills in Alaska. I keep expecting a flock of endangered herons to come staggering out from under the towel and die at my feet."

10 Hey, there's an image to drown out any ugly thoughts I might be having about my parental units.

I dove right in and helped with the cleanup by spraying even more bluish gunk all over everything (which, by the way, why IS every liquid cleaner some shade of blue-green? Just wondering.).
15 Pretty soon, the stain was mostly a lovely fluorescent greenish-brownish gray, if that's a color. And the smell was like what you'd get if you dumped a tub of toilet tank fresheners into a vat of melted Hershey's Kisses. Just then, my mom stomped down from upstairs, took one whiff, and fled back up with a hand over her mouth. I had
20 that "she'll be back" feeling, though.

---

2 **murmur** (n) ['mɜːmə]: sound of quiet talking   **blend into sth.**: mix with sth.
4 **desperate**: trying very hard and wanting to succeed very much   **vast**: very large
quantity: amount   5 **amoeba** [ə'miːbə]: very small living being that consists of only
one cell   7 **oil spill**: large amount of oil floating on water as a result of a shipping
accident   8 **flock**: group of birds   **endangered** [ɪn'deɪndʒəd]: (of animals)
belonging to a kind that may die out soon   **heron** [herən]: water bird with long legs
and a long neck   **stagger**: walk uncertainly, as if you are going to fall   10 **drown
sth. out**: (here) be stronger than sth. so you no longer notice it   11 **parental units**
(infml): (humorous) parents   12 **dive in**: start doing sth. quickly and eagerly
13 **gunk** (AE, infml): unpleasant, soft, dirty substance   17 **toilet tank freshener**:
chemical used in camping toilets to remove smells   **vat**: large container that holds
liquids   18 **Hershey's Kisses**: small chocolates sold in the USA

Boy, am I smart. About ten minutes later, while Laurie and I were feverishly brainstorming for either a solution or an excuse, Mom came down again, with a sheepish dad in tow. We stopped trying to figure out a way to smuggle the entire roomful of carpeting out of the house, and started wishing we'd smuggled OURSELVES out instead.

Since my social skills are so finely honed, I broke the ice. "Hi, Dad. Did somebody put the city of Philadelphia upstairs without my noticing?" The 'rents looked at each other, and I noticed they were – ugh! – holding hands. This was an unusual scene, to say the least.

"Well, we … that is, I … your mother … uh …"

"OK, Dad. Thanks for clarifying. Mom?"

"Can we talk about this later, Alex? Like maybe after some breakfast? After all, we have company here!"

We sure do, I thought. "All right, Mom. Let's eat."

"But wait, Alex. What's that stain on the carpet?"

I smiled like a choirboy. "Stain? Oh, you mean THAT little dot on the rug? I'll be glad to explain it to you after all the COMPANY leaves."

So we sat down to the ABC special: awkwardness, bagels, and coffee. All of which went down great with the lingering disinfectant and chocolate fumes. Laurie kicked me under the table and rolled her eyes as my parents chatted like two people who hadn't just spent twelve months and thirty thousand bucks battling each other tooth and nail through the legal system. I rubbed my shin and made faces back at her behind my coffee mug. When she got up to get more cream cheese, I caught myself checking out her legs again, and immediately made my first New Year's resolution: NO SCOPING LAURIE! And I didn't break that one for a good five minutes,

3 **sheepish**: embarrassed   **with sb. in tow**: with sb. closely behind you   7 **finely honed**: made perfect   9 **'rents** (infml): short word for parents   12 **clarify**: make sth. clear   17 **choirboy** ['kwaɪəbɔɪ]: boy who is part of a group of people that sing together, usu. in a church   20 **bagel**: bread shaped like a ring   21 **linger**: stay for a long time   22 **fumes**: strong-smelling gas   24 **buck** (AE, infml): dollar 24–25 **tooth and nail**: very hard (usu. to describe fighting)   25 **shin**: front part of the lower leg which is hard and bony   28–29 **scope sb.** (infml): look closely at sb. to see if you like them

although my parents must have been breaking their own resolutions left and right. Whatever. Laurie ate in a hurry, and didn't say anything else until it was time to say good-bye to my parents:

"Bye, Mrs. G. Bye, Mr. G. I have to go work out at the dojo.
5 Thanks for breakfast. Sorry about the rug!"

Off she went, looking chipper. Sure, she was feeling good – she was off to karate-kick things just for fun, and I wanted to karate-kick my parents, but couldn't do that OR have fun. Plus, I still had to cope with this weirdness, and the rug issue. "Hey, Mom, Dad. What's
10 going on?"

Oh, no. Dad put down his coffee mug, and pinched the bridge of his nose between his finger and thumb. Mom took a big swig of orange juice, pushed aside her glass, and nervously pulled her hair back away from her face. It had been a while since I had seen these
15 signals, but they were instantly familiar, and I knew a Big Talk was coming. It's always been exactly the same: When my grandfather got sick for the last time, when I asked my day care teacher why the classroom goldfish was floating faceup, when I did the little skateboard-roof thing – Dad pinches the nose and Mom does the
20 hair pullback. Plus, the longer and more elaborate the pinching and pullbacking are, the worse the talk is going to be.

So this time, when Dad fiddled with his nose for about half a minute until I was ready for his skin to start blistering from the friction, and Mom pulled her hair back so tight it looked like she
25 had just gotten face-lift surgery, I knew this Big Talk would be a doozy.

"Honey, do you remember yesterday morning, when I was a bit upset?"

"Uh, Mom, do you remember the *Titanic* movie, when the ship
30 hit a bit of ice?"

"Okay, fine, a lot upset. That was because your father and I had a long argument about his moving to Philadelphia. Then we agreed to

---

4 **dojo**: training place for martial arts such as karate, judo, etc.   5 **rug**: carpet
6 **chipper**: happy and cheerful   9 **cope with sth.**: deal with sth. difficult
11–12 **bridge of your nose**: top part of the nose   24 **friction**: action of one thing
rubbing against another   26 **doozy** (n, AE, infml): big event

have dinner and talk it over last night. There was this jazz trio playing in the corner of the restaurant, and they played our wedding song, and one thing led to another …"

"Stop right there, Mom. I don't need to hear any more, especially when I just ate. So you're telling me Dad paid these guys to serenade 5 you, and you took it as a sign from God that you should get back together?"

"It wasn't like that, Alex. Was it, Simon?"

"Well …"

Mom took that moment to demonstrate her unique mood- 10 switching abilities: "Wait, you PAID them to play that song? You SET ME UP?"

Oh, boy. Now things felt back to normal. "Yes, Janet, I did."

Mom took a deep breath and held it. So did Dad. I felt an instant cold sweat bursting out all over my back. Then Mom reached over 15 and squeezed Dad's hand on the table. "Thank you, Simon. That was really sweet!"

Wow, a double mood switch! I give up. Maybe things were NEVER normal in this family.

But Mom never stopped trying for normalcy, anyway: "Now, Alex, 20 about that stain …"

11–12 **set sb. up**: play a trick on sb.

ENTER THE CHA-KINGS

On January 2, which was a Tuesday, we went back to school. In homeroom, I was talking with Laurie about my problem with Sol when inspiration struck me like a ham-sized fist. Well, actually a ham-sized fist struck me like an inspiration. Or something. I got
5 punched, and inspired. Here's how it happened.

"Laurie," I was saying, "how am I going to show up at Sol's place today? What am I supposed to say?"

"I already told you he's not mad. That's just how he is – he blows off some steam once in a while."

10 "Oh, like you're the big expert on Solomon Lewis all of a sudden, O feet-washing genius."

"Don't get mad at me just because you befriended an old man under false pretenses. I'm just trying to tell you things will be okay, that's all."

15 And then came the fist, bashing into my right upper arm with three hundred pounds of semi-blubbery football player behind it. Bryan Gilson. "Hey, Lawn Boy. I missed you over the break. Why didn't you come to Jody Krasiloff's New Year's party? Oh, that's right, it's because you're a complete loser who's grounded for life."

20 He sat down on the edge of my desk while I struggled desperately against the urge to rub my arm where he'd clobbered me.

"Anyway, I couldn't help overhearing that you got your geezer friend mad at you. Since I know you'll go to jail if you blow off your probation, and since homeroom wouldn't be the same without your
25 sorry company, I'll give you some free advice."

Laurie was never much for staying quiet. "Free advice from you? You just learned to speak in sentences like, last week, and Alex needs YOUR wisdom? Anyway, he's trying to stay OUT of trouble, which

21 **urge to do sth.** (n): strong need to do sth.   **clobber sb.** (infml): hit sb. very hard   22 **overhear**: hear other people speaking without their knowledge   **geezer** [giːzə] (AE, infml): old man   25 **sorry** (adj): (here) bad, undesirable

isn't exactly your specialty. Why don't you go impress your friends by walking away AND chewing gum?"

"No, really. All you have to do, dorkwad, is make the old man feel special. You know, like, bring him a gift. The severed head of a lawn gnome, maybe?"   5

I crossed my eyes and pretended to think about it for a second. Then I really DID think about it for a second. Then I got an amazing idea, just as the bell rang for first period. I grabbed Bryan's hand and shook it profusely. "That's IT! You ARE smarter than your girlfriend told me you were last night! Thanks, Bryan. I owe you one."   10

As I ran off in triumph, Bryan and Laurie were shrugging at each other, trying to figure out why I was so excited. It was like a little pixie-bison bonding moment.

Bryan's "advice" had actually given me a great idea. This idea was amazing on about seventeen different levels: 15

1. It would impress the judge with my apparent selflessness and personal growth.
2. It would entertain and amuse dozens of oldsters.
3. It would make my mom think I might have some shred of redeemable goodness.   20
4. It was a chance to play guitar.
5. It might even shut Sol up for an hour.

Okay, so it was only amazing for five reasons. Still, they were mighty big reasons. The idea was this: I would stage a benefit jazz concert at the home, with profits going toward future cultural events there. It   25
would help people, and might even prove to Sol that he wasn't just

---

3 **dorkwad** (infml, derog.): stupid person   4 **sever sth.**: cut sth. off   6 **cross your eyes**: look with both eyes toward the nose   8 **period**: lesson   9 **profusely** [prə'fjuːsli]: very much   10 **I owe you one** (infml): thanking a person who has done you a favor, and implying you will one for them in the future   11 **shrug at sb.**: raise your shoulders while looking at sb. to show that you do not understand   13 **bond** (v): form a connection   16 **apparent**: obvious   19 **shred of sth.**: very small amount of sth.   20 **redeemable**: (here) able to be reformed or improved   24 **stage sth.**: organize sth. (concert, play, etc.)

my "punishment." It was a win-win situation all around. And I knew exactly the people I would need to make it happen.

The Cha-KINGS. These were two members of my high school jazz band. Steven was a superhuman drummer, and his eterna-
5 girlfriend Annette was a hellaciously gifted piano whiz. I called them the Cha-KINGS after the sound that happens in a sciencefiction movie when two spaceships' airlocks are slammed together by the nearly irresistible force of a magnetic tractor beam: cha-KING. That's how close Steven and Annette were. I needed the Cha-KINGS for
10 this project because of the three things they loved nearly as much as they adored each other, which were jazz, being do-gooders, and their constant quest to create the perfect benefit concert.

Why were they so into benefit concerts? Well, the obvious reason was that the concerts they put on together always involved playing
15 jazz and do-gooding. But there was more to it: Three years ago, they had fallen in love while planning and rehearsing a benefit concert to pay the hospital bills for Steven's little brother, Jeffrey, who had cancer. Even though Annette never got to play a single note at the concert, and Steven had to run out during intermission to take
20 Jeffrey to the hospital, the gig was a huge success. The bills got paid, Jeffrey became the unofficial town mascot, a position he holds to this day, and of course Steven and Annette got each other.

Really, it's so sweet I could hurl.

The Cha-KINGS are A students, of course. They are the most
25 beloved couple ever to walk the halls of a high school without wearing athletic uniforms. They are jaw-droppingly good musicians.

---

4 **superhuman**: with more powers than normal people   **eterna-** (Lat.): for ever
5 **hellacious** (AE): (here) extremely good   **whiz**: gifted person   7 **airlock**:
Luftschleuse 8 **tractor beam**: magnetic force (in science fiction)   11 **adore sb.**:
love sb. very much   **do-gooder** (infml, derog.): person who likes to help others all
the time   12 **quest** (fml): search   18 **cancer**: very serious disease causing cells to
grow unnaturally   19 **intermission**: longer pause in a concert, play, etc.   20 **gig**:
performance by musicians   21 **mascot**: person or animal that is believed to bring
luck and that represents a team, city, etc.   23 **hurl** (AE, sl): (here) *erbrechen*
24 **A student**: student who always gets the best grades   25 **beloved**: loved very
much   26 **jaw-droppingly** (infml): amazingly

And they are very, very nice. Kind to animals. Honor Society officers. Patron saints of the Key Club. Very, very different from the mediocre guitarist, the car-thieving lawn-gnome mangler, the convicted delinquent who would now be attempting to enlist their aid.

Good thing I'm so charming.   5

Oh, who was I kidding? These people LIVED for benefit concerts. If Steven's mom were choking on a chicken bone, he would start the Heimlich maneuver while Annette started designing the poster for "Bone Aid." They would jump on this opportunity. It was in the bag.

Right?   10

I thought about my approach all day. We all had jazz band practice right after school, and then I would be heading straight for the home. So if I did this right, I would have the news of the concert ready as ammunition for when I had to face Sol. I decided to leave my last class early, because Steven and Annette had an independent-   15
study music class at the end of the day. That's how amazing these people's lives were: They had convinced an entire high school to give them a special daily period built for two. As for me, I had to practically promise my firstborn child to my precalc teacher just so I could miss the last eight minutes of his valuable instructional droning.   20

So there I was, on the long hallway approaching the band room. As I got closer I could hear the tinkling of Annette's piano, along with something else: like a *clink, clink* sound, but with different pitches, and beautiful. I peeked in the little square window of the

1 **Honor Society** (AE): organization with only the best students as members
2 **patron saint of sth.** ['peɪtrən seɪnt]: holy person in the Christian faith responsible
for sth.   **Key Club** (AE): organization of high school students who do community
service   **mediocre** [ˌmiːdiˈəʊkə]: not very good   3 **mangle sth.**: damage sth. badly
by crushing it   **convicted**: found guilty of a crime by a court   4 **delinquent**:
person who has broken the law   5 **charming**: with a pleasant personality
8 **Heimlich maneuver** ['haɪmlɪk məˌnuvər]: treatment when a person is choking on
a piece of food (the helper stands behind the person and puts pressure on their
stomach very suddenly)   9 **in the bag** (infml): certain to be achieved   12 **head for
sth.**: go towards sth.   14 **ammunition**: (here) information that can be used in an
argument   15–16 **independent-study**: course in which students can work on a
topic of their choice   20 **instructional**: educational   **droning**: low sound that
lasts long and always stays at the same level   24 **pitch**: how high or low a musical
note is

door, and saw Annette playing chords, while this complicated single-note line of clinks was floating over the top. It hit me that I knew the melody: "Sunrise, Sunset." Well, that was fitting. Steven was playing the marimba, which is like a big xylophone thing with wooden bars
5 instead of the metal kind. I hadn't even known he played anything other than drums – I hadn't even known our school had a marimba – but I guess that's why he and Annette were music gods while I was sitting on my *tuchis* in math class. I poked my head in the door, feeling a bit weird about breaking in on the musical dance they had
10 going, especially when Steven suddenly started embellishing the melody with all sorts of fast little grace notes that I wouldn't have been able to pull off on the guitar, much less on a second instrument.

Annette was talking and playing at the same time, just in case her powers hadn't already been awesome enough. "Okay, Steven, that
15 sounds great for the melody. Now, do you think you can add in the harmony line?"

I was thinking, *Duh. How can he play extra harmony notes when he only has two mallets?* But then he did this amazing thing: He picked up an extra mallet for each hand, without even missing a beat, and
20 kind of spread the mallets between different fingers, so now it was like he was holding upside-down chopsticks or something. And sure enough, he started playing the melody and a harmony part at the same time. Finally, just when the insane skill level of these people was nearly too depressing to contemplate, he reached behind him to
25 a xylophone that was set up there, and finished his solo with one hand jamming away on each instrument.

---

4 **xylophone** [ˈzaɪləfəʊn]: musical instrument with a row of wooden or metal bars that are hit by special sticks   8 **poke sth. in somewhere**: stick sth. in somewhere quickly   10–11 **embellish sth. with sth.**: make sth. more beautiful by adding sth.
11 **grace note**: note that is added to another note in a piece of music as decoration
14 **awesome** (AE, infml): very good   16 **harmony line**: part of a piece of music added to the melody to make it sound more pleasant   17 **Duh** [dʌ] (AE, infml): sound made to express that you think sth. is stupid or impossible   19 **mallet**: (here) sticks with a soft ball on the end used to play the xylophone, etc.   **beat**: regular sequence of stresses that make up the backbone of the rhythm in a piece of music   21 **chopsticks**: wooden sticks used to eat with in some Asian countries
26 **jam** (v): (here) play music in an informal way which involves improvising

Annette and Steven gave each other a little grin at the last note of the solo, and then – in perfect unison – burst into the little coda that ends the *Fiddler on the Roof* medley. When they stopped, I applauded. Annette turned to Steven and said, "Show-off!"

"Wait, he wasn't showing off THAT much. I kept waiting for him   5
to light his mallets on fire and start juggling them during the solo, or play bass drum with his foot or something." They both just kind of stared at me like they had caught me beating a baby seal or something. I had forgotten that the Cha-KINGS are SERIOUS ABOUT MUSIC. "Oh, well. Maybe next time." More staring. "Hi, guys. You're   10
probably wondering why I'm here. I mean, why I'm here now, instead of after the bell rings. I mean, instead of in math. Because that's what I have now. Math. Precalc. Uh …" Still more staring.

"Would the two of you like to help some elderly people in need?"
Their eyes lit up. For a babbling idiot, I'm a pretty good salesman.   15

---

2 **in unison** ['juːnɪsn]: (in music) two or more musicians playing the same melody at the same pitch   **coda**: final part of a piece of music   3 **applaud**: clap your hands at the end of a performance to show you liked it   4 **show-off** (infml, derog.): person who wants to impress others by showing how good they are   6 **juggle**: throw several objects into the air and catch and throw them again quickly   8 **seal**: *Seehund*   14 **elderly**: polite word for 'old'   15 **babble**: talk quickly and in a silly way

HOME AGAIN

I walked into Sol's room that evening with good news and sweaty palms. I know Laurie had said Sol wasn't mad at me, but she was only ALMOST always right. He wasn't around, so I sat down in the chair and thought about the afternoon. Steven and Annette had
5 surprised me a little bit; they didn't think we could pull off a successful benefit concert without months of lead time, so we had agreed on just practicing for a few weeks and doing an informal, free concert at the home. They had also gotten me to commit to practicing every Monday and Wednesday afternoon until 4:30, which they
10 apparently did anyway just for fun like the mutants they were. So now I REALLY had no life, even if having no life with two other people and my guitar was better than having no life alone in my house.

Although it occurred to me that HAVING a life would beat both
15 of my options.

Just when I might have started to get depressed about the sorry state of my social status, I heard a resonant "HOO-hah!" from the elevator area. A few seconds later, Sol came in and the fun began.

"Hey, look! It's Mr. Um, my compulsory volunteer. Happy new
20 year. Did you have a nice New Year's Eve after you abandoned me to the lonely fate of the forgotten and the elderly?"

"Listen, Sol, I'm sorry I ran out, and I'm sorry I never explained why I was here. But I thought you KNEW."

"Alex, Alex. You'll learn one day that real apologies don't come
25 with a BUT in the middle. In the meantime, thank you. Are you going to maybe play for me today?"

"No, but I've got big news. In a few weeks, I'm putting on a jazz concert here, for everyone who wants to come."

6 **lead time**: (here) time to prepare   8 **commit to doing sth.**: promise very seriously that you will do sth.   10 **mutant** [mjuː'tənt]: (here) people with superhuman powers   17 **resonant**: loud and clear   19 **compulsory**: that must be done because of a rule   20 **abandon sb.**: leave sb.   21 **fate**: things that will happen to you

"YOU'RE putting on a concert? With what musicians?"

"Well, there are these two kids at my school who are like prodigies or something. There's a drummer named Steven and a piano player named Annette. And I'll play guitar. I think it will be great."

"Great, I don't know about. But it should be more entertaining   5
than sitting around waiting for my breathing treatment, and wondering whether anybody *pished* in the hydrotherapy pool."

"Wow, thanks for your enthusiasm."

Sol is either totally immune to sarcasm, or so good at counter-sarcasm that I can never even tell whether he's making fun of me.   10
"Don't mention it, *boychik*. But I hope you know how much work it is putting on a show."

"What do you mean? I've played in shows before. We'll practice, we'll show up, and we'll play, right?"

"Well, maybe. If you have the room reserved. And if you have   15
permission to get your event put on the schedule. And if the cheap bastards who run this place are willing to pay all the overtime for the orderlies to get us all down there and back up. AND if you have all the power you need, and microphones, and extension cords, speakers, lights ..."   20

Perhaps it would have been a good idea to ask how he knew so much about this stuff. But I had already used up my good idea for the day. "I get the point, Sol. Don't worry, I'll get it all done. Trust me."

"Heh. 'Trust me,' he says. My grandmother always used to tell   25
me, '*Nisht azoi gich macht zich vi es tracht zich.*'"

"And that would mean ... ?"

"Easier said than done, *boychik*. Easier said than done."

---

2 **prodigy** ['prɒdədʒi]: young person who is extremely good at something   7 **pish** (Yiddish, infml): urinate   8 **enthusiasm**: feeling of strong interest   9 **immune to sth.**: (here) not affected by sth.   **sarcasm**: saying the opposite of what you mean to be funny or cruel   9–10 **counter-sth.**: reacting to or opposing sth.

16 **permission**: officially allowing sth.   **schedule** ['ʃedjuːl]: list of planned activities   **cheap** (AE): not willing to spend money   17 **overtime**: time you spend working in addition to your normal hours   19 **power**: (here) electricity **extension cord**: electrical wire that you use to make your wire longer

"Uh, okay. Sol, there's another thing I wanted to talk about today. I'm really not a criminal or anything. The only reason I got in trouble was because, well, my parents are divorced, and my mom was going out on a date, so I took my mom's car and …"

"Wait a minute. What about the drinking?"

"Okay, I was drinking. But …"

"You see, Alex, again with the 'but.' But, but, but. Always with the but. A criminal, you're not. You might even be a nice boy. But you did something wrong, and you got caught. That's all I need to know. Everything else is just excuses."

"But …"

"See?"

"Aaarrrggghhh! You're so frustrating!"

"I know. Thank God I'm also handsome, or who knows how I would have gotten along in the world?"

January 3

Dear Judge Trent,

I am pleased to report a new breakthrough in my community service work. Much as I enjoy serving Mr. Lewis, I have come to realize that I could do even more if I set my mind to it. In light of this, I have decided to arrange and perform a concert of Mr. Lewis's beloved jazz music for the entire resident population at the home. I feel that this will provide an enjoyable cultural experience for the community members there, and also give Mr. Lewis something to look forward to as he recovers from some recent health difficulties he has experienced.

I told Mr. Lewis of my plan the other day, and he appeared enthusiastic. In just one visit, he wished me a happy new year, told me I was a nice boy, AND said the concert could be, and I quote, "entertaining." Yes, I suppose you could say we are really bonding now.

18 **breakthrough**: important event in a particular development

Thank you for a wonderful growth opportunity. Sincerely,

Alex Gregory

PS – There are only forty-two hours remaining in my sentence. Have you considered my earlier request to extend my time at the home? I really think Sol would miss me if I stopped visiting him.   5

4 **request**: polite question

AM I A GREAT MUSICIAN, OR WHAT?

My first practice session with Steven and Annette was like being dragged around by a fast horse.

Adding to my pleasure was the fact that Laurie was going to show up at some point to watch us. Because, let's face it, if there was a
5 possibility that I might be humiliated completely, Laurie wanted to be in the front row.

While we got set up with our instruments, I told Steven and Annette what I wanted us to play, basically a bunch of the easiest songs we already did in jazz band. Between the time crunch and the
10 fact that both Steven and Annette were so much better than I was, I figured simple was good. Both of them agreed that the list would work, so we were ready to go. They looked at me. Annette said, "Hey, Alex, call the first tune."

"Uh, how about 'Mercy, Mercy, Mercy'?"

15 They both took out the chart and put it on their music stands. Then they started giving me that "you are an idiot" look – Sol had once referred to it as "the fish eye" – again. Steven asked me, in the same voice that kindergarten teachers use with their slowest pupils, "Aren't you going to count it off?"

20 It's weird being in charge. "Sure. One – two – three – four." We started playing, but I knew right away something was wrong. Annette stopped.

"That's too fast, Alex. This song is supposed to have a groove."

Oh, excuse me, Hipster Girl. "Sorry. One – two – three – four."

25 Annette was right. The new tempo was better. Steven had this whole laid-back backbeat going on; Annette was doing a cool

---

9 **crunch** (AE): problematic situation   13 **call a tune**: decide which piece of music to play   14 **mercy**: not punish sb. you have the right to punish   19 **count sth. off**: count before playing sth. to set the tempo (in music)   20 **in charge**: in the position of responsibility   23 **groove** (infml): relaxed rhythm in popular music   26 **laid-back**: relaxed   **backbeat**: rhythm with stresses in unusual places

bass line with her left hand, and chording with her right. I had the
melody, and thought I was actually doing a good job with it. Then
we got to the solo section, and all hell broke loose. First Annette
soloed while I just played the chords, which should have been easy
enough. But then she started playing these funky accents all over the   5
place, and somehow I lost the beat. It was like when you're trying to
remember a number and your friend purposely yells out random
sequences of digits to mess you up.

Well, Annette messed me up. When she realized I was totally
lost, she glanced over and said, "eighteen-two-three-four, nineteen-   10
two-three-four," so I'd know what measure we were up to. Five bars
later, it was Steven's turn to make me look like a goon. All of a
sudden, Annette was playing the chords again, so I switched over to
the melody. But just as I was attempting to get my feel back, Steven
started doing all these weird odd-time rolls on the toms, with quick   15
little offbeat accents on the cymbals. I almost counted my way
through the chaos by concentrating on the steady boom-boom of the
bass drum, until he started messing around with that, too.

It was hopeless. I was lost in a vast, storm-tossed sea of shifting
rhythmic complexities. Of course, at my instant of deepest confusion,   20
Laurie walked in. So she got to see Steven whisper to me cuttingly,
"Psst! DROP OUT!" I stopped playing, and Steven and Annette
continued, playfully turning the rest of the song into a drum-and-
piano conversation. He would play a rhythm, she would play it back
at him. She would do a tinkling little run on the high notes, he   25
would somehow echo it instantly on the bells of his cymbals. He
would go nuts with his bass drum, she would suddenly fire back a

---

1 **bass line** [beɪs]: series of very low notes added to a melody   **chord** (v): play
chords   3 **solo** (v): play or sing alone in a piece of music   5 **funky**: with a strong
rhythm that is easy to dance to (in music)   8 **digit**: (here) number between
0 and 9   11 **measure**: (here) *Takt*   12 **goon** (infml, old-fashioned): stupid person
15 **odd-time**: (in music) stressed in unusual positions   **roll**: (here) long period of
very fast drum beats   **tom**: short for 'tom-tom': small drum usually beaten with the
hands   16 **offbeat accent**: stress on the beat that is usually unstressed   **cymbal**:
musical metal instrument shaped like a flat plate that makes a sound when hit
19 **storm-tossed**: very stormy   21 **cuttingly**: unkindly   25 **tinkle**: make a light,
ringing sound

flurry of wacky low notes. I was just sitting there, cradling my guitar in my lap. Laurie was shaking her head at the scene. And then, suddenly, Steven and Annette were playing the main theme of the song in perfect unison, and the song ended with a perfect fade-out.

5 Laurie applauded, I glared. Everyone's eyes were on me. I had to say something.

"Well, that one shows promise. What's next?"

"You're kidding, right? We need to do that one again from the top. Right, Steven?"

10 "Yeah. But maybe we should play simpler this time, until …"

"Until what? Until I develop mental telepathy like you guys have?"

"No, just until you learn the music. Are you always this touchy?"

Laurie had to pipe up. "Why, yes, Steven, he is."

15 So we took it from the top. Again and again. Until I was practically begging for some "Mercy, Mercy, Mercy" myself. But we did get to the point where I could play through the song without completely self-destructing, which was a plus. We ran through a couple of other songs, too, and I managed to fool myself into believing that I was

20 really holding my own. At the end of the rehearsal, Annette gave me a list of things she thought I should focus on while practicing at home. I was thinking, *Wow, and I thought Laurie was bossy. How does Steven stand it?* But they seemed so happy together, and I had the dating record of a leper, so maybe I was missing something.

25 On the walk home, I kept waiting for Laurie to bust on me about my performance, but she was in a really contemplative mood. Every once in a while this happened, like the time she made me camp out in her backyard when we were nine and we made up stories about the stars until we both fell asleep. Or once at the beach, when she

30 started wondering whether there were two other kids in Europe or

---

1 **flurry**: moment of very busy activity   **wacky** (infml): slightly crazy   **cradle sth.**: hold sth. gently   4 **fade-out**: music becoming quieter and quieter until it is no longer heard   5 **glare**: stare angrily   11 **mental**: of the mind   **telepathy**: communication via thoughts alone   13 **touchy**: easily upset   14 **pipe up**: speak suddenly   18 **self-destruct**: destroy oneself   **plus**: (here) one good thing   24 **leper** [lepə]: *Leprakranker*   26 **contemplative**: thinking deeply

Africa watching these same waves rolling away from their beach. Tonight's food for thought was whether it was possible to be happily married.

"Alex, do you think your parents are going to stay together this time?"   5

"I don't know, why?"

"Well, I was just thinking about it. I mean, won't the same stuff that drove them apart the first time just drive them apart again?"

"It depends, I guess. I'm not even sure what the problem was in the first place – but maybe they're different now. Don't you think   10 people can change for the better if they want to?"

"I'm not sure. My mom was a miserable wife and mother for us, but now she's trying again with a new husband. So SHE must think she's changed."

"Unless she just thinks it was all your dad's fault, and she'll be the   15 perfect mate for your stepdad."

"You know, Alex, she probably IS the perfect mate for my stepdad – they're both idiots!" She got quiet for a minute, and then blew the hair out of her eyes. "Men and women CAN be happy together, though, right? I mean, somehow, somewhere?"   20

"Sure, Laur. Look at Steven and Annette. I think she orders him around so much, she should have given him a tip at the end of the rehearsal, but he must love something about her."

"Alex, can I ask you something?"

"Just did."   25

"Ha-ha. Do you think Annette is pretty?"

I wanted to shout, "You're prettier!" But you never know how Laurie is going to respond to a statement like that, and there's always that "sudden use of karate" problem she tends to have. So I just said, "Yeah, I guess so. I mean, in a band-geek kind of way. Why?"   30

"I dunno. Steven just looks at her like she hung the moon or something. I think it would be great if a guy looked at me that way. I

---

12 **miserable**: (here) very bad   16 **mate** (AE): (here) partner   **stepdad** (infml): your mother's husband who is not your biological father   30 **geek**: person who is unpopular and unfashionable

could see staying together for life with somebody who cared about me that much."

"I care about you that much." Oops, dang! Did I say that out loud?

5   "Yeah, but I mean a real guy."

I must have had some facial reaction to that one, because Laurie backtracked. "I mean, you're a real guy, and you're good-looking and nice to me and funny and … umm … I dunno, great. But you're my ALEX. You know?"

10   "Yeah, I suppose so." But I was a little hurt anyway. "You know who I think is REALLY hot? That girl Stephanie Simon, from homeroom."

"The snotty cheerleader? For real?"

"Oh, yes. Absolutely for real."

15   "You don't think she's a little – I don't know – trashy with the tight clothes and everything?"

"Sure, but she has other good points, too."

"Chuckle, chuckle. And don't you think her face is a little odd-looking?"

20   "Stephanie Simon has a face? I don't think I ever noticed that before. Huh, who knew?"

At that point, I knew the chop was coming. But I couldn't stop it. That's why Laurie had a black belt and I just had lots of bruises. But when Laurie hit me this time, it felt extra-hard, even for her.

25   "OOWWW!"

"Oh, it hurts when I do that? Huh, who knew?" We were in front of Laurie's house at that point, so she just flounced away up her driveway, leaving me to wonder how we had gone from a philosophical discussion to me getting pounded on in just a few short

30   blocks. I watched her until she got inside. Just before she shut the door, she stuck out her tongue at me. Which is weird, because whatever had just happened, I was pretty certain she had started it.

---

7 **backtrack**: change what you said before because you didn't mean it   13 **snotty** (infml): rude (esp. because you think you are better others)   15 **trashy** (infml): (here) showing bad taste   22 **chop**: hit with the side of your hand, as in karate
27 **flounce**: walk somewhere quickly, showing you are angry

January 26

Dear Judge Trent,

It is with the greatest pleasure that I humbly extend my invitation for you to attend the first-ever Egbert P. Johnson Memorial Home for the Aged Winter Jazz Thingie, an event that will have a fancier title as 5 *soon as I think of one. This will be a spectacular concert, featuring me on guitar, and precocious jazz geniuses Steven Alper and Annette Watson on drums and piano, respectively. The festivities will begin promptly at six p.m. Eastern Standard Time on February 7, at the recreation hall on the first floor of the home.* 10

I would relish the opportunity to demonstrate to you the sincerity and strength of my newfound enthusiasm for assisting the elderly, as well as my organizational and musical skills.

If it is not too much trouble, please let me know as soon as possible whether you will be attending, so that I may reserve you a seat of 15 *honor in the front between my mother, with whom you are acquainted, and my good friend, Mr. Solomon Lewis.*

Thank you. Yours truly,

Alex Gregory

---

7 **precocious** [prɪˈkəʊʃəs]: with special skills at an early age   8 **respectively**: in the same order as the things mentioned before   11 **relish sth.**: enjoy sth. very much **sincerity** [sɪnˈserəti]: really meaning what you say   15–16 **seat of honor**: seat where the most important guest is seated

January 30

Dear Alex,

Your concert sounds like a wonderful event, as well as a marvelous learning experience for all involved. However, I am afraid I have to decline your invitation to attend, due to some unfinished private business of my own.

I look forward to hearing of your great success in this worthy endeavor.

Sincerely,

Judge J. Trent

5 **decline sth.**: not accept sth.   7 **endeavor** [ɪnˈdevə]: attempt to do sth. difficult

A NIGHT FOR SURPRISES

The month of January was a mind-numbing slog through hell. I had practice with the Cha-KINGS two days a week and visits with Sol on the in-between days. On the weekends,even if I hadn't been grounded, I would have had to ground myself to study for my midterms, which were the last week of the month. My parents were now 5
officially "dating" each other, which was odd and icky, so I just tried to completely ignore it, although at least my dad seemed to have forgotten about moving to Philadelphia for the time being. Oh, and to top it all off, things were awkward and strange with Laurie. I really wanted my old pal, Laurie, back, so we could laugh and make egg 10
creams, get kicked out of the mall restaurants together, and just generally hang. But instead I had this weird new Laurie, who smiled less, battered me more, and still somehow made me think of her constantly. I was tired all the time, and my dreams were a terrifying jumble of random, out-of-tune guitar noises, massive precalc prob- 15
lems, scrambled American history factoids, and images of my parents and Laurie; Sol and Laurie; Annette, Steven, and Laurie.

With some extra Laurie thrown in for good luck.

Somehow, I made it through the month, passed my midterms, and staggered into my last practice before the concert. I even 20
remembered my guitar and sheet music, which I thought was a nice touch. The Cha-KINGS were all set up, but had an odd, almost guilty expression on their usually eager faces. Annette dropped the bomb: "Alex, first of all, we want to thank you very much for the opportunity you have offered us to play at the home tomorrow. It's 25
always nice to be given a chance to help people, and you know we both love playing music. But …" She stopped talking and

---

1 **mind-numbing slog**: very boring period of hard work   4 **midterms** (AE): exams
in the middle of the school year   6 **icky** (infml): unpleasant   12 **hang** (infml):
short for 'hang out'   13 **batter sb.**: hit sb. hard again and again   15 **jumble**: things
that are mixed up untidily   **random**: without plan or system   **out of tune**: not
hitting the notes correctly (in music)   16 **scramble sth.**: mix sth. around   **factoid**
(infml): small piece of information

straightened out her very preppy band-geek skirt. It was hard to believe, but Annette seemed, well, nervous.

"Okay, but?"

"Uh … we don't think you're really ready to play with us tomor-
5 row. Steven knows his parts cold, and I certainly have a handle on what I'm doing, but your playing is still not really where it should be."

"I'm doing okay. We'll get through the concert. Listen, just last Tuesday, you said my solo on the Fiddler medley was 'nice,' and I
10 haven't gotten lost and had to drop out of anything for at least a week."

Steven took his potshot at the rapidly deflating target formerly known as my ego. "Alex, you're doing OKAY. But we want better than just OKAY. We want GREAT. We want EXCELLENT. And even
15 though you've been trying much harder than I'd thought you could, you're just … not … quite … there. I'm sorry."

"Wait a minute. Annette, Steven, listen to me. All of those people at the home, they're depending on us. They've been looking forward to this for weeks. They don't have much going on in their lives, and
20 they need a little inspiration. Maybe we could bring a smile to their faces. Who knows? Maybe our little concert could even help some-body to … hey, wait. Why are you laughing?"

Laurie popped up from behind the piano, and growled, "Gotcha!" Actually, it was a pretty respectable imitation of Sol, although I was
25 NOT pleased that Laurie had added this newest weapon to her arsenal of Alex-torture methods. "Wow, Alex, you sounded like a guy who *cares* for a moment there. It scared me."

Steven and Annette were cracking up now. I had always thought the Cha-KINGS were stiff and dull, but I guess you can just add that
30 to my long list of misjudgments. "I DO care!" And I did. I mean,

---

1 **preppy** (AE, infml): resembling a pupil at an expensive private school   5 **know sth. cold** (infml): know sth. extremely well   5–6 **have a handle on sth.** (infml): understand sth. very well   12 **take a potshot at sth. or sb.** (infml): criticise sb. or sth.   **deflate**: (here) become smaller   26 **arsenal**: collection of weapons **torture**: act of causing great pain   28 **crack up** (infml): laugh   29 **dull**: boring 30 **misjudgement**: incorrect opinion

Laurie had a point. I used to not care. And Sol still bugged me, and irritated me, and even got me furious pretty much every time. But I wanted this concert to go right.

Annette said, "We know, Alex. Just because we're the Cha-KINGS doesn't mean we can't tell when a person is serious about a project. 5 Don't worry, we're going to play the job. How could we miss it? Laurie told us your friend Sol is the most entertaining man on earth."

Wait just one cotton-pickin' minute! They knew I called them the Cha-KINGS? I was going to KILL Laurie. Right until she took the surprise cake out from behind her back. 10

"Congratulations, Alex. You're really going to pull this thing off. And it will be an event to remember." Laurie was right, too, although not quite in any way we could have imagined. The concert was a success in all the ways you'd want. The stage got set up. The orderlies transported everyone to the right place at the right time. The oldsters 15 loved the music. Steven and Annette got a big kick out of playing. My parents sat together in the front row with Laurie and Sol, and didn't make any kind of fighting scene whatsoever. And I got through the whole first half of the program without any major embarrassments.

I admit, I was a little tense at the start of the show. The big 20 manager lady of the home said a few words about how wonderful it was to see young people being active in the community, blah blah blah. Then she handed the microphone to me. I had been so focused on the musical part that it never crossed my mind that I'd have to speak in public, too. I looked at my mom and dad, who were leaning 25 forward a bit, waiting to hear my brilliant words. I looked at Sol, who was coughing hard into a napkin, totally oblivious to the onstage festivities. I looked at Laurie, who was crossing her eyes and sticking her tongue out at me. I took a breath.

"Uh, ladies and gentlemen, thank you for coming today. I mean, 30 not coming exactly, since most of you live here, but ... well, you know what I mean. Anyway, I'm Alex, and the drummer is Steven. Annette over there is playing piano. Well, she isn't playing piano

---

1 **bug sb.** (infml): annoy sb.   2 **irritate sb.**: make sb. angry   **furious** ['fjʊəriəs]: very angry   8 **cotton-pickin'** (AE, infml, old-fashioned): used to express surprise and anger   27 **oblivious to sth.**: not noticing sth.

right NOW, but she will be once I shut up. Okay, here's a song called 'Mercy, Mercy, Mercy.' "

    I'm man enough to face the fact that my little blurb wasn't going to win me any speaker-of-the- year awards, but at least I hadn't

5 tripped and fallen off the stage, crushing and killing three elderly jazz fans. Whatever. It was time to play and we did. I could have been looser and more relaxed, but I didn't make any glaring errors. Plus, the Cha-KINGS were so devastatingly skilled that I could probably have been reading my sheet music upside down, playing in

10 the wrong key, and setting my guitar on fire while juggling five enraged cats without anyone particularly noticing. I just basically stayed out of their way, played chords when it was chord time, played melodies when it was my turn to do that, and kept my solos simple. Steven was a subtle tornado. His arms barely even moved,

15 but somehow he played these super-quick fills that always stopped EXACTLY on time. His bass drum danced through the tunes, twining into Annette's bass notes and propelling all of us along with a gliding feel I had never quite heard him achieve before. And Annette. Holy cow! I had once heard Steven say he thought she was most beautiful

20 when she played, and at the time, I hadn't seen it. But she really was striking to watch now. Her fingers had that same light, darting thing going on that Steven's hands did, and her face was totally serene – like she had been born to do this, just exactly this, totally and only this. And then once in a while, when she and Steven did one of their

25 mental- telepathy accent runs together, she locked eyes with him in a way that almost made me blush. But instead of blushing, I found myself turning away from Annette to gaze at Laurie.

---

3 **blurb**: (here) short speech   7 **glaring** (adj): very bad and easily noticed
8 **devastatingly**: (here) extremely   11 **enraged**: very angry   14 **subtle**: only
noticeable when you look very closely   15 **fill**: passage of music that fills in a gap in
the melody   16–17 **twine into sth.**: wind around and mix with sth.   17 **propel
sb. along**: make sb. move along with you   **glide**: move easily   18–19 **Holy cow!**
(infml): expression of surprise   21 **dart**: move very quickly   22 **serene** [sə'riːn]:
peaceful and calm   25 **run**: series of musical notes that quickly move up or down
the scale (*Tonleiter*)   **lock eyes with sb.**: look at sb. who is looking at you
27 **gaze at sb.**: look at sb. for a long time

Okay, I'm making it sound dreamier than it was. For one thing, I was sweating the whole time, sweating like a pig at the International Bacon Festival. For another, I dropped my pick a couple of times, and my music fell off the stand once – which was the one time I was totally sure Sol was watching, because I could hear him clearing his throat like he was covering up one of his little barking laughs as I was frantically reaching down for the pages I'd dropped. And, of course, since it was the home, I kept being conscious of a nearly constant stream of coughing emanating from the audience whenever we got to a quiet part.

But I was feeling pretty good when we walked offstage for intermission after my witty announcement of "We're going to … uh … take a break now and then … um … play some more if you're still here." Laurie told me how great she thought it was, the manager gave me a thumbs-up, and my parents smiled and started to walk over to me. But Sol grabbed my arm first. "Alex, I need you to do something for me."

"I'm kind of busy right now, Sol. And I have to play again in a few minutes. Are you having a good time?"

"Sure, sure. You're magnificent, Alex. But can you run up to my room and get my other eyeglasses?"

"What's wrong with the ones you're wearing?"

"They chafe me and I can't see right. If the night nurse hadn't been such a *schmegegge* and moved everything around in my room last night, this wouldn't have happened. Look, would you just go?"

By now, I felt like everyone in America was staring at me, the mean kid who wouldn't get an old man a pair of glasses.

"Fine. Where should I look for them?"

"If I knew where to find them, I would have worn them in the first place. I don't know, they're the only pair of glasses in my room. How hard can it be for a talented young guy like yourself?"

---

3 **pick** (n): small piece of plastic or metal used to hit the strings of a guitar
7 **frantically** (AE, infml): (here) with stress   9 **emanate from sth.**: come out of sth.
23 **chafe sb.**: make sb.'s skin sore by rubbing it   24 **schmegegge** (Yiddish): person who upsets you

I looked around for Steven and Annette to tell them where I was going, and that I'd be right back, but they must have run out to the bathroom or something. Laurie saw, and said, "Don't worry, Alex. I'll tell the Cha-KINGS where you went."

5 I turned to go, just as my clueless father asked Laurie, "What's a Cha-KING?"

Sol's floor was eerily deserted, because everybody was downstairs. It kind of felt like I was in one of those dreams where you show up at your school, and there's nobody in the halls. So it gets darker and 10 darker, and you try to run out, screaming. But it's too late, because a hand reaches out and ...

Well, anyway, I started to get a little creeped out. In the room, I didn't see anything in the open that looked remotely similar to eyewear. I quickly opened each drawer of Sol's dresser, but no dice 15 there either. By this point, I kept waiting for the inevitable masked killer to grab me, which added to the intensity of my search. I got down to the bottom drawer, which contained nothing but billowing mounds of Sol's underwear – boxers, by the way. I knew the glasses might be beneath the piles in there, but actually moving the boxers 20 was a horrific thought on its own. So I found an unused, wrapped tongue depressor on top of the dresser, popped it open, and sort of stirred the undies around. I hit something solid, and forced myself to reach in. A case! I pulled it out and pushed the little latch device that opened the lid.

25 But there were no glasses inside, just a big old key. Hmm. Where were the glasses? Were there any glasses? Was this a ... a ... a trick? *Oh, my God!* I thought. *Sol's up to something. How could I be so gullible?*

---

5 **clueless**: not understanding   7 **eerie**: scary   12 **creeped out** (infml): scared
13 **remotely**: (here) slightly   14 **eyewear**: eye-glasses   **no dice** (AE, infml, old-fashioned): no luck   15 **inevitable**: not to be avoided   17 **billow**: be blown up with air, thus looking bigger (usu. of clothes)   18 **mound of sth.**: (here) large amount of sth. in a pile   20 **horrific**: terrible   21 **tongue depressor** [tʌŋ dɪˈpresə] (AE): long flat wooden instrument that doctors use to press down your tongue when looking at your throat   22 **undies** (infml): underwear   23 **latch**: metal device used to hold a lid or door shut

I launched myself out the door and down the fire stairs, still holding
the case. When I came out of the stairwell, my fears became a reality.
Okay, not the slaughter ones, but the trickery ones. I could hear
Steven's drums start up on a fast Latin tune. When Annette jumped
in, I recognized it as a Tito Puente chart called "Para Los Rumberos"   5
that I knew Steven loved. What on earth were they doing?

Then I heard my beloved Tele jumping into action. But I had
never played it like this. The notes were rippling forth in a torrent,
faster than I would have been on my best day, and with the kind of
timing I would have killed for. I came screeching around a corner   10
into the rec room, and saw a tableau I'll never forget. The nurses
were up on their feet, swaying. The orderlies were getting down.
Even many of the residents were standing and shimmying like
people with actual, biological hip joints. And in front of this frenzied
hotbed of party power, a man was wailing on MY guitar.   15

A man whose glasses were chafing him.

Sol looked all the way to the back of the room at me, and mouthed
the word that I absolutely knew was coming: "Gotcha!"

What was I going to do? I walked up to the front, and stood
between my mom and Laurie, in Sol's seat. Laurie had a huge grin   20
going, and whispered to me, "This is amazing. He's incredible!"

I didn't say a word. I could feel the redness of my face, but Laurie
didn't notice. My mom put her arm around my shoulder and said,
"Oh, Alex. What a wonderful surprise! I don't know how you did it,
but it's like you've brought Mr. Lewis back to life!"   25

---

1 **launch yourself somewhere**: go somewhere with a lot of energy   **fire stairs**:
stairs built onto or inside a building to help people escape in case of fire
2 **stairwell**: place where stairs lead from one storey to another   3 **slaughter**
['slɔːtə]: (here) violent act of murder   8 **ripple**: move in small waves   **torrent**:
large amount of sth. moving very fast (usu. water)   10 **screech**: make a loud,
unpleasant sound as you move   11 **rec room**: room in an official building where
people can play games, relax, etc.   **tableau** ['tæbləʊ]: (here) scene   12 **sway**: move
slowly from side to side   13 **shimmy** (v): move your hips and shoulders as you
dance   14 **frenzied**: fast and hectic   15 **hotbed of sth**: place where sth. is
happening a lot   **wail**: make a long sound   17–18 **mouth sth.**: move your lips
as if you are saying sth.   21 **incredible**: unbelievable

Yeah, excellent. And easy for her to say. She wasn't going to have to get up there and play the guitar when Sol was through demonically possessing it. The song ended to wild applause. I glanced around, and saw that Mrs. Goldfarb was in a state of transformation – she
5 looked like she might write her phone number on an article of clothing and fling it Sol's way if he played much longer. This just kept getting more and more surreal. I decided right then and there that if an MTV film crew rolled up, I was going to hurl myself out the window.
10 Sol played a few more tunes with Steven and Annette. After his version of the "Fiddler" medley got everyone all misty-eyed, he bowed. Then he walked over to the microphone. Oh, man. Laurie reached over and squeezed my hand. I was sure my miserable scowl and sweaty palm must have been a real turn-on for her, but somehow
15 she resisted sweeping into my arms and kissing me deeply. Short of me getting struck by lightning, I didn't know how the day could have gotten worse.

"Ladies and gentlemen, thank you for your kind applause. Now I would like to invite back onstage the young man who made this all
20 possible, the real star of today's show – Mr. Alex 'The Um' Gregory!!!" Everyone clapped, although my puzzled dad had to whisper to my mother, "What's an Um?" Then Sol continued, "Remember to tip your waiters, your waitresses, and bartenders before you leave. That was a joke, Mrs. Goldfarb. Would it kill you to maybe laugh a little?
25 Oh, by the way, folks: Whatever you do, don't let Alex drive you home."

Some people laughed, others looked puzzled. As I took the longest ten-step walk of my life back onto the stage, Sol gave me a weird smile – triumphant and angry at the same time. Then he
30 handed me the guitar. I had a panicked little huddle with Steven and

---

2 **demonic**: wild; like an evil spirit   7 **surreal**: very strange   8 **roll up**: (here) arrive   **hurl yourself**: throw yourself with a lot of force   11 **misty-eyed**: with tears in your eyes   12 **bow**: bend your head or top part of your body down to thank your audience   13 **squeeze sth.**: press sth. hard with your hand   **scowl**: angry expression   15–16 **short of sth.**: unless sth. happens   22–23 **tip sb.**: give sb. money to thank them for their services   27 **puzzled**: confused   30 **huddle** (n): standing close together to discuss further plans

Annette. (Well, I was panicked. They were still all juiced up from the thrill of playing with Sol.) Then I stepped to the mike. "For our last number, we would like to play a little number called 'All Blues.' This is a Miles Davis tune about how it feels to … uh … play guitar right after Solomon Lewis."   5

It was the simplest jazz piece I knew, which would help me get out of this nightmare without too much additional damage. Annette came in on the piano, then Steven started playing a really cool little pattern with his brushes instead of drumsticks, and finally I came in with the parallel sliding melody and harmony lines that move in   10
sixths through a haunting minor scale. Somehow the beauty of the song gradually crept into my bones and I forgot all about the audience, Sol's performance, everything but my fingers slipping up and down the fretboard. Annette played the first solo, which was so good I nearly forgot to keep playing. Then Annette nodded at me,   15
and I burst into my last solo of the night. I did look up at Sol then, and the sadness on his face found its way into the notes I was playing. So did the flash of Laurie's eyes, while the link between my parents' intertwined hands became the elastic lockstep of the harmony. Plus, my anger found its way in there when I played some   20
dissonant clusters of jarring flatted fifths for a few bars. And when I resolved all that tension back into the melody, I wasn't mad anymore.

Sure, Sol had showed me up in front of a crowd that included the most important people in my life. But they were surely clapping

1 **juiced up** (AE, infml): excited   2 **thrill**: great excitement   4 **Miles Davis**:
famous American jazz trumpeter (1926–1991)   7 **nightmare**: very bad dream
10 **parallel melody**: melody that accompanies the main melody   11 **sixth**: *Sexte* (in
music)   **haunting**: sad and beautiful in a way that isn't easy to forget   **minor**: *Moll*
(in music)   **scale**: series of notes going up or down (in music)   12 **creep**: (here)
move slowly and subtly   14 **fretboard**: long wooden board on the neck of a guitar
against which your fingers press the strings to determine the pitch   19 **intertwined**:
twisted together and hard to separate   **lockstep**: when two things are done in
exactly the same way   21 **dissonant**: musical notes that don't sound pleasant
together   **cluster**: group of similar things arranged closely together   **jar**: have a
strange or unpleasant effect   **flatted fifth**: *verminderte Quinte* (in music)   **bar**: *Takt*
(in music)   22 **resolve sth. into sth.**: change sth. into sth. else

for me now. If Sol didn't say anything to rub the soreness in, I'd be okay.

And if it got breezy and rainy in the Sahara Desert, they'd change its name to the Sahara Palms Resort.

5 We finished. People clapped. We packed up. Annette and I helped Steven get his drums out to his mom's car while all of the residents except Sol went back to their floors for the night. After my last trip to carry out my guitar and amp, I walked over to where the Cha-KINGS were chatting with my parents, Laurie, and Sol. Annette

10 said, "Wow, Mr. Lewis, Alex never told me you played."

"I don't play. I haven't played in twenty-seven years and three months. Before that, I played." Sol's words kind of tapered off, and I realized he was very short of breath.

"But you have so much skill. How could you have just given it

15 up?"

"Sweetheart, there's more to life than skill. You're very young. Maybe one day you'll know what I'm talking about."

"But I mean it. You're really brilliant!"

"Thank you." Sol was pale and maybe a little shaky, plus I could

20 tell he didn't want to talk about whatever his secret was. He saw me and changed the subject. "Mr. Um! Did you find my glasses?"

"No, I didn't find your glasses – you don't have another pair of glasses, Sol."

He thought, and breathed, for a moment. "Oh, well, I guess I

25 only have one face anyway. Who needs extra glasses?"

"I found something else, though." I held the key up to the light. "Any idea what it's for?"

"I think maybe one day I'll show you. For now, just keep it very safe." His last few words turned into a titanic cough, and he suddenly

30 sat down on the nearest chair, hard. He was gripping his chest and turning a deep red. A nurse I didn't know appeared out of the blue

---

1 **rub sth. in**: remind sb. about sth. they don't want to think about   **soreness**: (here) feeling of painful embarrassment   3 **breezy**: windy   4 **resort**: place where people spend their holidays   12 **taper off**: become weaker   29 **titanic** (AE): very big and strong   31 **out of the blue**: unexpectedly

and called for oxygen. A transport guy shuffled over with a wheel-chair that had an air tank attached, and they got Sol into the chair and attached the nose-clip thing to him. Within a couple of moments, while everybody stood around not knowing what to do or say, Sol's color returned and he leaned back in the chair. He turned   5
to me and the orderly and said, "Would you take me upstairs, please? An artist needs his beauty rest. You think I was born looking this lovely?"

I said good-bye to my parents and Laurie. Steven gave me a high five and said, "Some show, huh?" Yup, it had been some show. One   10
way or the other, it had been some show. Annette shook my hand in both of hers, and spoke so only I could hear. "You played well, and that Miles Davis tune was great. Will ... will your friend be all right?"

I mumbled something that sounded vaguely affirmative, but as I followed Sol's wheelchair to the elevator, I couldn't help thinking   15
that Annette had been zero for two: Sol wasn't exactly my friend, and he wasn't ever going to be all right.

1 **shuffle**: walk, dragging your feet on the ground   7 **beauty rest**: (used humorously) the amount of rest you need to look well and attractive
14 **affirmative**: positive   16 **zero for two**: baseball term meaning that you have made two mistakes

DARKNESS

I stayed with Sol until he was in his checkered flannel old-man pj's and back in bed. With the oxygen flowing, he seemed fine, but you had to wonder what the exertion of playing had done to him. He turned to me, but didn't quite make eye contact. "*Boychik*, that wasn't
5 a bad concert. Your friends are very talented. And you really worked hard."

How could this man get me so mad so fast? "So they're talented, and I worked hard? Thanks, Sol. You worked hard, too. I especially liked the way you tricked me into leaving my own concert, took
10 over, and made me look like a *schlemazzel*!"

"Hey, take it easy, Alex. At least you're learning some Yiddish from me, right? And I didn't make you look like a *schlemazzel*. I just played better than you did."

"Yeah, you played better than me. That's all. Except you also
15 never told me you played. So I made an idiot of myself for months playing in front of you. And you acted like you liked it while you were laughing in my face! Why didn't you tell me?"

"You never asked, Alex. You've been coming here since the autumn already, and you've never asked me a thing about myself.
20 You think I was born with a hose clipped to my face?" He flicked at his nasal cannula, sighed, and continued lacing into me. "You young people never think anybody over the age of sixty ever did anything. Well, I'll tell you something, Mr. Um, Mr. Drunk Car-Crashing Hot-shot: I DID PLENTY!"

25 He took another breath break, and I bit my lip so hard I could feel the salty blood oozing in between my front teeth. "You know

---

1 **checkered**: with a pattern made up of squares in different colors   **flannel**: type of soft cloth that is used for clothes   3 **exertion**: great effort   20 **clip sth. to sth**: attach sth. to sth. else   20–21 **flick at sth.**: hit sth. quickly (esp. with your finger and thumb)   21 **nasal cannula**: thin tube attached to the nose through which a patient receives oxygen   **lace into sb.**: criticize sb. harshly   23–24 **hotshot**: very successful person   26 **ooze**: flow slowly

Mrs. Goldfarb down the hall? She was the principal of YOUR high
school for thirty-two years. Mr. Moran, in three-twenty? He ran a
bank with his brother, Albert. For forty years, they built that
business. Then they sold it for millions of dollars, and their kids
shoved them in here three months later. Albert was dead before   5
winter, but Mr. Moran vowed he'd outlive his no-good sons. He
might just do it, too."

Sol emitted a sound that was like what you'd get if a laugh and a
wheeze struck each other head-on in a freeway accident, took a sip
of water from the cup on his nightstand, and started in yet again.   10
"And you sit there counting out the hours until you can put me
behind you forever. But I'll still be here, *boychik*. When I leave this
place it's going to be feet first. So don't tell me I didn't tell you, I
didn't tell you. Why should I have to tell you when you already
know everything?"   15

He got quiet, sipped his water, and then lay back. He was
breathing harder again, so I had a chance to yell at him for a bit
while he got his wind back. But I didn't take it. "Fine, I'll ask a
question: Why don't you play guitar anymore? Why did you stop?"

His eyes were closed, and he was silent for so long that I thought   20
he must have fallen asleep. Then his lips moved, and I had to lean all
the way over his bed to hear him. "Alex, Alex. I played guitar for a
living. Thirty years, six nights a week. New York, Miami, California.
The casinos, cruise ships, the Poconos, the Catskills. You name the
room, Lou Solomon played it. That's what they called me then, Lou   25
Solomon. I don't know why, but my promoter thought it sounded
less Jewish. Like the audience wouldn't take one look at this enor-
mous *schnoz* on my face and figure it out anyway."

---

5 **shove sb. somewhere**: put sb. somewhere in a thoughtless manner   6 **vow sth.**:
promise sth. very seriously   **outlive sb.**: live on after sb. has died   8 **emit sth.**:
release sth. (usu. sound, gas, etc.)   9 **head-on**: when the fronts of two cars crash
into each other (in an accident)   **freeway** (AE): large road on which you can drive
fast   13 **feet first** (infml): dead   18 **wind**: (here) breath   22–23 **do sth. for a
living**: do sth. to earn money   24 **cruise ship**: large ship on which people spend
holidays   **Poconos**: Pocono Mountains; region in Pennsylvania where people go on
holiday   **Catskills**: Catskill Mountains; region in New York where people go on
holiday   26 **promoter**: person who organizes concerts   28 **schnoz** (Yiddish): nose

Pause, breathing, sip.

"What the hell was I talking about? Oh, the guitar. I had a wife back then. Her name was Ethel, and she was beautiful. I know, a name like Ethel maybe doesn't sound so gorgeous, but my Ethel
5 was. She was small and bright, like a little bird. Your Laurie reminds me of her."

I interrupted, "Laurie isn't …"

"I'm speaking here. Do you mind? Anyway, we had a daughter, too – Judy. Cute, with a smart mouth. Always with the smart mouth.
10 I was gone too much playing the damn guitar, but I spent enough time at home to know Judy was going to be SOMETHING someday. It was a decent life. I traveled, I met all the great ones – Monk, Dizzy, Buddy Rich, I even sat in with Miles once at the Half Note. But after a while it got old, you know what I mean? Like lobster, maybe. You
15 eat it once in a while, it's a delicacy. You eat it every day, soon it's just a giant bug with claws in butter sauce. And Judy was in high school, Ethel wanted to go back to work – she was a librarian – and me working nights was tough for them."

Cough, breathe, sip.

20 "So what happened? You retired from playing to be with your family? I think that's really …"

"No, I didn't retire to be with my family. I should have, but there was always one more big gig coming up, you know? So one day, Ethel drives up to Mountain Laurel, in the Poconos, to watch me
25 play – which she didn't do that often, but Judy was sleeping at a friend's house, and maybe she was lonely. Anyway, Mountain Laurel wasn't such a great jazz room, but it was a bread-and-butter gig. Three of those in a month, and you paid the mortgage. Whatever. In

---

4 **gorgeous** ['gɔːdʒəs]: very beautiful   9 **with a smart mouth** (sl): clever in a rude way   12 **Dizzy**: Dizzy Gillespie, famous American jazz trumpeter (1917–1993)
13 **Buddy Rich**: famous American jazz drummer (1917–1987)   **sit in with sb.**: play music with sb.   **Miles**: Miles Davis   **Half Note**: famous New York jazz club, closed in 1972   14 **lobster**: *Hummer*   15 **delicacy** [delıkəsi]: expensive or rare food that tastes very good   27 **bread-and-butter** (adj, infml): basic work, not very exciting, that provides the money you need   28 **mortgage**: money you borrow to buy a house and which you pay back every month

the middle of the gig, I get called to the hotel phone – Judy was at the emergency room back home with a high fever. Ethel wanted me to walk off the gig to drive to the hospital with her. But I said, and it's true, 'Ethel, I've never blown a gig. Never. And people know when they book Lou Solomon, they're getting a sure thing. You go. I'm   5 sure it'll be fine. It's only a little temperature.' We had a big argument. She said some things she maybe shouldn't have said, I said some things, too. But what was I going to do? I just couldn't walk off the gig. Ethel grabbed her purse, gave me one last look – the worst look I ever got from her – and ran out of the ballroom. The bandleader   10 told me I should go after her, but I couldn't find her anywhere. I even sent the girl singer we had then into the ladies' room, but Ethel wasn't anywhere to be found. She must have headed straight for the car and just zoomed away. I had to go back onstage, so I did. I don't know, maybe I should have run outside or something, jumped in the   15 band truck, and tried to catch up. But who knew what was going to happen? And Lou Solomon never blew a gig. So I went back on."

Breathe, sip, cry. Cry? Sure enough, Sol's shoulders were trembling, and tears were rolling down his cheeks. "Sol, you don't have to tell me if …"   20

"You asked, so I'm telling. It's fine. You should know this, I think. Ethel never made it home, Alex. Some drunken driver in a big truck fell asleep at the wheel on the Pennsylvania Turnpike, and knocked my Ethel's car right off the road. Right off a cliff. Bam! The highway patrol said she probably never even saw it coming, so at least there   25 wasn't any pain. No pain? Ha! I never played again, until tonight. I painted houses instead. I was good at it, and I could be home at night for Judy. So she spent another couple of years at our house, and then moved away for school as soon as she could. Now I'm alone, and she's the big-shot lawyer who never even picks up her   30 Hanukkah flowers."

---

2 **emergency room** (AE): hospital department where badly ill or injured people can be treated immediately   3 **walk sth. off**: leave sth. before it is finished   4 **blow sth.**: leave sth. suddenly   23 **turnpike** (AE): large road on which you can travel fast

I wasn't sure if this was the right move, and I'm not the most comforting guy in general, but I put my hand on Sol's arm. We stayed like that for a really, really long time, until both Sol and my left leg were fast asleep. Now I knew why Sol had gone ballistic over
5   my little gnome episode. I pulled his blanket up to cover him, turned off the lamp over his bed, and tiptoed out of there. Just as I hit the doorway, I heard Sol turn over and mumble, "I liked 'All Blues,' kid. Keep the key."

I dozed off on the bus home, with my hand clenched tight around
10 the key in my pocket. It had been a long day.

---

2 **comforting**: making you feel less upset   4–5 **go ballistic over sth.** (infml): get very angry about sth.   9 **doze**: sleep briefly and lightly   **clench your hand**: press your fingers tightly together

THE VALENTINE'S DAY MASSACRE

In case I might have accidentally had a moment of relaxation or contentment, my high school scheduled a Sadie Hawkins dance for Valentine's Day. For those of you who haven't endured the nearly medieval torture of this particular event, a Sadie Hawkins dance is one where the girls have to ask the guys out. Now, I have very little   5
skill in the man-woman-type area anyway, so I probably would have just stayed home in slightly depressed peace on V-day in a normal year, because the chances of my asking out a human female with any degree of success were right up there with the odds of the Chicago Cubs winning the World Series. No, worse – the Cubs winning the   10
Super Bowl. But this Sadie Hawkins thing meant I couldn't even just give up and sulk, because at any moment some random girl might snatch me up as a partner. Granted, there wasn't exactly a waiting list to ask out semiproficient band geeks with criminal histories, but as long as there was the slightest hope, I would be sitting on pins   15
and needles.

And of course, there was the dreaded, yet slightly exciting, prospect that Laurie might choose me. So every time I was with her I had that to add to my agony. Every day at lunch, I sat across from Laurie, choking down my oddly congealed school cafeteria pizza, watching   20
her eat her inevitable salad, and waiting for a word from her about the dance. Of course, at least three guys would stop by the table, one by one, to talk to her, and I'd have to sweat over whether she would pop the question to them right in front of me. Seriously, I'd perspire

---

2 **contentment**: satisfaction   **schedule sth.**: plan sth. for a specific time
4 **medieval** [medi'i:vl]: of the Middle Ages (ca. 600–1500 A.D.)   9–10 **Chicago Cubs**: American baseball team   10 **World Series**: series of seven baseball games played to determine the best US baseball team of the year   11 **Super Bowl**: most important game in American football   12 **sulk**: show your anger by being silent
14 **semiproficient** ['semiprə'fɪʃnt]: only slightly talented   15–16 **be on pins and needles** (AE): be nervously waiting   17–18 **prospect**: (here) possibility
20 **congealed**: having become solid or stiff (of liquid or soft food)   23 **sweat over sth.**: (here) worry about sth.   24 **perspire**: sweat

and pray, Not in front of me. *Please, dear Lord, not right in front of me.*
Then they'd leave, and I'd be vainly trying to dry off my soaked
palms while awaiting the next potential suitor.

But nothing happened, nothing happened, nothing happened. It
5 was like watching the world's greatest relief pitcher. Three up, three
down. Every lunch period, three up and three down. Until one day,
this girl Sarah walked up to me. Sarah was a quiet, mousy little
trombone player whose most distinctive features were a massive
retainer that made her sound like she was gargling marbles, and the
10 ability to write endless pages of horrendous love poetry that she read
out loud daily in our English class. Here's my impression of Sarah
reading Shakespeare:

"Womeo, ah Womeo, where faw ot dow, Womeo?"

Sarah reading Elizabeth Barrett Bwowning (sorry, Browning):

15 *"How goo I lub vee?*
Wet me cout the ways."

And here's Sarah, asking me to the Sadie Hawkins dance right in
front of Laurie:

"Hi,Wauwie. Hi, Awex. Hey, Awex, goo you what to go wiv me to vhe
20 *Sagie Hawkins Gance?"*

I just sat there, sweating and panicking. What does one say in a
situation like this? There are really no guidelines whatsoever, because

---

2 **vainly**: unsuccessfully   **soaked**: very wet   3 **suitor**: man who wants to marry (or
here: go out with) a specific woman   5 **relief pitcher**: baseball player who replaces
the pitcher (the one who throws the ball)   8 **trombone**: *Posaune*   9 **retainer**: wire
and plastic device that you wear in your mouth to keep your teeth straight   **gargle**:
put liquid in your mouth and move it around in your throat   **marble**: small glass
ball   10 **horrendous**: terrible   13 **Womeo** …: imitating a quotation from
Shakespeare's Romeo and Juliet: "Romeo, Romeo, wherefore art thou Romeo?"
15–16 **How goo** …: quotation from a famous poem by English poet Elizabeth Barret
Browning (1806–1861): "How do I love thee? Let me count the ways."

this is the kind of thing that only happens to ME. After a few moments of unbearable silence – I mean, silence from me; it's not like the whole lunchroom got quiet, which is a small blessing – Laurie kicked me under the table like I was a pile of pine boards and she was really going for a trophy. I wasn't sure what she meant to   5
convey, other than a painful bruise, but she succeeded in prodding me into action. "Sure, Sarah, I'd be glad to."

While Sarah and I were working out the details, and I was trying to rub my shin without being too pathetically obvious, Laurie somehow left the cafeteria. By the time I said a fond farewell to my   10
new hot date and hobbled out into the hall, Laurie was long gone.

While I was making these swell plans, my parents were getting their own warped ideas for the upcoming holiday. They were in "couples therapy" together, because, as Dad put it, "We want to start fresh, and not make the same mistakes again that we made last   15
time." They could have saved seventy-five bucks an hour if they had just come to me instead. It was no big mystery: I would have just told Dad to stop getting it on with my teachers. But anyway, their therapist had this great idea that they should try to have a big, ceremonial, perfect "first date" on Valentine's Day. So they had a   20
whole elaborate scenario worked out, with fancy clothes, flowers, dinner, dancing, and God knew what else. Every time I went to Dad's (which I was grudgingly doing maybe twice a week now), he would try to get me to tell him what Mom was going to wear. Then I'd get home, and Mom would interrogate me about Dad's wardrobe   25
choice for the evening. Like a) I cared, and, b) I paid attention to the weird sounds that came out when their lips were moving. I hoped things would go well for them, or at least I mostly did, but I wanted

---

3 **blessing**: lucky thing   4 **pine boards**: flat pieces of wood that are hit with a hand or a foot and broken in two (in karate)   5 **trophy** ['trəʊfi]: prize for winning a competition   5–6 **convey sth.**: make sth. known   6–7 **prod sb. into sth.**: encourage sb. to do sth.   11 **hobble**: walk as if your feet or legs are injured
12 **swell** (AE, infml, old-fashioned): great   13 **warped**: strange in a negative way
18 **get it on with sb.** (AE, infml): have sex with sb.   21 **elaborate**: complicated and detailed   23 **grudgingly**: unwillingly   25 **interrogate sb.**: ask sb. many questions to make them tell a certain piece of information

nothing to do with any of it, because even if they were forgetting, I remembered how peachy their romance had turned out to be the first time around. Whatever, it was just another interesting V-day plot twist.

5   The day after my first disastrous lunch with Laurie, I was treated to the pleasure of another. I lurched over to the table with an exaggerated limp so Laurie would know she had probably hobbled me for life with her vicious kick, and said, "Hi. Salad today? A bold choice."

10   She fired right back, "Verbally challenged bandgeek date? A bold choice."

"What's your problem? She came over. She asked me out. When I didn't immediately jump up and start kissing her instantly, you kicked me under the table. So I said yes, just like you wanted me to."

15   "I didn't want you to say yes, I wanted you to say no."

"Gee, too bad you didn't give me the ankle-kicking Morse code translation kit so I could figure that out. I guess I'm a little rusty on distinguishing the yes kick from the no kick. And why did you want me to say no?"

20   "Well, because you don't *like* Sarah. At least, you've never mentioned her before. It just seems kind of cruel to lead her on. She's obviously been longing for you in her heart, pining away, her tragic tears dripping down her face and rusting her adorable little retainer."

25   "Oh, *I'm* cruel? You're busting on her orthodontic issues, but I'm the cruel one? And what if I had said no? Then I would have sat at home, miserable, and she would have, too."

---

4 **plot twist**: surprising change of events in a story   5 **disastrous**: very bad; unsuccessful   7 **exaggerated**: done in a way that is more extreme than necessary 7–8 **hobble sb.**: stop sb. being able to walk   8 **bold**: brave   10 **verbally challenged**: unable to speak properly   16 **gee** (AE): exclamation expressing surprise or slight anger   16 **ankle**: joint connecting the foot to the leg   17 **kit**: set of tools   17–18 **be rusty on sth.** (infml): not be very good at sth. anymore 21 **lead sb. on**: make sb. believe that you love them   22 **pine away**: miss sb. so much that you become weak and ill   25 **orthodontic**: related to the treatment of teeth that aren't in the right positions

Laurie chewed her lip for a moment. "Alex, you weren't going to be sitting home on Valentine's Day."

"What do you mean?" "Well, I kind of thought …"

Before she could finish, a huge shadow fell over us. We both looked up at the tanklike form of Brad Hunter, the star offensive lineman on our football team. Like a heavily armored attack vehicle, he towered above the table with an air of menace. Unlike a heavily armored attack vehicle, he started talking to Laurie. "Listen, Laurie, I know this is supposed to be a girls-asking-guys thing, but I think you're really special, and I'd like to take you to the dance. I mean, if you don't have other plans."

Laurie gave me yet another of her deadly and accurate kicks, and smiled sweetly at Brad. "No, I don't have any other plans."

Women! Can't live with 'em, can't walk.

*   *   *

The night of the dance, I was all set to make the most of the situation. My mom had graciously ungrounded me, perhaps so she could be home alone when my dad arrived to pick her up. I had on a nice pair of black pants and a dark green sweater that Laurie had bought me because she said it "set off my eyes." I had shaved, which, okay, maybe I didn't technically have a massive growth of facial hair, but hey! It allowed me to feel entitled to splash on some aftershave. I had brushed my teeth – twice – and rinsed with mouthwash until my mouth was a veritable garden of minty freshness. I had combed my hair so it didn't quite have the usual "brown Q-Tip" thing happening. I was just about to set out on the short walk to Sarah's house, which was only a block from school, when the phone rang.

---

5 **tanklike**: very large   5–6 **offensive lineman**: player in a front position in American football   6 **armored vehicle**: vehicle with a strong metal covering used by the military   7 **tower above sth.**: be much taller than sth.   **menace**: threat
16 **gracious**: kind and generous   21 **feel entitled to do sth.**: feel you have the right to do sth.   23 **veritable**: real   24 **Q-tip** (AE): brand name for thin sticks with cotton wool (Watte) at each end

My mom jumped about seven feet sideways and almost yanked the phone out of the wall – not that she was tense or anything, right? I only heard her end of the convo, obviously, but it didn't have a good ring to it:

5   "Hello. This is she. He WHAT? He can't? When did this happen? Where is he? He asked for … ? Okay, I'll see what I can do. Thank you."

She turned to me. I was all ready to hear my dad had suddenly fled the country with my gym teacher or something, but I've never 10 had a big gift for premonition. "Alex, I have some bad news. Mr. Lewis … Sol … is in the hospital. He has pneumonia. I know the timing is bad , but he asked to see you."

Oh, crud. "All right, I'll go tomorrow morning. Can I skip school?"

15   "Alex, you don't get it. Sol has pneumonia. Pneumonia kills people, especially old people. Especially old people with emphysema. He might not be … around … tomorrow morning."

I thought fast. "Mom, can you drive me right now? We'll have to stop at Sarah's house to tell her what's going on."

20   Mom sighed. This wasn't exactly the vision she had had for this evening. "Okay, get your coat. I'll call your father from the car."

At Sarah's, I ran up and rang the bell. I'd been expecting her mom or dad to answer the door so we could have one of those awkward predate Spanish Inquisition rituals, but Sarah must have beaten 25 them to it. She looked really, really pretty. I'd never seen her in anything except jeans and T-shirts before, but she was wearing some kind of silky green dress thing that suited her, somehow. Her eyes were green like mine, which had never registered with me before. Something else was different, too, but it didn't click for me until she

---

1–2 **yank sth.** (AE, infml): pull sth. quickly and hard   3 **convo** (infml): short for 'conversation'   10 **premonition**: feeling that sth. bad is going to happen   13 **crud** (sl): (here) expression of being annoyed   13–14 **skip school**: not go to school when you should   24 **predate** (adj): happening before or at the beginning of a date **Spanish Inquisition**: severe questioning, often involving torture, of people of a different faith from the main church, as happened in Spain between 1478 and 1800 24–25 **beat sb. to it**: be faster than sb.   28 **register with sb.**: be clear to sb.   29 **it didn't click for me** (infml): I didn't realize it

shouted, "Bye, Mom. Bye, Dad. I'll be back by midnight. I have my
cell if you need me!" When she smiled shyly at me, I had visual
confirmation: The retainer had been deep-sixed for the night. Sarah
could speak! So now I had a date who had basically transformed
herself into a princess, but our gala ball had turned into a bedside   5
vigil. I had to 'fess up to the facts, so on the way back to the car, I
stopped walking and gave her the update. "Sarah, I have some bad
news. I volunteer at the nursing home …"

"For that old man, Sol, right? I know all about it – you got in
trouble for drunk driving, and then you got sentenced to work at the   10
nursing home. But then you really bonded with this old guy, and
you put on a concert with Steven and Annette, and your guy played
guitar, right? I think it's heroic the way you're helping an old man in
need!"

How did she know all this? I had to ask. "How do you know all   15
this?"

"Didn't Bryan Gilson tell you? He told me all about you. I mean, I
knew you from jazz band, and I knew you were cute… ." God, my
mom must have been smirking if she was hearing this through the
open car window. "But Bryan was the one who told me how deep   20
and sensitive you are. And then I wasn't going to ask you out anyway,
because of your – you know – relationship with Laurie, but Bryan
said it was okay, and that Laurie was going with one of his jock
friends anyway. So here we are, and I'm glad. I'm sorry, you were
saying?"   25

"Um, well, it's like this: Sol – the old man – is in the hospital. I
just got the call, and he's really sick. He asked for me, and this might
be, like, his deathbed. So I have to go right now to see him. You can
come, if you want. Or my mom can probably drop you off at the
dance, and I could meet you there after …" Sarah stopped me with a   30
hand on my forearm. Her hand was warm and dry. And she was

---

3 **confirmation**: (here) proof   **deep-six sth.** (AE, infml): not use sth.   6 **vigil**: time
during which you stay by a sick person's bed   **'fess up to the facts** (infml): tell the
truth   21 **sensitive**: (here) open to other people's feelings and needs   23 **jock** (AE,
infml, derog.): sporty student who is considered stupid

looking at me with weird googly eyes. "Alex, I'd be honored to go visit your friend with you. Let's go there."

So we jumped in the car, and that's what we did. When Mom dropped us off, I told her to go ahead with her date. She gave me a
5   twenty and told me to call a cab when we were ready to go from the hospital to the dance. As we walked up to the hospital's information desk, Sarah grabbed my hand and squeezed it. This was a weird night for sure. And I couldn't decide whether I should thank Bryan or kill him.

10   Sol's room upstairs was "semiprivate," which is hospital code for "not private." So there was a guy in the bed by the window all hooked up to tubes and wires. Sol was by the door, propped partway up on pillows, with two different IV bags dripping into his arm and a cannula clipped between his nostrils. His glasses weren't on, which
15   made his nose look both bigger and sunken at the same time. His lips were blue.

God, his lips were blue. I'm no doctor, and the ninety-one I got in biology freshman year probably didn't qualify me as a diagnostic expert, but I was fairly certain blue lips were not one of the top ten
20   signs of robust health. I said hello, and he turned toward my voice.

"Alex, *boychik*, is that you? I knew you'd come." His voice sounded like he was trying to speak through a mouthful of coffee grounds. BOILING coffee grounds. I went right over and put my hand on his shoulder – his blue, IV-punctured hand was just a little
25   too scary for me. While he was catching his breath after this long speech, Sarah stepped up next to me.

"Sol, this is …"

"I know who this is. What, I get a little cough and take off my glasses and you think I'm suddenly a complete *schmeggege*? It's
30   wonderful to see you again, Laurie."

---

1 **googly eyes**: eyes that express that you love or admire a person   5 **cab** (AE): taxi
12 **be hooked up to sth.**: be connected to sth.   15 **sunken**: hollow and unhealthy
looking   17 **ninety-one**: (here) refers to how well you did in an exam: ninety-one
out of a hundred possible points   18 **freshman year**: first year of high school or
college   24 **IV-punctured**: with an IV stuck into it

Uh-oh. Sarah stiffened and pulled her hand away. Sol grabbed her hand. "Let me have a good look at you, dear." For what seemed like maybe the length of – oh, I don't know – a year on Pluto, he squinted up at her and breathed raggedly. "Alex, va-va-voom! She's all dressed up tonight. So where is your husband taking you this 5 evening, Mrs. Um?"

She didn't know how to reply to that, and neither did I, but Sol seemed to catch the look that passed between us. "Oh, I know, I know. You aren't married YET. But I might die tomorrow, so I'm using the present tense – HOO-hah, excuse me – for the future." 10

"Sol, uh, she isn't …"

"Oh, I know. She isn't comfortable talking out loud about this, are you, Laurie, honey? Don't worry, then – we all understand exactly what's going on here, right?"

Sarah's eyes were flashing danger signals at this point, but I 15 couldn't work out a way to stop Sol from digging the hole even deeper. You had to give me credit for trying, though. "Sol, listen to me. This isn't …"

"Oh, I don't think it's the end for me either. You don't have to try to cheer me up, Alex. And there's no need for crying, Laurie. I'll pull 20 through fine. These doctors are excellent. And I think this one nurse likes me. She winked at me before. I told her I was too old for her, but these women just can't resist a man with his *tuchis* hanging out – sorry, Laurie – with his *tuchis* hanging out of a robe like this."

I gave up on my attempts to correct Sol, which meant that Sarah 25 sulked and fumed through the rest of the visit. Sol and I talked for maybe fifteen minutes more, and then a nurse came in and told us that visiting hours were over. As soon as we stood up to go, Sol launched into the longest, deepest coughing fit I'd ever heard. I mean, even for him, this was something special. There was har- 30 rumph-ing, and HOO-hah-ing, and barking, then more of all three. When he suddenly grabbed a cup from the nightstand and spat into

---

4 **squint**: partly shut your eyes in order to see better   **raggedly**: (here) with difficulty   20–21 **pull through**: survive and get better   26 **fume**: be very angry

it, he got his wind back for a second. He said to Sarah, "Laurie, sweetie, can you please get me a glass of water from the nurses' station? I appear to have *schmutzed* into my drinking cup."

When she cleared the doorway, I saw my chance: "Sol, that's not Laurie. Her name is Sarah. She's a trombone player in my school jazz band, and she's my date for a dance tonight."

He gave me such a deadpan look that I wanted to shake him. "Of course, she's not Laurie. Do you think pneumonia makes a man blind? What school do you go to again?"

"Well, I mean, you said … she isn't … you're not wearing your glasses, so I thought …"

"*Boychik*, haven't you ever heard of contact lenses? You really need to get with the times here."

"Then you knew this whole … ?"

Sol's malicious, yet radiant, smile told me everything I needed to know: "GOTCHA!"

Sarah came in with the water at that point, just as Sol doubled over in another spasm of coughing. But it sounded to me like there might have been just a touch of laughter mixed in. I apologized profusely to Sarah all the way downstairs, and while we waited outside for our cab, AND on the whole ride over. AND as we headed into the dance. She kept telling me over and over that it was no problem, she understood, yada yada. But it didn't take a genius to realize Sol had a better chance of running off to Aruba with his nurse than I did of getting anywhere with Sarah.

And the odds didn't get any better inside. The first people we ran into on our way to the dance floor were Laurie and her monolithic side of beef, Brad. She was wearing – and I couldn't believe my eyes – a fire-engine–red dress that fit her like the designer had run out of fabric in the middle and switched over to spray paint to finish the

---

3 **schmutz** (Yiddish): make sth. dirty   7 **deadpan**: not showing any emotion or humour in your face   15 **malicious**: unkind; cruel   **radiant**: expressing joy and happiness   18 **spasm**: painful tightening of muscles   23 **yada yada**: words used to show that you are not repeating everything that was said because it was boring or repetitive   24 **Aruba**: Caribbean island   27 **monolithic**: very large and inflexible 28 **side of beef** (sl, derog.): (here) large, muscular person

job. Brad was sporting baggy slate-colored pants, a slate-colored shirt, and a slate-colored sweater. I don't want to insult the guy, but all I'm saying is this: If you had been mugged by an African water animal, and the safari police placed Brad in a lineup with four rhinos, it would have been pretty hard to disqualify him as a suspect.   5

He was almost incomprehensibly bigger than she was. Approaching them from a distance, the view reminded me of a picture book I used to love when I was around five, called *The Little Red Lighthouse and the Great Gray Bridge*. But this story was a lot less entertaining for me. And when we got close enough that I started worrying we   10 might get caught up and sucked into Brad's gravitational field, we had to actually communicate.

"Hi, Laurie. Hi, Brad."

"Hi, Alex. Hey, Sarah. *You're* fashionably late."

(Yeah, and your partner is fashionably rectangular. So?)   15

"Well, we ran into a little obstacle."

Brad's nearly subsonic voice lumbered into the fray. "Oh, like a lawn gnome, maybe?"

I thought, *Wow, we ARE really late. Laurie had time to teach Brad to SPEAK!* But I didn't say it, because I'm above that sort of thing. Oh,   20 and because Brad could basically reach out one granitelike finger and smear me into a thin paste. So I just chuckled. "Good one, Brad. No, actually we had to stop at the hospital on the way over."

I stopped and waited for that to sink in. While Brad was probably still struggling to cope with my daunting use of a three-syllable   25 word, Laurie asked, "The hospital? Why? What's going on?"

"Uh, Sol has pneumonia."

---

1 **sport sth.**: wear sth. proudly   **slate**: (here) dark grey   3 **mug sb.**: attack sb. and steal their money   4 **lineup** (AE): line of people including a criminal, whom a witness is asked to identify   5 **rhino** (infml): (short for 'rhinoceros') large grey animal with one or two horns on its nose   **disqualify**: (here) not consider   **suspect**: person thought to have committed a crime
6 **incomprehensible**: hard to understand   8 **Lighthouse**: tall tower on the coast that flashes a strong light signal for ships   11 **gravitational field**: *Gravitationsfeld*
15 **rectangular**: *rechteckig*   17 **subsonic**: (here) very slow and deep   **lumber**: move very slowly   **fray**: fight   21 **granitelike**: like granite (a very hard type of stone)   25 **daunting**: making you feel scared and less confident

"Oh, my God! How is he? Can he speak? Is he coherent? I have to go see him."

Sarah saw her opening. "Don't worry, Laurie. He thinks you already did!"

5 Laurie raised an eyebrow, and reached out to grab my arm. Sarah was probably about ready to reach into her bag and spray me with Mace, and it might have been my imagination, but I think Brad was actually RUMBLING at me. Laurie said, in that totally characteristic, I-don't-care-what-anybody-else-thinks way, "Alex, take me to the

10 hospital!"

Who knew that three people from such different backgrounds, and with such varied emotional needs and perspectives, could all say, "BUT …" at exactly the same instant?

"No buts. I'm sorry, but this is a life on the line, not some cheesy

15 high school theme dance. Look, Sarah, was your date with Alex going well?"

"Uhh …"

"My point exactly. And Brad? Do you feel we've made an immortal, transcendent soul-to-soul connection tonight?"

20 "Huh?"

"See? Brad, meet Sarah. Sarah's a very talented musician. And Sarah, meet Brad. Brad does the most amazing impression of a Himalaya! Alex, get your coat back on and let's blow this Popsicle stand."

25 Twenty minutes later, we were sneaking up to Sol's floor on a service elevator. A nurse busted us, but Laurie did this whole Oscar-winning performance as Sol's frantic granddaughter, and she granted us a small exemption from the visiting-hours rules. There are times when I have to admit Laurie is very nearly a superhero of some sort,

---

1 **coherent**: able to think and speak clearly   7 **Mace**: (brand name) chemical used for self-defense that can be sprayed into a person's eyes   8 **rumble**: make a long, deep sound   14 **on the line**: in danger of being lost   19 **transcendent**: (here) better than anything else   22 **impression of sth.**: imitation of sth.   23–24 **let's blow this Popsicle stand** (AE, infml): let's get out of here   26 **service elevator**: lift used by employees, not usually by visitors   **bust sb.**: (here) catch sb.
28 **exemption from sth.**: permission to not follow sth. (e.g. rule)

although it would have been tricky for her to conceal a costume under the particular dress she was wearing. Sol noticed the outfit right off the bat. "Laurie, it's wonderful to see you again so soon. You changed your dress. This one is a lot nicer. I hope Alex told you that."   5

I blushed and bit my lip.

Laurie went through a big Q&A about Sol's whole health situation while I tried not to check out her whole skintight-dress situation. He assured her that he was fine, and his color definitely DID look better than it had even an hour and a half before. Then he asked Laurie if   10
he could speak to me for a moment alone, man to man. She raised the old eyebrow, but kissed him good-bye without a peep of protest and walked out into the hall. Sol patted the edge of his bed, and I sat there. "*Boychik*," he intoned in a manly-man-giving-another-manly-man-advice voice, "That's the girl for you. *That's* your dance partner,   15
not some tuba-honking mouse."

"Sol, Sarah plays the trombone."

"Whatever, do what you want. Go, date your little Sousaphone player. I'm old, what do I know? But when you're done messing around, I hope Laurie is still going to be waiting for you. From the   20
look of her in that red dress, I wouldn't count on it."

It had been an odd day, so maybe my guard was down more than usual. "Sol, I wouldn't mind going out with Laurie. But SHE doesn't notice ME that way."

"Alex, you really are a *meshuggener* sometimes. This girl follows   25
you around, she worries about you all the time, she even plays nicely with your grumpy old friend Sol. She notices you, all right. And she notices you noticing her. You just don't notice her noticing you. Oy, this is giving me a headache. But the point is, time is precious, and a girl like that is precious. Now stop wasting both of them and let me   30
get some sleep. On second thought, maybe call that beautiful nurse

---

7 **Q&A**: question and answer   12 **peep**: (here) single comment   13 **pat sth.**:
touch sth. several times in a row; (here) invite a person to sit down on sth.
18 **Sousaphone**: very large brass instrument (*Blechbläser*)   22 **my guard was
down**: I was not as careful as usual   27 **grumpy** (infml): bad-tempered
29 **precious** ['preʃəs]: valuable

in here and see if it's time for my next dose of cough medicine. I love that stuff!"

As Laurie and I left, Sol had another huge paroxysm of coughing. It was almost as if he had been putting the cough aside in order to
5 concentrate on his advice to me. And when Laurie leaned her head on my shoulder in the elevator, I was really hoping the advice had been right. "Where should we go now?" she asked me. "I don't think Sarah and Brad will be so excited to see us back at the dance, do you?"

10 "No, and I'd rather be with you tonight. I mean, all the time. I mean …"

She put a finger to my lips and I noticed that her short, bitten-down fingernails were polished red to match the outfit. "Shh," she whispered, and tilted her head up to me. Did she want me to kiss
15 her? How weird was this going to be? Should it be like a real kiss, with passion and stuff? Or more of an experimental, pecking kind of deal? And why did this elevator smell like month-old cabbage?

Putting aside my deep thoughts, I made my move.

Suavely, with one deft motion, I reached behind her and pushed
20 the red stop button on the elevator's control panel. And an alarm started blaring at a bone-shattering volume. Laurie jerked up off my shoulder so fast that we banged teeth. As I slapped frantically at the controls to pull the button back out, Laurie started cracking up. My blushing reflex was sure getting a whole lot of practice for one day.
25 When I got the button released, there was a shocking silence. Laurie reined in her guffaws, and was just sort of letting off a random giggle every couple of seconds as she stared at my lip. "Alex, you're bleeding! Let me – GIGGLE – help you." She fished a dubious-looking tissue out of her purse and dabbed at my face. She leaned
30 closer to get a better look, and it was almost starting to look like

---

3 **paroxysm of sth.**: sudden fit of sth.   14 **tilt sb.'s head up**: move sb.'s chin up
16 **peck**: kiss lightly and quickly   19 **deft**: skilful   20 **control panel**: metal board
with buttons and switches on it   21 **blare**: make a loud noise   **bone-shattering**:
shocking   26 **rein sth. in**: control sth.   **guffaw** [gəˈfɔː]: loud laugh   28 **dubious**
[ˈdjuːbiəs]: possibly not good   29 **tissue** [ˈtɪʃuː]: soft paper in which you blow
your nose   **dab at sth.**: touch sth. lightly and repeatedly

Round Two, when we reached the ground floor. The doors opened
onto a packed lobby, with two aging security guards right in front.

"Everything okay, kids? We heard the alarm."

"Yes, sorry, sir. I just … uh … needed to stop the car for a second.
Because …"   5

"Yeah, I can see the 'because' with my own two eyes, son. Hey,
aren't you the kid with the lawn gnome?"

"Uh, Sarge? Is that you?"

He gave me a long glare, which relaxed into a grin. "Yeah, I
moonlight here – hey, I got two daughters in college. You're looking   10
a little better than the last couple of times I saw you. I asked your
judge, and she said you're keeping your nose clean. Anyway, you'd
best be moving on now – and stay out of trouble."

Laurie and I walked through the crowd, as Sarge's partner said,
"Wow, did you see the way she looked at him? If that boy stays out   15
of trouble tonight, it'll be a miracle."

---

2 **packed**: filled with people   10 **moonlight**: have a second job, usu. without your
main employer's knowledge   12 **keep your nose clean**: not get into trouble

GOOD MORNING, WORLD!

The day after the dance was interesting. Because V-day had fallen on a Sunday, and our school's Student Council was a bunch of idiots, the dance had been held on the actual evening of the fourteenth, and we were all staggeringly tired at school on Monday morning. When
5   I collapsed into my homeroom seat, all I wanted was to slump there and pray the gigantic cappuccino thing I'd guzzled en route would start waking me up soon. But Bryan Gilson must have had a quicker metabolism, because he was totally alert and all ready to gloat. "So did you have fun with Sarah last night? You owe me one, buddy.
10 Somebody had to get tired of watching you drool all over yourself in front of Laurie every day and get you a woman. And somebody had to spare Laurie the inconvenience of denying your sorry booty if you finally ever got the courage to be a man and ask her out. So I got my boy Bradley to help her out, too. And now you and the ninja master
15 can settle down and be normal friends, right?"

   Laurie walked in, sort of sashayed and glided her way past Bryan, and leaned over me. She put her arms around my neck from behind and kissed the top of my head. "Mmm," she purred. "You smell like French vanilla. How was your very short sleep, sweetheart?"
20 NOW I was awake. Considering that nothing had happened after the hospital except one of our usual three-hour frozen talks on my

---

1 **V-day**: (here) Valentine's Day   2 **Student Council**: group of students whose task it is to share students' opinions with teachers, and to organize social events
4 **staggeringly**: very   5 **collapse**: sit or fall down because you are very tired
slump: (here) sit down heavily because you are too tired to sit up straight
6 **guzzle sth.** ['gʌzl] (infml): drink large amounts of sth. quickly   **en route**: on the way   8 **metabolism** [mə'tæbəlɪzəm]: bodily process responsible for changing food into energy   **gloat**: show pleasure at your own success or at the bad luck of another person   10 **drool**: (here) show you like sb. in an exaggerated way
12 **spare sb. sth.**: save sb. from sth. (e.g. an unpleasant experience)
inconvenience [,ɪnkən'viːnɪəns]: troublesome thing that you have to do   **booty** (AE, sl): *Hintern*   14 **ninja** [nɪndʒə]: very skilled martial-arts fighter   16 **sashay** ['sæʃeɪ]: walk confidently, swinging your hips, wanting to be noticed   18 **purr**: (here) speak softly and pleasantly

front porch while we were on a stakeout for my mom's return, this was news to me. But even though Bryan couldn't see Laurie's battle-hardened fingers digging into my abdomen, I could feel them. And for once I actually got the hint. "Great, honey. I was dreaming about you all – night – long."   5

"Mmmm … that wasn't a dream, sweet boy. It was a telepathic promise."

Did you ever play Ping-Pong in front of a cat? They sit right down as close to the net as they can, and watch in astonishment as the ball pings and pongs back and forth. And they look rather astonished   10 every time a new volley starts, like it is just an almost unbearable source of wonderment that this hollow plastic sphere is flying in a pattern before their very eyes AGAIN. Well, that was basically the vibe Bryan was giving off as he tried to make sense of this exchange.

The bell rang for the end of homeroom, and Laurie squeezed my   15 bicep, bumped me with her hip, winked, and slipped around Bryan out the door. He and I walked out into the hall together, with him squawking little sounds like, "Wha-huh? Umm-urk. Lau-you-I-huh? Ugg."

I said, "Yup, you really did fix me up. Thanks, bud. By the way, I   20 think it's great that you're now relaxed enough around me to reveal your inner caveman."

And then the shadow fell. Brad! Astonishing. He actually dwarfed Bryan. In case I'd been wondering what astronauts feel like when

---

1 **stakeout for sth.**: watching a place and waiting for sth. to happen   2–3 **battle-hardened**: made hard through lots of fighting   3 **abdomen**: belly   4 **get a hint**: understand a suggestion that has not been said directly   9 **astonishment**: great surprise   11 **volley**: act of hitting a ball back and forth   **unbearable**: too much to accept   12 **source**: *Quelle*   **wonderment**: feeling of pleasant surprise   **hollow**: empty   **sphere** [sfɪə]: round object   14 **give off a vibe** (infml): convey a particular impression or mood   **exchange**: (here) conversation   16 **bicep**: muscle of your upper arm   18 **squawk**: make short, unpleasant sounds   20 **fix sb. up** (infml): help sb. find a romantic partner   **bud**: buddy; friend   21–22 **reveal sth.**: show sth. you had kept hidden   22 **your inner sth./sb.**: sth./sb. that represent your true personality   **caveman**: historic man who lived in caves and had not developed speech   23–24 **dwarf sb.**: be so big that you make sb. seem smaller than they are

they come around the dark side of the moon, and see the Earth taking up the entire sky, now I knew. His hand fell on my shoulder, and if my knees hadn't already been weak from Laurie's advances, they sure were wobbly under his massive body force. His tremendous
5 head was mere inches from mine. And there was this twisted grimace on his face. "Hey, Gregory!"

Whoa, I thought, here comes the killing part of my morning.

But then a strange realization came over me:

The contorted expression was what happened when a football
10 lineman attempted to smile. He thundered, "Thanks!" And I noticed that crunched in under his other redwoodlike arm was a petite little shape with brown hair on top.

The voice of Brad's new girlfriend reverberated from his right armpit: "Yeah, Awex. Fanks!"

15 Walking home from school that afternoon, Laurie was in an exuberant mood. "Did you see how I got Bryan going? He really thinks we hooked up last night!"

Of course, her act had been so good that I, myself, had been halfway caught between wanting that, and believing it. But if she
20 could be casual, I could be casual-er. More casual. Whatever. "Yeah, we're a great team. We should be secret agents. You could be the deadly martial-arts assassin …"

"Great! I love those slinky black Kevlar outfits they wear."

---

3 **advances**: attempts to start a romantic relationship   4 **wobbly**: weak and shaky **tremendous**: very large   5 **mere**: only   9 **contorted**: pulled into a different, abnormal shape   10 **attempt to do sth.**: try to do sth.   **thunder** (v): (here) speak with a low, loud voice   11 **crunched in**: (here) pressed so hard that you are almost crushed   **redwoodlike**: like a redwood (the world's largest tree)   **petite** [pəˈtiːt] (French): small and thin   13 **reverberate** [rɪˈvɜːbəreɪt] (v): be heard several times like an echo   14 **armpit**: place under the arm where it is attached to the body   16 **exuberant** [ɡˈzjuːbərənt]: very happy and excited   17 **hook up**: start having a romantic relationship   20 **casual** [ˈkæʒuəl]: relaxed   22 **assassin**: professional murderer (e.g. of important or famous people)   23 **slinky**: skin-tight in an attractive way (of clothes)   **Kevlar**: strong material used in clothes to protect you from fire or gunshots   **outfit**: clothes worn together

"Yeah, me, too. And I could be the … uh …" "Slightly deranged ex-convict? Elevator saboteur?

Drunken getaway driver? Lawn Gnome Terminator?" Really, with a life as entertaining as mine, who needs caffeine?

February 16   5

Dear Judge Trent,

I just realized that I never wrote to fill you in on the results of the big concert at the home. All of the attendees had a wonderful time, and several people commented on the excellent guitar playing.

Not my guitar playing, though. The big surprise of the night was that   10
my friend Solomon Lewis used to be a professional guitarist. Evidently,
he swore off playing many years ago because he blames himself for a
drunk-driving accident in which his wife died.

It's really sad, and I am starting to understand why Mr. Lewis is some-
times rather bitter. He has a grown- up daughter who is a lawyer   15
somewhere, and she doesn't speak to him. It's pretty horrible, really,
because he wasn't even in the car with his wife when she crashed, but
somehow the fault falls on him anyway.

I guess I would be snappish, too, in Mr. Lewis's place.

Anyway, we gave Mr. Lewis a chance to play at the concert. I felt great   20
that he got an opportunity to entertain people in such a positive way,

---

2 **ex-convict**: person found guilty of a crime in the past   **saboteur** [ˌsæbəˈtɜː]:
person who damages things on purpose   3 **getaway driver**: person who drives a
car to get criminals away from crime scenes   **terminator**: (here) murderer; killer
8 **attendee**: person who goes to an event   11 **evidently**: as it seems   12 **swear off
sth.**: decide not to do sth. any more   12–13 **blame sb. for sth.**: think or say that
sb. is responsible for sth. bad   19 **snappish**: easily upset and showing anger

especially because now he is in the hospital with pneumonia. This may have been his last chance to play the guitar for an audience, and I am proud to have provided it for him.

Sincerely, Alex Gregory

February 19

Dear Alex,

I am glad your event went well. What you have discovered about your client's tragic past is very interesting. Perhaps, given the nature of your offense, you were deliberately assigned to Mr. Lewis so that you could 5 *learn some lessons together.*

That is, after all, the point of the Full Circle program. Do keep up the good work, and continue to keep me informed of your progress. Sincerely,

Judge J. Trent   10

---

4 **client** : person you serve professionally   5 **deliberately**: done in a planned way, for a particular reason   7 **Full Circle program**: project in which Alex takes part as his punishment

THE MISSION

Later that week, Sol pitched a plan to help me out. He was back at the home, and was having a postpneumonia burst of energy. "Hey, Alex, you haven't played guitar for me in a while."

"Well, Sol, don't hold your breath. I can't play in front of you now
5   that you blew me off the stage. It would just be stupid."

"Stupid, schmupid. What's stupid is to quit when you have a good thing going."

"I'm not quitting, I'm just not playing here. And besides, I don't have a good thing going. I have a mediocre thing going. *You* had a
10   good thing going. And come to think of it, *you* quit."

"For this, I came back from the hospital? *Boychik*, I'm not trying to fight with you here. I'm trying to help you out, to make you an offer, to give your life a meaning and a purpose. So you don't just stumble around like a *schmegegge* all the time, drinking too much,
15   stealing cars, and who knows what other hooligan foolishness."

"Wow, I'm glad you're not trying to fight. But where's the help part?"

"Here's the help part, Mister Smart Aleck. Next time you come, you bring your guitar here, and I'll teach you some things you need
20   to know. Then you'll practice them and come back for another lesson. I figure if you really set your mind to it, and don't get all distracted chasing around everything in a red dress, you'll be ready for your next concert in six weeks."

"What next concert?"

25   "Well, the one I set up in April."

"April? I don't even know whether the other musicians are available in April."

---

1 **pitch a plan**: present a plan   2 **burst of sth.**: short period of an increased amount of sth.   4 **don't hold your breath** (infml): it might never happen   15 **hooligan**: noisy and violent person   **foolishness**: stupidity   18 **smart aleck** (infml): annoying person who tries to be clever

"You mean, Steven and Annette? You just missed them the other day. They visited when you left, and we picked a date for you to play again. And not to compare you to anybody, but Annette brought a lovely fruitcake. You brought me *bupkes*."

"I don't believe you, Sol!"   5

"What? It's true. When was the last time you brought me a little snack? I don't expect much, but some baked goods once in a while would be a nice gesture."

"Not about the fruitcake. I can't believe you set this up without asking me."   10

"I'm asking, I'm asking. Of course, I'm asking for maybe some cookies next time you come, too, but what are my chances?"

"You're not asking me, you're telling me. And the answer is no. I don't want to be embarrassed again."

"You know what, Mr. Sensitive? When I was coming up, if a guy   15
got shown up on the bandstand, he woodshedded. He went back home and practiced. Then he practiced. Then he practiced some more. Then he got back up onstage and – maybe, just maybe – he was ready the second time around. So what are you going to do, cry in a corner forever, or be a man and take some free guitar lessons?"   20

"I'll tell you what, Sol: I'll play the concert… ."

A smile began its slow spread across his wrinkled cheeks.

"… as long as you play it with me. So how about it, Mr. Jump Back in the Saddle? Are you with me?"

Sol thought it over through the course of a moderately gross   25
coughing fit. After he spat, drank, and took a few really slow breaths, I got my response. "I'll tell YOU what, *boychik*. I'll see you in two days. Bring a guitar, some sheet music, maybe some blank paper. And would it kill you to stop and pick up a Danish or two?"

*   *   *

---

4 **bupkes** (Yiddish): absolutely nothing   16 **show sb. up** (infml): make sb. feel bad
in public because you are more talented   **woodshed**: go home and practice your
instrument   25 **gross** (infml) [rəʊs]: unpleasant   28 **blank**: with nothing written
or printed on it (of paper)   29 **Danish**: (here) sweet cake made of light pastry

At home, I found my dad in the kitchen, wearing an apron and cooking for my mom. I asked whether he was officially moving back in, and he smiled. "I don't know, bud. You know we're trying to go slow and easy with this, but I almost think it might be time to try
5   being under one roof again. Here, try this."

"What is it?"

"Alfredo. It's a creamy cheese sauce."

"Since when do you know how to make ANYTHING, much less a so-called 'creamy cheese sauce'?"

10   "Oh, Alex. Gimme a break. People can change, right? Now, taste it already."

"I don't know, Dad. I've been burned before."

"Hmm, is that a resentful little metaphor?"

"No, it's a statement about something that sometimes happens to
15   the roof of my mouth when I consume hot foods." I took a wincing little mini-sip off of the wooden spoon my dad was holding out to me. "Hey, not bad. Maybe an old dog can learn new tricks."

"Or at least new recipes. I'll just add a little more Parmesan, turn up the heat a bit, and …"

20   Just then we heard a big clattering crash upstairs, followed by a piercing screech from my mom. I charged up the steps right behind my father, who was still holding the spoon in his right hand. He was ready for action, in a chef-style kind of way. "What is it, Janet?"

She was standing over a shattered picture frame, sucking her
25   thumb. "Oh, Simon, look at this! I was trying to hang our wedding portrait back up; I thought it was time. But I banged my finger with the hammer, and dropped everything. The frame is broken, and the picture is probably scratched up. I'm afraid to move. Can you look?"

---

1 **apron**: *Schurz*   3–4 **go slow**: (here) not be too romantic too quickly (of a relationship)   10 **gimme a break** (infml): stop annoying me!   12 **have been burned**: (here) have had bad experiences   13 **resentful**: angry about unfair things that happened to you   15 **wince**: make a facial expression showing pain   16 **sip**: small amout of liquid that you drink   17 **old dog …**: referring to "You can't teach an old dog new tricks", meaning that an old person cannot learn anything new   21 **piercing**: high and unpleasant (of sounds)   **screech**: high, unpleasant sound   23 **chef** [ʃef]: professional cook   24 **shattered**: broken

Dad handed the spoon off to me, got down on his hands and knees, and crawled through the chaos of shattered glass. The picture was flipped upside down, and was resting against my mom's bare foot. Dad gingerly lifted it off, and I saw that the actual photo looked fine – but something had cut the top of my mother's foot pretty hideously. Since Mom is a nurse, once there was a bloody wound she took control right away. "Simon, pick me up. No, under the arms. Now carry me to the bed. Alex, don't just stand there – go get the vacuum and a garbage can, and start picking up the broken glass. All right, Simon, watch out for the bedspread. We'll need – uh – two towels and some gauze."

While Dad and I scrambled around like we were on an Easter-egg hunt, Mom sat hunched over on the bed and pressed a wad of tissues to the gushing slit in her foot. "This is going to need stitches. Oh, Simon. I'm sorry. I broke our portrait and ruined your big dinner plans."

He rushed back into the room and gently – oh, so gently – wrapped her foot in gauze. "It's okay, Janet. Broken things can be fixed. And I'm glad I'm here for you."

Oh, how freaking romantic. Gory, yet freaking romantic.

Three minutes later, Apron Man and Gimp Lady were on the way to the hospital. I realized I was hungry, and walked into the kitchen. That's when I noticed the bitter smell. And when I lifted the lid of Dad's creation, I got a face full of acrid brown smoke. The sauce was now a thin wafer of charred carbon.

Here was a lesson I could tell the judge I'd learned: Some people get the romance, and some people get coal for dinner.

6 **hideously** ['hɪdiəsli]: terribly   9 **vacuum** ['vækjuəm]: (short for vacuum cleaner) device that sucks up dirt from the floor   10 **watch out for sth.**: be careful of sth. **bedspread**: large blanket you put on top of a bed to make it look nice   11 **gauze**: very light cloth used to wrap around wounds   12 **scramble around**: move quickly to get sth. difficult done   13 **wad**: lump of soft material that is pressed together 14 **gush**: flow thick and fast (of a liquid)   **slit**: long, narrow cut   **stitches**: piece of string pulled through the edges of a wound to hold it together and help it heal 20 **freaking** (infml): (here) very   21 **gimp** (AE, infml, derog.): person who cannot walk well   24 **acrid**: with a strong, unpleasant smell or taste   25 **wafer of sth.**: (here) very thin, hard piece of sth.   **carbon**: *Kohlenstoff*

THE SAINTS GO MARCHIN' IN

"No, no, Alex! Jazz has to have a swing to it. All the time, a swing."

"But this is a sad song."

"All the more reason it should swing, then. Listen: Do you know
how jazz started out? As funeral music. In New Orleans, when
5 somebody would die, they would all walk down to the cemetery
with a band playing sad songs. But on the way BACK from the
cemetery, they danced. The band played fast, they played happy.
And the people danced. Even in sorrow, jazz should sound like
there's dancing in it. Have you ever heard 'When the Saints Go
10 Marching In?'"

"Uh, I'm not sure."

Sol held out his hands for my guitar, and I handed it over. I was
ready for a break anyway. It was our first day of official practice, and
he had shown me some new scale patterns first. After I had played
15 those for maybe twenty minutes, he'd shown me some finger
exercises, some new chords, and now a brand-new song. My fingers
felt like they were going to shrivel up and die, and apparently, I
hadn't done anything right yet.

He took the guitar and played a simple little melody. First he
20 played just the melody, with no bounce to it at all, like this:

Ding-ding-ding-ding.

It was the corniest thing I had ever heard. Like, if Mister Rogers had
played guitar, this would have been his big solo feature. Then Sol
played just the melody again, with a swing:

---

saint: holy person of the Christian religion   4 **funeral**: ceremony in which the body
of a dead person is buried *(begraben)*   5 **cemetery**: place where dead people are
buried   17 **shrivel up**: become smaller and wrinkled *(verschrumpelt)*   20 **bounce**:
(here) jazzy, energetic rhythm   22 **Mister Rogers**: main character in the American
children's TV series Mr. Rogers' Neighborhood, in which there is no conflict and
everything is nice

Ding-a-ding-a-ding-ding.

This was starting to sound a little hipper. Next, he played the chords on the low strings, and the melody on the high strings, all at the same time. Suddenly, it was so bouncy I couldn't sit still. When he played it again, and added a call-and-response part, I found myself 5
tapping along on my legs and smiling:

Dinga-dinga-ding-ding. (Dinga-dinga-ding-ding.)

Finally, he played the chords, but sang the words to the tune AND answered them with the response part on the high strings:

"Oh, when the saints (dinga-dinga-ding-ding.)   10
Go marching in (dinga-dinga-ding-ding.)
Oh, when the saints go marching in, (deet-deet-deet-dooby-doo-wah)
Oh how I want to be in that number, when the saints go marchin' in."

When he stopped, he was wildly out of breath. Claudelle was standing in the doorway clapping, but he was too wrapped up in 15
catching up on oxygen to notice. She said to me, under her breath, "He sounds good. But that's goin' to get harder and harder for him now. You watch. You'd better be careful not to push him too hard, or he's goin' to *be* in that number soon enough."

On the way to my third or fourth lesson, I realized something 20
that should have probably hit me much sooner: We had one guitar, and two guitarists. How were we both going to play at this concert? I came up with a plan, and told Sol about it right away. "Hey, Sol, listen. We have a little problem, but I think I have it all figured out."

"YOU have it all figured out? THIS I've got to hear."   25

---

5 **call-and-response**: musical pattern typical of African and African-American music in which the call of a singer or player is answered by a choir, another player or a choir   15–16 **wrapped up in sth.**: focused on sth.

"Ha-ha. Look, we've got two of us, but only one guitar. I have a feeling that will add a bit too much challenge to the duet portion of the concert program."

"So I won't play. That's fine, *boychik*. I've been pretty tired lately
5 anyway." Which he had.

"No, you'll play. Here's the thing: My hundred hours of mandated public service are almost up. After that, I'll get to keep the five bucks an hour I earn for being here. I was planning to use that money to save up for a car, but we all know that, thanks to my brilliance, I
10 have a few years to do that anyway. So I have a schedule I just made, and if I can get Annette and Steven to practice here sometimes, I think I can make about three hundred bucks in the next few weeks. Then I'll buy a cheap jazz guitar used somewhere. I can play that, and you can have my Telecaster. And, um, you don't have to pay me
15 back or anything. Consider it payment for these amazing lessons. I've never improved this fast in my life."

"Wait a minute, Mr. Um. You're telling me you'd play a used, old, dusty guitar and let me use your beautiful Telecaster? Are you really sure?"

20 "Sol, I'm sure. Why?"

"Wait, wait. Are you SURE you're sure? You'll play the old thing, I'll play the Tele, and you're even willing to pay the bill?"

"YES, that's what I'm saying."

"Hmmm. Do you still have the key I gave you?"

25 "Yeah, it's on my key chain." I took it out. "See?"

"Okay, Alex, it's time for my breathing treatment. Why don't you take a walk down to the storage lockers at the end of the hall? That key fits my locker, number three-forty-four. Just like the room number. Anyway, bring me what you find."

30 "Is there only one thing in there, or will I know what I'm looking for?"

---

2 **duet**: piece of music performed by two people   7 **be up** (infml): (here) be
finished   10 **schedule** ['ʃedjuːl]: plan   27 **storage locker** [stɔːrɪdʒ]: place where
you keep things while you do not need them

As the respiratory therapy guy strapped the little mask on his head, Sol said, "You'll know, *boychik*. Believe me, you'll know."

I took my walk then. Down the hall, around the corner, chat with the nurses, buy a candy bar, hang out with Mrs. Goldfarb. Killing time, because I was kinda nervous to see what was in the locker. But when I saw the respiratory therapist leave Sol's room, I figured that was my cue. I walked down the long hall to the locker, not knowing what would be in there. A jug of water, rigged to dump on my head? A spring-loaded pie-throwing device? I definitely felt a "GOTCHA" coming on, but Sol hadn't had quite the usual gloating smirk on his face. I shoved the key in the lock, took a deep breath, and turned it. The mechanism was creaky; I could tell nobody had been in the locker for a long time. Okay, that meant the pie-thrower was probably not a realistic threat, anyway. When I opened the door, there wasn't much to see, just a few big boxes, labeled RECORD COLLECTION, FAMILY PHOTOS, MUSIC PHOTOS, and JUDY. But when I pushed the top box aside a bit, I saw a black shape sticking up from behind the pile, a shape I knew. It was a very, very dusty guitar case. Choking on the dust, I pulled it up and over the boxes, then straightened the pile back up. As I closed the locker and headed back to Sol's room, I was dying to see what was inside. I was also dying of a sudden allergy fit, so I stopped by the nurses' desk and rubbed down the outside of the case with a cleaning wipe Juanita gave me. I figured the big surprise wouldn't be quite right if Sol keeled over and died from the dust.

Sol was sitting up in bed in the usual position, but his posture was different somehow. He looked taller, straighter, more alert. And I realized that the guitar in this case was something he really wanted

---

1 **respiratory**: to do with breathing   2–3 **strap sth. on sth./sb.**: use a long, narrow piece of material to fasten sth. onto sth./sb.   4–5 **kill time**: do unimportant things while waiting   5 **kinda** (infml): kind of; quite   7 **cue**: signal   8 **jug**: container for liquid   **rig sth.**: set sth. up   **dump**: (here) turn over and empty in an untidy way 9 **spring-loaded**: fixed with a metal spring   11 **shove sth.**: push sth.   12 **creaky**: making unpleasant sounds when moved   14 **threat**: (here) possibility of danger 19 **dusty**: staubig   21 **be dying to do sth.** (infml): want to do sth. very much 25 **keel over**: fall over suddenly   27 **alert**: ready to think and notice things quickly

to see again. I set it on the bed, with the latches facing him. He spun
it around toward me. "You open it, *boychik*. I already know what's in
there."

   Click. One latch. *Click*, the second. *Click*, number three. I tried to
5 swing the lid up. Doh! This was one of the old-fashioned kind of
cases that has the extra latch by the bottom. *Click*. Deep breath for
me. Shallow breath for Sol. Slowly, I started to lift that lid again. I
sort of squinched my eyes up so I wouldn't see too much too soon,
but I knew I was looking at a special instrument. The body was a
10 gleaming blond wood, with cream-colored binding around the edges
and F-holes. The hardware was gold, with one of those fancy harp
tailpieces you see on guitars in old, old movies. The neck was,
literally, a work of art, with gorgeous slanted, parallel blocks of pearl
inlay at the first, third, fifth, and seventh frets. The headstock of the
15 guitar had the word "D'Angelico" in beautiful, flowing script, over
an elaborate art-deco design. And inlaid into the twelfth fret in
gleaming mother-of-pearl was a single word: gotcha!

   My voice was shaky. "Sol, is this what I think it is?"

   "What am I, a mind reader? If you're thinking it's a toaster, you're
20 wrong. However, if you're thinking it's a very valuable 1954 D'Angelico New Yorker archtop with a custom inlay, you're smarter than
you look."

   "And I'm supposed to PLAY this?"

---

7 **shallow**: not deep   8 **squinch your eyes up**: press your eyelids together without
fully closing them   10 **gleaming**: shining beautifully   **blond**: pale yellow color
11 **F-hole**: hole shaped like the letter 'f' that is cut into some instruments (e.g.
violins, guitars)   **hardware**: (here) metal components   **harp**: *Harfe*   12 **tailpiece**:
piece of metal which fastens the strings to the body of string instruments
13 **gorgeous**: very beautiful   **slanted**: *schräg*   14 **inlay**: decoration of a wooden
surface made by putting another material into it   **fret**: thin metal bar on the long
piece of a guitar that shows you where to put your fingers   **headstock**: piece of
metal or wood at the end of the long piece of a guitar to which the strings are
attached   15 **D'Angelico**: jazz guitar made by the famous New York guitar maker
John d'Angelico (1905–1964)   **script**: (here) style of letters   16 **art-deco**: style of
architecture, design and decoration popular in the 1920s and '30s   17 **mother-of-
pearl**: shiny, white substance on the inside of some sea shells used for decoration
21 **archtop**: jazz guitar with a hollow body whose wooden top is bent outward
custom: specially made for a specific person

"Alex, it's yours. You could strap it to your feet and use it for skiing if you want to, but I personally think that would be wasteful."

"Why me?"

"You gave me your Telecaster, and you can't go up onstage next month and play the washboard. So now you have a real jazz guitar." 5

"But I'm not a real jazz guitar player."

"So you'll grow into it. Or you'll wait until I die, sell it, and pay for two years of college. Whatever. Now, tune that thing up and let's play."

Holy cow, holy cow, holy … freaking … COW! 10

My hands were starting to tremble, but I picked up the D'Angelico, sat in the big chair, and tuned it (the guitar, not the chair). Even with decades-old strings, the thing sounded like a heavenly choir of angels. Well, all right, a heavenly choir of tone-deaf angels – at least until I finished tuning. When everything sounded good, I played a 15 few chords. Then I played a few more chords. Then a single-note run. Then some of the call-and-response chord-melody stuff Sol had been showing me. I looked up, and Sol was grinning from ear to ear, but his eyes were watery, too. He growled, "Nice-sounding hunk of wood, eh? Think you can work with it?" 20

"It'll have to do, I suppose."

"Good. Now let's see how you're doing with the chord-substitution exercises from last time. And remember to keep your right wrist loose. If you lose the swing, it doesn't matter if you're playing a solidgold guitar with diamond inlays – nobody's going to be happy. 25 All right, then. One-two-three-four!"

---

5 **washboard**: board used in the past for washing clothes, and used as a musical instrument in some types of folk music 8 **tune sth. up**: adjust the parts of a musical instrument so that it makes sounds at the correct pitch 11 **tremble**: shake 13 **decade**: period of ten years 14 **tone-deaf**: not able to hear differences in pitch 19 **growl** (AE): make a low sound like an angry dog 19–20 **hunk of sth.** (AE): large piece of sth. 22 **chord-substitution**: advanced jazz technique in which you replace one chord with another to make the piece sound more interesting 23 **wrist**: joint that connects the hand to the arm

THE WORK OF BREATHING

The next time I went to visit Sol, I was bearing gifts, but he wasn't in the room. Leonora was walking by, and came over to me. "Hello, Alex. I haven't seen you in a while, but I hear you and Mr. Lewis have been exchanging instruments. If someone had told me three
5 months ago that I'd see the day when Sol started sharing his things with others, I wouldn't have believed it. You and he have quite a special relationship, young man. My hat's off to you."

"Thank you. Uh, where is he?"

"Just at the doctor's for some tests. You know, it's becoming more
10 difficult to manage his CHF, so the medical folks here have been consulting a lot with the cardiologists over at the hospital."

"CHF?"

"Congestive heart failure. He is doing remarkably well for a man with so little remaining lung capacity, but after all, his emphysema is
15 terminal."

I had a lump in my throat all of a sudden, like someone had snuck down in there with a chicken bone, some crazy glue, and a bad grudge. "Yes, I know he's in bad shape. Will … when … when will he be coming back?"

20 "You have about an hour or so, at the least. Why don't you go on into his room and play your guitar for a while? That way, you will be ready to impress him when he arrives. Oh, he so enjoys your time together."

"Sure. Thank you, Leonora." She strode off to depress somebody
25 else, and I walked down to Sol's locker to get the guitar – I still

---

1 **bear sth.**: (here) carry sth.   7 **my hat's off to you** (informal): Well done!
10 **CHF (congestive heart failure)**: heart disease when the heart doesn't have enough strength to pump blood through the body   11 **cardiologist**: doctor specializing in heart diseases   14 **lung capacity**: ability of the lung to work properly   15 **terminal**: unable to be cured and eventually leading to death
17 **sneak** (infml, AE) (past: snuck): go somewhere secretly   **crazy glue**: (brand name) extremely strong glue

couldn't even begin to think of it as MY guitar. I reached in for the
handle of the case and missed. The boxes tipped, tumbled, and
crashed, although I made a spectacular diving save and grabbed the
guitar case before it had a chance to hit the ground. Then I spent a
few minutes panting and choking on the cloud of grimy dust I'd   5
raised. After about a thousand rapid-fire blinks, my eyes cleared to
the point where I could see again, and I found myself standing amid
a heap of jumbled photos. Well, I figured out really fast that I wasn't
going to get any guitar practice in, because getting the pictures back
into the upside-down box labeled judy was going to be a slow   10
process even if I didn't have an asthma attack from the allergen-
laden air. I sat down, creating a little secondary mushroom cloud
around myself, and started sorting through Solomon Lewis's great
disappointment.

An hour later, I was in Sol's room, randomly picking out a sad   15
little blues progression on my Tele – it would have been almost
sacrilege to play the down and dirty blues on Sol's D'Angelico, like
sketching over the Mona Lisa with watercolors – and trying to
process what I'd seen in the "Judy box." It was hard for me to even
imagine all the pain Sol had gone through in his life. And the pain   20
was going to get worse before it was through. When they wheeled
him in, Sol's skin was the shade of ashes in oatmeal, and his chest
looked all puffed up. He grinned at me, but distantly, and you could
just tell that it cost him some effort somehow.

His voice was breathy and scratchy at the same time.   25

---

3 **diving save** (n): sudden downward movement by which you catch sth. that is
falling   5 **grimy**: dirty   6 **rapid-fire**: repeated several times very quickly   **blink** :
act of closing and opening your eyes quickly   7 **amid sth.** (fml): surrounded by
sth.   11–12 **allergen-laden** ['æləd͡ʒən 'leɪdn]: containing a large amount of allergens
(substances that cause allergies)   16 **blues progression**: melody that follows the
typical chord pattern of blues music   17 **sacrilege** ['sækrəlɪd͡ʒ]: being disrespectful
towards a holy thing   **down and dirty**: (here) rude and shocking   18 **sketch**:
draw or paint quickly and without much detail   19 **process sth.**: (here) try to
understand and deal with sth.   22 **oatmeal** (AE): Haferbrei   23 **puffed up**: full of
air   25 **breathy** ['breθi]: speaking with the noticeable sound of breathing
scratchy: sounding rough and unpleasant

"So, *boychik*, what's with the blues? Is that mean old no-good Mrs. Um doin' you wrong again?"

"No, just thinking. How are you feeling? You look tired."

"Well, you know, I have my good days and my ... not-so-good
5 days. This one isn't necessarily in my top ten."

"Hey, I brought you something." I took out the two huge black-and-white bakery cookies I had stowed under my chair, but he barely even glanced at them.

"Leave them. Maybe I'll ... be ... hungry later." "No problem, Sol.
10 What do you want to work on with me today?"

He was lying all the way back in bed, and while he pondered my question I could hear the air rattling and whistling through his lungs. The guy was suffocating while his genius protégé was offering him cookies. "Like you said, I'm tired right now. Just ... play some-
15 thing nice. Okay?"

So I played and played: whole songs, half songs, chord progressions, whatever wound up under my fingers. Sol's breathing noises would get louder for maybe a minute at a time, and then so quiet that I almost wanted to stop playing and take his pulse to make sure
20 my playing hadn't carried him off to the Great Beyond. Then at some point, Claudelle came in and stood next to me. She put a hand on my shoulder, and gestured with the other to the doorway. "Come on out, baby," she whispered. "Your friend needs his rest now."

In the hallway, all I could say was, "Why is his chest so loud now?
25 And why does he look all puffed up like that?"

Claudelle sighed before she answered. "Work of breathing, Alex. The doctors call it 'the work of breathing.' You and me, our lungs do all the work the way they should, so it doesn't look hard. But a man like Sol, his lungs are all scarred up and swollen on the inside. So he
30 has to *work* for his oxygen."

---

2 **do sb. wrong** (infml): act unfairly towards sb.   7 **stow sth. somewhere** [stəʊ]: put sth. somewhere until you need it   11–12 **ponder sth.**: think deeply about sth.   13 **suffocate**: die because you can't get enough air to breathe   **protégé** [prɒtəʒeɪ] (French): younger person who is taught and helped by an older, more experienced person   17 **wind up** (past: wound up): get somewhere, usu. without planning   20 **Great Beyond** (fml): death   29 **scarred up**: with marks of former injuries or illnesses

"Always? Every breath? Why now?"

"Oh, baby. Your friend in there is a tough old fighter. But you see how hard it is. And nobody fights forever. Nobody."

I had to get out of there, and I did. I needed Laurie, so I went to her house. Her dad answered the door, and warned me: "Her High- 5
ness has retired to her royal bedchamber. She's in a serious mood, Alex. She got ultrasound pictures from her mother today, and ripped them into tiny black-and-white confetti. You can go up if you want, but I think I'm just going to stay out of Laurie's way for a while, like, until she turns thirty. I've been hearing sounds, like boards breaking." 10

"Well, I think breaking her karate boards is a healthy way to get out some aggression, Mr. Flynn."

"So do I, Alex. I just wish she *had* some karate boards at home."

"Oh. Uh, well, I guess I'll be going up the stairs now."

"All right, son. Just in case things don't go … well up there, let 15
me just take this time to tell you what a great kid I think you were
– I mean, are."

Is the guy just a total riot, or what?

I listened outside of Laurie's door for a few minutes, and couldn't hear any blatantly dangerous noises, so I knocked. She grunted 20
something, which I took as an invitation, and I entered the Chamber of Raging Sorrow. The room was definitely trashed, but I ignored the wreckage, or at least the nonhuman wreckage. Laurie was curled up on her bed with a wad of tissues in one hand and a folded paper in the other. She wasn't actively crying, but she was still in that sniffly 25
post-weep stage. I swept a damp cluster of tissues off the bed onto the floor, and sat by her knees. I gave her one of those weird little pats that old-fashioned country doctors give in the movies when

---

5–6 **Highness**: title for a king or queen   6 **be in a serious mood**: (here) be in a
seriously bad mood   7 **ultrasound**: medical procedure used to take pictures of
inside your body (e.g. a fetus)   8 **riot** (infml, old-fashioned): (here) funny person or
thing   20 **grunt**: make a low sound like an animal, because you don't want to
speak   21 **chamber** [tʃeɪmbə] (fml): room   22 **raging**: very strong and forceful
sorrow: great sadness   23 **wreckage** ['rekɪdʒ]: what is left after sth. has been
destroyed   26 **weep** (fml): cry because you are very sad   26 **cluster**: number of
things pressed together

they're delivering horrendous news, and her red-rimmed eyes focused on mine.

"She's really going to have the baby, Alex. She's really going to spawn. Look at this!" She unfolded the paper, and waved it in my
5 face. It was the ultra- sound photo her dad had mentioned.

"Hey, your father told me you ripped that up."

"He's such an exaggerator. He probably told you I was breaking things up here too, right?"

I took in the dumped drawers, the beauty supplies scattered
10 everywhere, and the massive diagonal crack in her headboard. I raised an eyebrow.

"Well, he exaggerated about the stupid paper, anyway. I only ripped up the envelope and the cute, annoying card she sent."

I grabbed the ultrasound picture, which basically looked like a
15 radar image of a space alien. The odd being had a gigantic head, a teeny body, little floppy arms and curled-up legs. And, looking more closely, I couldn't help but notice that it appeared to have a tail.

"Whoa," I exclaimed, "Monkey city!"

"Must be from the father's side of the family."
20 I twisted over Laurie and looked down at her back. "Yup, you appear to be tail-free."

"Thanks for noticing."

Suddenly I couldn't be on the bed, so I started pacing – which was tricky in a room that was maybe eight feet long and had random
25 objects covering its floor to varying depths. "So, uh, you're pretty upset, I guess. But why now? You've known this was coming."

"I know, it's just … the picture and the card make it so real. Like this new person really is going to come, and be my half sister, and my mother's whole daughter, so I'll be just her half daughter."

---

1 **deliver news**: describe what has happened (usu. sth. unpleasant)   **horrendous** [hɒˈrendəs]: very bad   **red-rimmed**: with reddened edges   4 **spawn** (derog.): have a baby   7 **exaggerator**: person who makes things seem larger, worse etc. than they really are   9 **beauty supplies**: lipsticks, eye-shadow, etc.   **scattered**: dropped in a messy way   10 **headboard**: upright board at that end of your bed where you put your head   15 **being**: (here) human   16 **teeny** (infml): very small   **floppy**: hanging loosely   25 **depth**: (here) distance from the top of a pile of things to the ground on which they lie

"Uh, Laur, remember how I beat you on the math PSAT? I think the logic section may have been your downfall."

"Uh, Alex, remember when we were eleven, and you tried to blow up that huge anthill with firecrackers, and all the ants landed on you, and they bit you everywhere, and you were in the hospital for three days? Don't talk to me about logic, buster!"

"Okay, first of all, that would have worked if the Raid can had just detonated on time. But anyway, all I'm saying is that you're still your mom's whole daughter. Look, she invited you to stay there this summer, right? Doesn't that tell you anything?"

"Yeah, it tells me she's seen *Cinderella*, and she knows cheap labor when she sees it. Maybe I just won't go at all."

"I don't know, Laur. It seems to me like she's reaching out to you. Don't you think that might just burn your bridges with her completely?"

"Maybe I *want* to burn my bridges with her. That way she can't keep jerking me around like this for years at a time!"

She kicked her headboard rather mightily to emphasize her point, and also succeeded in emphasizing the titanic crack in the wood. I strode over to her, insofar as it was possible to stride under the conditions, and put my hand on her shoulder. Her eyes had that little prism thing going, where the tears are just brimming up but not yet running over. We didn't say anything for a long time, until finally I started feeling too nervous with the silence.

"You know, I just think a child and a parent should speak with each other, that's all."

---

1 **PSAT**: 'Preliminary Scholastic Aptitude Test': test taken by high-school US students preparing for college entrance exams   6 **buster** (derog.): annoying boy or man   7 **Raid**: (brand name) chemical used to kill insects   8 **detonate** [detǝneɪt]: explode   11–12 **cheap labor**: workers who aren't paid a lot of money   13 **reach out to sb.**: make contact with sb. to show that you like them   14 **burn your bridges with sb**: break off contact with sb. permanently   17 **jerk sb. around** (AE, infml): treat sb. in a way that makes life difficult for them   22 **prism**: object through which light flows and is broken up into different colors   **brim up**: fill up to the edge

She just stared, so I filled the convo gap again. "I went to Sol's today, and he … he wasn't around, so I was in the locker. You know, where I got the guitar from? Because I was going to take it out again and play. But then I knocked everything over – well, I caught the
5 guitar, but – and a box of pictures and stuff fell out. So I was putting them back in, and they were of Judy, his daughter. And she hasn't spoken to him in forever, but he has EVERYTHING of hers in there. I mean, there was a baby tooth in there, and her second-grade report card, and even some news clippings from her grown-up life. And
10 you can just tell he loves her so much … but he can't …"

Suddenly there were four welling-up eyes in the room. Laurie asked, "How's he doing? What's wrong?" So I told her what Leonora had said, and Claudelle, and about the horrible noises in his lungs, and how he hadn't even wanted the cookies, even though he had
15 practically twisted my arm to make me bring them. And by then I was completely crying, and so was Laurie, and we were practically swimming in a sea of freshly utilized tissues. Then we were on the bed, and my arms were around her, and hers were around me, and there was a whole long interval of progressively closer eye contact.
20 So we both started leaning in for real, and I could tell this was going to be the big kiss, because I was so sad and so happy at the same time. And I closed my eyes and waited for the gentle brush of her lips on mine …

And then there was a tremendous *CRACK*, like a gunshot. I mean,
25 not like some tiny little .22 caliber jobbie either, but like a crazy huge hand cannon from an ultra-violent military-type movie. And Laurie and I tumbled into each other, and we banged teeth AGAIN.

We were on the mattress, which was on the floor, because Laurie's entire bed frame had split down the middle where she'd kicked it. I
30 suppose I recovered first. "Wow, Laurie, you sure do rock at karate!"

---

9 **news clipping**: article cut out of a newspaper   11 **well up**: fill up with tears (of eyes)   15 **twist sb.'s arm** (infml): force sb.   17 **utilize sth.** (fml) ['juːtəlaɪz]: use sth.   19 **interval**: period of time (usu. between two events)   **progressively**: increasingly, more and more   30 **recover**: get better (after an illness or injury) **rock at sth.** (infml): be very good at sth.

She grinned at me adorably through her split lip. "Wow, Alex, you sure do have slick man moves!"

I should write this stuff down some day. But honestly, who on God's green earth would believe it?

1 **split**: (here) cut   2 **slick**: skilful and elegant

PEACE IN MY TRIBE

All the way home from Laurie's house, I thought about two things: my painful, swelling upper lip and my relationship with my parents. If I could cry over Sol's estrangement from his daughter, and if I could tell Laurie to bury the hatchet with her mother, then maybe
5 there were some things I should say to my mom and dad so I didn't have to walk around knowing I was the world's largest hypocrite.

They were sitting at the table, having a late-night cup of herbal tea. It was a scene so normal that I could barely comprehend how a year and a half of insanity could have crept in since the last time I
10 had seen my parents do this. I put a hand on each parent's shoulder. "Mom, Dad, there's something I want to talk to you about."

My father looked worried, so I continued. "Relax, I didn't smash up anybody's car this time. And I'm not failing my classes, and I didn't get anybody pregnant. Or pawn my guitar for crack money.
15 Or …"

Mom was sort of laughing, but she squeezed my hand. "We get the point, Alex. So what DO you want to tell us?"

"Well, I was at Sol's tonight, and he's not doing well, and I found a box of old pictures and stuff of his daughter, the … his daughter,
20 Judy. So I was thinking about how much he's done for her, and how she doesn't appreciate it. And I know I've been – uh – not so easy with the whole divorce thing. I think you may have noticed."

---

3 **estrangement** ['streɪndʒmənt]: state of not being in contact or friendly with people who used to be close to you   4 **bury the hatchet**: stop fighting and become friends   6 **hypocrite** ['hɪpəkrɪt]: (here) person who doesn't do the things they say other people should do   7–8 **herbal tea** ['hɜːbl]: caffeine-free tea made from plants that are thought to have a healing effect   8 **barely**: hardly   **comprehend**: understand   9 **insanity**: craziness   14 **pawn sth.**: *etw. verpfänden*   **crack**: strong illegal drug similar to cocaine   16 **squeeze sth.**: press sth. with your hand
21 **appreciate sth.** [ə'priːʃieɪt]: be thankful for sth.

Mom wasn't going to let that opening pass her by. "Oh, so the whole lawn-gnome incident would have been kind of, oh, I don't know, an anger thing?"

Dad took a shot, too. "And that whole not-talking-to-my-father-for-months routine, would that have been part of a larger pattern?"   5

"Look, you are both just a raging hotbed of wit, okay? Yes, you both know how angry I was. And how weird it is for me now, to see you back together, only not ALL the way back together. Plus, even if you, like, remarry or whatever, I don't know how I'll ever really be sure it's permanent again."   10

They shared a pretty awkward little glance over that bit, but I needed to continue.

"But I know you both love me, and I love both of you. I'm sorry if I've been a problem. That's all."

"Problem?" Dad asked. "Did you notice a problem with the boy,   15
honey?"

"No, no problem," Mom replied. "I might have maybe encountered an *issue* or even a *situation*, but not a *problem*, per se."

My mom stood up and hugged me then, and my dad got his arms around both of us. It was weird, because we hadn't necessarily been   20
such a big huggy kind of family before. But it felt good, too. Then Mom broke the mood. "Okay, boys, some of us have a twelve-hour shift tomorrow. I have to get to bed."

Dad asked me if I wanted a cup of tea, and I said yes, even though I secretly think herbal tea tastes like fermented dishwater. When all   25
the shuffling around the kitchen was done, and we were sitting side by side at the table, Dad had something to get off his chest. "Alex, remember when I told you that I didn't run out on Mom, that she told me to leave?"

---

4 **take a shot**: (here) make a critical remark   9 **remarry**: marry again
10 **permanent**: continuing forever   18 **issue**: (here) small problem   **per se**: by
itself; not in connection with other things   23 **shift**: time period during which a
group of people work (e.g. at a hospital, factory, etc.)   25 **fermented**: (here)
chemically changed over a long period of time   27 **get sth. off your chest**: talk
about sth. that has been bothering you in order to make yourself feel better

I took a long sip of my tepid and yucky beverage. "Yeah?"

"I think maybe I should tell you about what happened between your mother and me last year."

I took another sip, stalling for time while I considered this. "You
5   know what, Dad? I don't really want to know. You gave me enough of an answer in December."

"Really? What did I say?"

"You told me, 'Things aren't so simple. People are complicated and contrary.' And you were right. And that's all I need to know.
10 Really."

Dad looked relieved. "Well, all right, if you're really okay with all this now."

"I am, Dad. I really am."

He started to get up from the table, and it occurred to me that I
15 did have one other question. "Wait. I do have just one more thing I'm curious about, since you asked."

"Okay, shoot."

"Uh, why did you break up with Mrs. Simonsen?" "I don't know, bud. I just couldn't see spending the rest of my life with a woman
20 who smelled like chalk." Yes, friends, that's right: Another marriage saved by chalk dust.

April 3

Dear Judge Trent,

This letter has two purposes. The first is to inform you that I feel I have
25 *nearly met the requirements of my pretrial intervention assignment. I
have now worked over a hundred hours at the Egbert P. Johnson
Memorial Home for the Aged. Additionally, and perhaps more important, I think I have learned and applied a life lesson.*

---

1 **tepid**: slightly warm in an unpleasant way   **yucky** (infml): disgusting   4 **stall for
time**: take a long time (e.g. to answer a question) in order to get more time to
think   17 **shoot** (infml): (here) Tell me!   28 **apply sth**: make use of sth.

The lesson I learned was taught to me by an old man, a vase of flowers, and a box of old mementos. Do you remember how I wrote in an earlier letter that Solomon Lewis has a daughter who doesn't speak with him? Well, he leaves her these flowers every year at Hanukkah time, even though she never comes to get them. Also, he has this storage locker at the home, and I came across a big box of photos and things, labeled "Judy." Of course, he has all of her childhood stuff, like report cards and baby teeth. But he also has a bunch of news articles and things about her adult life that he has found and saved over the many years since their estrangement began. Even with all of the difficulties he has, even though he is terminally ill, he keeps track of his child. It's like, if Sol's daughter would show up, even after all this time, he would be totally ready to pick right up with her again. So the lesson Sol has taught me is this: Most parents love their children, no matter how mad the children get, no matter what the children do or say. Most parents love their children, and everybody deserves a second chance at happiness. 5 10 15

So I told my best friend, who has a very messy relationship with her mother, to give daughterhood another try. And then I went home and put my money where my mouth is: I forgave my parents for their marital problems. Wow. I probably deserve some sort of juvenile delinquent merit badge. 20

The other purpose of this letter is to invite you to what will probably be Sol's last concert. His emphysema has taken a bad turn, but he insists on going through with one more jazz performance at the home, this Saturday at three p.m. in the home's rec room. The performance will 25

---

2 **memento**: object you keep to be reminded of a person, a place, or a time in your life   13 **pick up with sb.**: (here) continue a relationship with sb. after a period of no contact   18 **messy**: (here) unpleasant and complicated   20 **put your money where your mouth is** (infml): act in a way that supports what you say   21 **marital** ['mærɪtl]: to do with a marriage   22 **merit badge**: small piece of cloth or metal that young people are given as a reward for their achievements   24 **take a bad turn**: become worse   25 **go through with sth.**: do sth. to the end although it may be difficult or unpleasant

be really special, because first of all, Sol recently gave me a very
valuable and exquisite-sounding jazz guitar, and this will be my first
gig with the new instrument. Also, Sol has been giving me guitar
lessons for six weeks, and he is an incredible teacher. Plus, he and the
5   *other two musicians from my last concert are all brilliant players. So*
this concert should be a great event musically.

I almost didn't invite you to this event, because you didn't attend the
first one. However, as Sol has taught me, we all deserve a second
chance!

10 *I hope to see you there.*

Alex Gregory

2 **exquisite** ['ekskwɪzɪt]: very beautiful

April 6

Dear Alex,

I will attend. Sincerely,

Judge J. Trent

FINALE

Imagine this: You are a musician. Not a bad musician, but also not a supernaturally great one.

    You find yourself on a stage in front of a couple hundred people, many of whom you know personally – and one of whom could
5 theoretically send you to jail if your playing is TOO horrendous. You look around the stage and take in the view of your fellow instrumentalists: the teenage drum wizard looking calmly explosive in khakis and a white button-down shirt; the high school priestess of the piano, clad in a silky-looking dress, cracking her knuckles in a
10 way that is somehow ladylike when she does it; the elderly grand master of all things guitar, looking dapper in an ancient checkered tan blazer with lapels like highway on-ramps. And you try to forget your nervousness and the fact that you are unquestionably the smallest gun up there – that even though you have been working at
15 this harder than you've ever worked at anything, any one of these people could blow you off the stage faster than you can say, "Bebop!" Plus, there are three of them.

    You think back to a time when you didn't have to be on this stage, when the throngs weren't all massed in front of you, watching
20 your every move. A simpler time, a quieter time. A time twenty-five minutes earlier, when you were sitting around talking with your bandmates in a little back room.

---

6 **fellow** (adj): people who are doing the same thing as you   7 **wizard** (infml): (here) talented person   8 **khakis**: greenish or brownish trousers (often used for soldiers' uniforms)   9 **clad**: dressed   **knuckle**: finger joint between the finger and the rest of the hand   11 **all things guitar** (fml): all things connected with guitars   **dapper**: nicely dressed (usu. of a man)   **ancient**: very old   12 **tan**: (color) light, yellowish brown   **lapels** [lə'pels]: front part of a jacket that is folded back   **highway on-ramp**: road that leads onto a motorway   14 **smallest gun** (infml): (here) least important person   16 **Bebop** [biːbɒp]: type of jazz music from the 1940s considered the beginning of modern jazz   19 **throngs**: crowds of people   **massed**: gathered together in a large group   22 **bandmate**: person who plays in your band

"Uh, guys, I'm nervous."

"Why?" asked Annette, as she sat holding hands with Steven. "We did a concert just like this one just a couple of months ago."

"I know, but back then, I thought playing well meant just getting through the songs. This time, you guys and Sol have opened me up   5
to vast new horizons of self-criticism."

"But you've been playing great. Really. Steven was just saying last night how far you've come in this short time."

"And it's true. I was telling Annette that you're much more sensitive now. It's like you have a whole new set of ears. Even at the last   10
concert, when you and Annette were both playing accompaniment, you were banging out these huge chords on all six strings, so there wasn't much left for her to play. But two days ago at rehearsal, I noticed on 'I Got Rhythm' that you were only chording on three strings – and it sounded excellent. Plus your strum has gotten a lot   15
lighter and bouncier, too; you've been locking into my beats a lot better."

"Well, that's only because Sol has been yelling at me about that stuff. The other day we were running through the Fiddler medley, and he reached over and started banging on my head in time,   20
shouting, 'Not like that, *boychik*. You sound like a herd of elephants charging through a music store!' The only thing that saved me from permanent brain damage was that he had a big coughing fit and I moved my chair away from the bed before he could recover."

They smiled, and Annette said, "He's really changed you, you   25
know."

"What do you mean? Just because his innovative use of fear as a teaching tool has been ..."

"No, seriously. You're not just more sensitive as a musician – you're a more sensitive person. Everybody has noticed. Look how   30
you always used to make fun of me and Steven behind our backs."

---

12 **bang sth. out**: play sth. (melody, rhythm etc.) loudly and with little skill
15 **strum**: play a guitar by moving your fingers up and down over the strings
16 **lock into sth.**: (here) play in harmony with sth. (e.g. the other musicians in your band)   22 **charge** (v): run   27 **innovative**: interesting and new

"Oh, about that. Listen, I just want to …"

"See? You were almost going to apologize. A year ago, you would have denied the whole thing, then started making up jokes about us as soon as I stopped talking. Then Laurie would have told me
5 afterward how misunderstood you were, he's a nice guy if you get to know him, blah blah blah. But now you're just, I don't know, better. Nicer."

I could feel the heat of a spectacular blush suffusing my face. I WAS standing there at that very instant, trying to make up a joke or
10 two. But what came out of my mouth was no joke. "Thank you, Annette. Thank you."

Just then, Sol burst into the room in a wheelchair, which was being pushed by a laughing orderly. "Thank you for the ride, my friend. I haven't had that much fun traveling since Rose Friedman
15 took me to the backseat of her Buick in nineteen forty-seven. Hello, kids! I hope you all brought your playing fingers with you today, because this is going to be GREAT!"

He was all rigged up with dual air tanks and a full-face oxygen mask hanging down next to his cannula, which was clipped in place
20 under his nose. Nobody else would be able to play even "Mary Had a Little Lamb" with all this equipment strapped to their head, but this was Sol. Still, his color was horrible, and his voice was ragged. He looked for a moment like he was going to cough, but grabbed the air mask and sucked deeply on it instead.

25 "Uh, Sol, what's that for? Are you really okay to play?"

He pulled the mask aside a bit. "What – this little thing? I'm fine. I'm just getting ahead on my oxygen." He stopped and took two big puffs from the mask again. "I figure this way, when I stop breathing, I'll have a couple days of life saved up, just in case I'm not done yet!"

30 Steven and Annette didn't quite know how to take this, but I knew it meant Sol was going to make it through the day. He was

---

8 **spectacular**: very impressive   **suffuse sth.** [sə'fjuːz]: spread over sth.
completely   12 **burst into sth.**: enter sth. (e.g. a place) suddenly and noisily
14 **Rose Friedman**: fictional woman that Sol knew in the past   15 **Buick** [bjuˈɪk]:
American car brand   18 **dual**: with two parts   20–21 **"Mary Had a Little Lamb"**:
English nursery rhyme (*Kinderlied*)

definitely ready for business, too. "Hey, Alex. Are the guitars tuned up?"

"Yes, Sol. They're out there, and Laurie is watching the whole stage while we're back here."

"Good. If that Mrs. Goldfarb gets down here early, there's no   5
telling how much damage she could do with a stage full of instruments. And how is Mrs. Um today? I hope she's not wearing her red dress, or you might have a heart attack and fall off the stage."

"She's wearing jeans, Sol." I put my hand on his. "And you just worry about yourself, okay? I don't want any surprises out there."   10

"Worry about myself? Why? I'm fine. I've played a million gigs before this one, kid. Nothing can really surprise me onstage anymore. I'm ready for action. You just watch those old ladies checking me out up there, and try to learn a thing or two."

So there I was onstage, twenty-five minutes later, trying to learn a   15
thing or two. We'd played through four tunes, and everybody else was doing their usual top-notch job. Sol wasn't playing the fastest runs I had ever heard from him, but each note was exactly perfect – as though he were carving the melodies into clay tablets so they would last a thousand years. Steven and Annette were just ridiculous   20
– an octopus of rhythm and harmony. As for me, I was mostly just staying out of the way, although I was turning into a fairly accomplished out- of-the-way-stayer, if I do say so myself.

The fifth tune was to be the last one before intermission, and Sol called it: the Fiddler medley, which was my big duet with him. If   25
ever there had been a time for me to screw up on a grand scale, this would have been it. I looked out at the front row, and Laurie was perched on the edge of her seat, chewing her lip – she knew how big this duet was for me, since I had played her my part over and over

---

13 **check sb. out** (infml): look at sb. with interest because you find them attractive
17 **top-notch** (infml): of the highest quality   19 **carve sth. into sth.**: cut sth.
(e.g. a pattern or letters) into sth. (e.g. a surface)   **clay**: material that can be
shaped and is often used for making pots or bricks   **tablet**: flat piece of stone or
clay into which letters are cut   21 **octopus**: sea animal with eight long arms
23 **accomplished**: talented   26 **screw up** (infml): make a bad mistake   **on a
grand scale**: very much   28 **perch** (v): sit like a bird

again for weeks. She gave me a little thumbs-up signal, and I was
glad I had her as my supportive whatever-she-was thing. My parents
were next to her, happily oblivious, Mom's head on Dad's shoulder. I
was glad I had them, and that they were being supportive whatever-
5 they-were things for each other, too. On the far side of my dad was
the judge. She had made it!

Sol spoke into the microphone, which some staff member had
handed to him while I was staring into space. "Hello. This one is a
special song for me. My young protégé here, Alex, will be playing a
10 lot of the melodies. He's worked really hard on the whole thing. He's
a good kid. I'd like to dedicate the piece, for both of us, to the lovely
girls in the front row."

He counted us in, and we played. At this point, I honestly can't
remember anything about how most of the medley went. I must
15 have played it, because we got to the last part somehow. But that
part was so mind-blowing that it has wiped out everything else from
my memory.

Now, in the fifteen or so times that Sol and I had run through this
number, and in the hundreds of run- throughs I had done at home,
20 I always played just the chords for "Sunrise, Sunset" while Sol played
the melody. This time, I got through the little intro part, and when it
was time for Sol to come in, my eyes were closed in concentration.
But his guitar didn't come in. His VOICE did:

Is this the little girl I carried?
25 *Is this the little boy at play?*
I don't remember growing older,
When did they?

When did she get to be a beauty?
When did he grow to be so tall?
30 *Wasn't it yesterday when they were small?*

---

11 **dedicate sth. to sb.**: say that you are doing sth. for sb. specific (of a book, piece
of music etc.)   16 **mind-blowing**: extremely impressive

Sun-rise, sun-set, sun-rise, sun-set,
Swiftly flow the days;
Seedlings turn overnight to sun-flow'rs,
Blossoming even as we gaze.

Sun-rise, sun-set, sun-rise, sun-set,   5
Swiftly fly the years;

One season following anoth-er,
Laden with hap-pi-ness … and tears …

Claudelle was standing next to Sol, holding the microphone in front
of his mouth. I went with the flow, played my parts, and tried to be   10
as quiet and unobtrusive as possible so everyone would hear Sol's
voice, which sounded tremendously fragile. At some point, I noticed
that the microphone was actually shaking: Claudelle was crying.
Anyway, we got through the song, and when the last note faded, Sol
immediately grasped for his air mask. There was no applause at all,   15
just total awed silence.

And the judge was walking toward us, with her face behind her
hands. She was crying, too. When she was about a foot away from
Sol, she leaned over him and said one word, which got picked up
loud and clear by Claudelle's microphone: 20

"Dad."

Sol had the strangest expression behind his mask. "Judy."

---

11 **unobtrusive** [ˌʌnəbˈtruːsɪv]: remaining in the background; subtle   15 **grasp for
sth.**: reach for sth. with your hands   16 **awed**: full of respect   18 **foot**: unit for
measuring length (ca. 30 cm)

CODA

Boop. Boop. Boop.

I'm sitting next to the old man's hospital bed, watching the bright green line spike and jiggle across the screen of his heart monitor. Just a couple of days ago, those little mountains on the monitor were
5   floating from left to right in perfect order, but now they're jangling and jerking like maddened hand puppets.

I know that sometime soon, the boops will become one long beep, the mountains will crumble into a flat line, and I will be finished with my work here.

10   I will be free.

You're probably wondering what happened in the second half of the concert, whether Sol and the judge reconciled, and how we got here. But the truth is, those aren't the most important parts of the story. Of course Sol and his daughter made up, and she visited him
15   daily for two weeks straight, and they talked for hours on end, and laughed a lot, and cried a bunch, too. She also talked a lot with me, and told me how my mom had pulled a "Gotcha" on her by getting me assigned to Sol, of all people. And then one day, we were sitting in Sol's room – me, Laurie, Sol, the judge, and Mrs. Goldfarb, who
20   was stopping in regularly now that Sol was a "star." Just sitting there, just talking. Sol sneezed, then sneezed again, and coughed one short little bark. Then he looked around at all of us and said, "Pneumonia. Get the nurse."

We did, and it was. They took him over to the hospital right away,
25   but you could just tell it was already too late – that this was it, the end, circle-the-wagons time. Within a few hours, he had a high fever, his breathing sounded like he was underwater, and he couldn't really do anything but cough. They put the mask on him full-time,

---

12 **reconcile** ['rekənsaɪl]: become friends again   14 **make up**: reconcile   17 **pull a "Gotcha" on sb.**: play a trick on sb.   26 **circle-the-wagons time**: (here) time to get together with close friends and family to deal with a crisis

and gave him IV antibiotics and painkillers galore. But he was too tired, simply too tired. I remembered Claudelle saying, "Nobody fights forever. Nobody." I sat there, and tasted my tears on my tongue, and watched Sol sleep until they kicked me out for the night.   5

In the next three days, which were also the past three days, Sol only woke up twice. A doctor told me and the judge that terminal emphysema patients almost always sank into a coma at the end, that this was nature's way of making the end easy. It didn't always look easy, though. Sometimes Sol would just lie there, slumped all the   10 way down, panting. Other times he'd stop breathing for a moment, and then take a series of huge gasps. Once he quickly sat straight up, looked at the judge, and said, "Hey, Judy, you think I could get maybe a cup of coffee in this dive?" in a totally normal Sol voice. Then he slumped over again.   15

And about an hour ago, Sol turned on his side, right in the middle of a gasping fit, opened his eyes, and peered at the judge. "Be happy, Judy. I loved your mother, and we both loved you. I'm very proud of my girl." Then he locked eyes with me and Laurie. "You're good kids. Alex, *boychik*, one day you will kiss her. And she will kiss you   20 back. Am I right?" When he laid himself back again, we thought he was finished, that all we could do was sit there and cry.

But then he opened his eyes again and gave me some parting advice, his last words on this earth: "*Boychik*, when you finish playing a gig, wipe your strings down with a soft cloth. They'll last longer."   25

That was it. That was all.

And now the monitor is going nuts, and soon I'll be free. But I guess somewhere in the course of this weird year – my junior year of high school, my senior year of childhood, Sol's last lap around the sun – I figured out that we're all free, in the only way that matters   30 anyway. We're all free to choose some people to love, and then do it.

---

1 **galore**: in large amounts   14 **dive** (infml, derog.): low-quality bar or restaurant
27 **nuts** (infml): crazy   29–30 **lap around the sun**: one year

THE SAINTS GO MARCHIN' IN AGAIN

I have one last thing to do for Solomon Lewis before I can let him go. We're at his memorial service, back at the home, in our little concert hall. The judge – who now insists I call her Judy – has asked me to end the festivities with a guitar rendition of "Taps." I get there early,
5 pull the stage curtain across in front of the piano, do some other setting up, pick a seat in the front row, and wait for all the people to come in. Claudelle is there, Leonora, Juanita. Mrs. Goldfarb – teeth, wig, and all. My parents. Laurie. The judge. Steven and Annette. The oxygen guy. The clarinet player from All-City Jazz Band.
10   They all sit down, and all the talking happens. There's a podium in front of the stage curtain, and various people use it. I'm sure the speeches are very nice, very appropriate, very touching. I'm also sure that if Sol were here, he'd be saying, "What a load of *chazzerai*! Who wants to hear this stuff now that I'm DEAD? Get out of here, go eat
15 some babka or something!" Finally Laurie is squishing my hand in her deadly Ninja claw grip, and I realize they have called my name. I walk up to the single chair set up to the right of the podium, whisper to the orderly who has been waiting by the stage for this, and get comfortable with Sol's – my – D'Angelico. And then, as slowly as I
20 can, with almost no swing to it whatsoever, I play the tune:

> *Day is done, gone the sun,*
> *From the lake, from the hills, from the sky;*
> *All is well, safely rest, God is nigh.*

2 **sb.'s memorial service**: ceremony held in memory of sb. who has died
4 **festivities**: all the events of a celebration   **rendition**: performance   **Taps**:
melody played at night in military camps, and at the funeral of a military person
10 **podium**: place on a stage from which a speaker delivers a speech
12 **appropriate**: correct and suitable for a particular situation   15 **babka** (Yiddish):
sweet yeast (*Hefe*) cake filled with chocolate and cinnamon that was introduced to
the USA by Jewish immigrants from Eastern Europe   16 **claw**: sharp, long nail on
an animal's foot   23 **nigh** (old use, literary): near

I don't look up, but I can hear three sets of footsteps approaching and then passing behind me. When I get to the last note, I hold it out as long as I can with vibrato, mentally thanking Sol for teaching me the trick. And while I'm wiggling that left third finger to keep the sound alive, the orderly opens the curtains. Steven and Annette are there, with drums and piano at the ready. So is the clarinetist, and he jumps in first. I play the sad, sad chords of "Sunrise, Sunset" under his lead, and in the middle I look up. We're wiping everybody out here. The whole first three rows are crying openly; Leonora is handing a tissue to Juanita, who is leaning on Claudelle. And the judge – forget about it. Mascara stripe city. We get to the last note of THAT.

And I say, "One-two-three-four!" We burst into "When the Saints Go Marchin' In." Steven is swinging like there's no tomorrow, Annette is playing such dirty barroom piano that you almost want to blush, and I'm playing chords on three strings, just like Sol would have wanted – I can almost feel his callused palm smacking the beat out on top of my head. The clarinet guy plays through the melody once pretty straight. We go back to the top, and he plays it really funky. Back again, and this time Steven and Annette are trading four-bar phrases back and forth with each other. I look up, and see that we've got the New Orleans vibe going strong. The tears are drying, smiles are coming out, and some feet are even tapping around the room. We repeat the head of the tune once more, while Steven is in full flow, I'm throwing phrases back and forth with Annette's right hand, and the clarinet is sailing over all of us, maybe all the way to Sol's new home.

5

10

15

20

25

---

3 **vibrato** [vɪˈbrɑːtəʊ]: playing a note in a slightly shaky way to make it sound fuller (in music)   **mental**: in your mind   4 **wiggle**: move back and forth quickly
11 **mascara** [mæˈskɑːrə]: dark make-up you put on your eyelashes (*Wimpern*)
16 **callused** [ˈkæləst]: made hard and thick, usu. from working hard (of skin)
smack: hit   19–20 **trade sth.**: give sth.; swap sth.   20 **back and forth**: *hin und her*
23 **head**: (here) main theme within a piece of jazz music

Oh, when the Saints (Oh, when the Saints!)
Go marching in (Go marching in!)
Oh, when the Saints go marching in,
I'd like to be in that number,
5 *When the Saints go marching in!*

We stop. The applause is deafening. I mean, people say that all the time, but in this case, it's literally true. Laurie is out of her seat, and my parents and the judge are headed my way, too. I look up at the ceiling, picture what's beyond it, shake my fist once upward in
10 triumph, and say it under my breath: "Gotcha!"

June 27

Dear Judge, or Judy, even though that still feels weird to me, I know you took some time off from work, and I wanted you to have a letter when you came back from wherever you went. So I'll update you on
15 *some things, notably my future.*

I got my SAT scores back right after the memorial service, and did quite well on the tests. So I shouldn't have any trouble getting into a great college. I may sell your father's guitar at some point to pay for some of the education I need, or maybe – just maybe – I can keep it
20 *and gig my way through school. I have been practicing a ton, because when I play I feel like my friend Sol is there. So my chops are up, and anything is possible. Steven and Annette even keep giving me brochures for music schools!*

My parents are looking more and more like they will marry each other
25 *again, which would be great. But whatever happens, happens. Each of them has been amazingly there for me this month, and I will be there for them if and when they ever need me.*

---

6 **deafening** ['defnɪŋ]: extremely loud   9 **picture sth.**: make a picture of sth. in your mind   14 **update sb. on sth.**: give sb. the most recent information on sth. 20 **a ton** (infml): a lot   21 **my chops are up** (infml): I'm happy

Laurie's mother had her baby the last week of school, and Laurie went down to help out for a few weeks. We talk pretty much every day, and Laurie sounds like she's doing well there. She even found out her stepdad used to do karate, so she's been getting him to spar with her a little, the poor man. I miss her, but I have a feeling we will be in each 5 other's lives for a good long time.

As for my summer plans, I have decided to work full time at the Home. It's not the same without Sol there, but I've grown close to some other residents and staff, which has been very rewarding. Plus, the pay is good, so I will be able to sock money away into my "car & college 10 fund."

Besides, somebody has to make sure Mrs. Goldfarb keeps her teeth in her head.

Love,

Alex   15

4 **spar with sb.**: practice fighting with sb. without hitting seriously   9 **rewarding**: making you feel good because you are doing important and valuable things
10 **sock money away** (AE, infml): save money

ADDITIONAL TEXTS

1. DRINKING TOO MUCH, TOO YOUNG

This American article attempts to find an answer to the persistent habit of binge drinking among young people that worries the nation's lawmakers.

The stories have been shocking, abruptly reminding a nation of a problem that remains unsolved: in the last hall of 2004, six college-age students in Colorado died as a result of binge drinking.　　　　5

Although each fatality was different in its circumstance – Samantha Spady, 19, a sophomore at Colorado State University, died after drinking vanilla vodka and more than two dozen beers, while Benett Bertoli, 20, also a CSU student, was found dead on a couch at an off-campus party from a combination of alcohol, methadone and benzo-　10 diazepene – the events leading up to the deaths were maddeningly familiar.

In almost every case, the fatalities were the unexpected ending to a boisterous party almost always involving large gatherings of young people on weekend nights consuming prodigious amounts of　15 alcohol, sometimes for two days straight.

The number of Colorado deaths from binge drinking in late 2004 was exceptionally large, but the state is not alone. It killed Thomas Ryan Hauser, 23, a student at Virginia Tech in September. Blake Hammontree, 19, died at his fraternity house at the University of　20 Oklahoma, also in September. Bradley Kemp, 20, died in October at his home near the University of Arkansas, where he was a student.

---

2 **binge drinking**: drinking a lot of alcohol in a short period of time　3 **abruptly**: suddenly　6 **fatality**: death　9–10 **off-campus**: not on land belonging to the university　10–11 **methadone and benzodiazepene**: drugs　11 **maddeningly**: making you angry　14 **boisterous**: wild　15 **prodigious**: large and powerful

Steven Judd died celebrating his 21st birthday with fraternity friends at New Mexico State University in November.

Those deaths did not occur in a vacuum. According to statistics from the National Institute for Alcohol Abuse and Alcoholism, more than
5 1,400 college students die from alcohol-related deaths each year including motor vehicle crashes. Unfortunately, that number has remained constant even though both high school and college-age drinking has decreased.

"The numbers have been going in the right direction," says Peter
10 Cressy, the president of the Distilled Spirits Council of the United States. "There is today less regular use of alcohol on college campuses than there was 20 years ago. There has been a drop in the number of college students both of age and not of age who drink at all during any given month. And the data for eighth, 10th, and 12th graders
15 who consume alcohol has also shown a downward trend."

But what hasn't changed, industry, health and alcohol experts all agree, is the stubborn number of young people who continue to engage in destructive behavior.

"The issue is not the 30,000 kids on the campus of the University of
20 Colorado, of any other school, who drink legally or illegally, but somehow manage to do it without any great peril," says Ralph Blackman, the president of the Century Council, a not-for-profit organization dedicated to fighting drunk driving and underage drinking.

"The issue is binge drinking and the continuing large numbers of
25 kids who insist on over consumption to a level that has a very decided risk for a dangerous result," continues Blackman. "That is a phenomenon that very much remains with us."

---

3 **occur**: happen   10 **distilled spirit**: strong alcohol (e.g. vodka, rum, etc.)
14 **any given**: any particular   17 **stubborn**: (here) not changing   18 **destructive**:
dangerous   21 **peril**: danger   25 **insist on sth.**: (here) do sth. no matter what
others say   26 **decided**: (here) real

Trying to find a specific reason for the persistence of binge drinking among the young is a subject that both vexes and causes great debate among the nation's policymakers. Do younger people just naturally like to get drunk, or in some cases, very drunk? Is it a matter of upbringing of income? Is it a reflection of a troubled and anxious   5
society? "You could ask questions like that all day, and not really get any solid answers," says Paul Hanson, a professor emeritus of sociology at the State University of New York, Potsdam.

"The only thing you could be sure of is that no matter how many different ways we approach it with different solutions, binge drinking   10
continues among the very young, generation after generation."

But some experts believe one thing that is different with those who are a part of what demographers call the Millennials – those born in 1980 of after – and their predecessors, is that binge drinking today is out of the closet and celebrated on almost a worldwide basis due to   15
the Internet.

"There is a huge difference from when many of us went to school in the 1960s and '70s and today," says Stephen Bentley, a coordinator of substance abuse services at the Wardenberg Health Center at the University of Colorado.   20

"Back in our day we really did not want any attention of any kind, we did not want adults of the world to know that we were drinking and partying excessively," continues Bentley.

"But today young people who engage in this kind of behavior are actually very proud of what they are doing, they post their own Web   25
sites about their parties so that everyone else can see what they did."

---

2 **vex sb.**: worry sb.   3 **policymaker**: lawmaker   5 **upbringing**: how you are raised when you are a child   7 **professor emeritus**: professor that no longer works in education   14 **predecessor**: person who went before you   23 **excessively**: too much

[…]

For Julia Sherman, field director with the Center on Alcohol Marketing and Youth, binge drinking self-promotion is almost a natural outgrowth of what she says is the alcohol industry's "preoccupation
5 with the young."

"The ads that are being put out there today are not your Mom and Pop, 'Mabel, Black Label,' ads of another era, but ads that ate very much geared toward an exceedingly young demographic," she says.

"The whole ad focus of the alcohol industry has changed both in
10 tenor and in numbers," says Sherman. "Their Web site ads now feature computer games and premiums for downloading music. They run ads in what are called the 'laddie magazines,' that are edgier than anything adults are seeing in their magazines. It is all part of a non-stop, never-ending pitch for the youth market."

15 […]

In Connecticut, Senator Biagio "Billy" Ciotto, a long-time advocate of programs that educate high school students on the harmful effects of both drinking and driving and binge drinking, says he remains convinced that lawmakers should concentrate on what he calls the
20 "realistic goal of reduction" vs. the "impossible idea," of elimination.

"You are never going to get rid of this kind of drinking completely," Ciotto says. "But I have no doubt in my mind that you can reduce the abuse simply by staying with it, never giving up, always trying to let kids know, without lecturing them, about the harmful effects of
25 alcohol abuse."

---

2 **field director**: specific job title   4 **outgrowth**: (here) consequence
preoccupation: obsession   6–7 **Mom … Label'**: old fashioned   7 **ad**: advertisement   8 **exceedingly**: very   **demographic** (n): section of the population
13 **edgy**: cool and controversial   20 **reduction**: making sth. less   **elimination**: completely getting rid of sth.

Ciotto's efforts have even won the support of the Connecticut Coalition to Stop Underage Drinking, which named him "Outstanding Legislator in Reducing Underage Drinking" in 2004.

"I think they and just about everyone else recognize that we have to work on the big majority of kids who will not abuse alcohol if they know the dangers, and just figure that there is always going to be a minority that will do what they want to do no matter what, he says." 5

Arizona's Downing agrees: "It would be very foolish for any state representative or senator to feel that you can propose a bill that will somehow magically get rid of the problems of binge drinking or underage drinking." 10

"You can't," says Downing. "And we have to admit that. All you can really do is nudge things in a certain direction, which is what so many of our laws do anyway. If people are going to behave in the wrong way no matter what, there is only so much we can do. But we can help those who want to do the right thing, or don't want to break any laws just to have a little fun. That is the group we need to appeal to." 15

[…]

Traffic accidents are the leading cause of death for 15- to 20-year-olds, and alcohol is a factor in 36 percent of traffic fatalities involving drivers under age 21. In fact, young drunk drivers are twice as likely to be involved in fatal accidents as are adult drunk drivers. 20

In 2003, more than 3,600 drivers under age 21 were killed in motor vehicle crashes, and 25 percent of those young drivers had a blood alcohol content (BAC) of .08 or higher. That's considered legally drunk in every state. 25

---

3 **legislator**: lawmaker   4 **just about**: almost   13 **nudge sth.**: push sth. lightly
17–18 **appeal to sb.**: (here) make sb. understand your point of view

As young drivers get older, they are even more likely to drink and drive. Almost a third of 20-year-old drivers who were killed in crashes in 2003 were legally drunk at the time. Those are alarming figures, particularly for an age group that isn't even legally allowed to
5   drink. It also factors into a disturbing pattern: Studies have shown that the younger a person is when they start to drink, the more likely they are to drink and drive throughout their lifetime.

[…]

Zero tolerance laws have been effective. Alcohol involvement for
10   drivers aged 15 to 20 years dropped by 6 percent nationwide from 1993 to 2003. The experience of individual states has varied depending on how long their law has been in effect and on how low they set their youth BAC standard. Despite the improvement, far too many young drivers are still hitting the road after hitting the bottle.
15   Reducing their access to alcohol is critical in saving lives.

Jeanne Mejeur, NCSL & Garry Boulard
COPYRIGHT 2005 National Conference of State Legislatures

http://www.thefreelibrary.com/Drinking+too+much,+too+young%3A+trying+to+find
+an+answer+to+the...-a0131086576

2. THE FAULT IN OUR STARS: SUPPORT GROUP

John Green's novel The Fault in our Stars tells the story of Hazel, a seventeen-year old cancer patient. In this excerpt she describes the support group she visits to spend time with other teenagers with cancer.

Late in the winter of my seventeenth year, my mother decided I was depressed, presumably because I rarely left the house, spent quite a 5
lot of time in bed, read the same book over and over, ate infrequently, and devoted quite a bit of my abundant free time to thinking about death.

Whenever you read a cancer booklet or website or whatever, they always list depression among the side effects of cancer. But, in fact, 10
depression is not a side effect of cancer. Depression is a side effect of dying. (Cancer is also a side effect of dying. Almost everything is, really.) But my mom believed I required treatment, so she took me to see my Regular Doctor Jim, who agreed that I was veritably swimming in a paralyzing and totally clinical depression, and that 15
therefore my meds should be adjusted and also I should attend a weekly Support Group.

This Support Group featured a rotating cast of characters in various states of tumor-driven unwellness. Why did the cast rotate? A side effect of dying. 20

The Support Group, of course, was depressing as hell. It met every Wednesday in the basement of a stone-walled Episcopal church

5 **presumably**: probably   6 **infrequently**: not regularly   7 **devote time to sth.**: spend time on sth.   **abundant**: much; many   13 **require sth.**: need sth.
14 **veritably**: absolutely; indeed   15 **paralyzing**: making you unable to move
clinical depression: depression as an illness that can be diagnosed by a doctor
16 **meds**: medication   18 **rotating**: (here) changing   **cast**: group

shaped like a cross. We all sat in a circle right in the middle of the cross, where the two boards would have met, where the heart of Jesus would have been.

I noticed this because Patrick, the Support Group Leader and only
5 person over eighteen in the room, talked about the heart of Jesus every freaking meeting, all about how we, as young cancer survivors, were sitting right in Christ's very sacred heart and whatever.

So here's how it went in God's heart: The six or seven or ten of us walked/wheeled in, grazed at a decrepit selection of cookies and
10 lemonade, sat down in the Circle of Trust, and listened to Patrick recount for the thousandth time his depressingly miserable life story – how he had cancer in his balls and they thought he was going to die but he didn't die and now here he is, a full-grown adult in a church basement in the 137th nicest city in America, divorced,
15 addicted to video games, mostly friendless, eking out a meager living by exploiting his cancertastic past, slowly working his way toward a master's degree that will not improve his career prospects, waiting, as we all do, for the sword of Damocles to give him the relief that he escaped lo those many years ago when cancer took both of his nuts
20 but spared what only the most generous soul would call his life.

AND YOU TOO MIGHT BE SO LUCKY!

Then we introduced ourselves: Name. Age. Diagnosis. And how we're doing today. I'm Hazel, I'd say when they'd get to me. Sixteen. Thyroid originally but with an impressive and long-settled satellite
25 colony in my lungs. And I'm doing okay.

---

2 **board**: piece of wood   9 **graze**: eat   **decrepit**: pathetic   **abundant**: much; many
12 **ball**: (here) *Testikel*   15 **eek out a living**: not earn much money   **meager**:
(here) depressing   **sword of Damocles**: (here) death   19 **lo** (fml): (here) all
20 **nut** (sl): (here) *Testikel*   24 **thyroid**: organ in the neck   25 **lung**: *Lunge*

Once we got around the circle, Patrick always asked if anyone wanted to share. And then began the circle jerk of support: everyone talking about fighting and battling and winning and shrinking and scanning. To be fair to Patrick, he let us talk about dying, too. But most of them weren't dying. Most would live into adulthood, as   5
Patrick had.

(Which meant there was quite a lot of competitiveness about it, with everybody wanting to beat not only cancer itself, but also the other people in the room. Like, I realize that this is irrational, but when they tell you that you have, say, a 20 percent chance of living five   10
years, the math kicks in and you figure that's one in five ... so you look around and think, as any healthy person would: I gotta outlast four of these bastards.)

The only redeeming facet of Support Group was this kid named Isaac, a long-faced, skinny guy with straight blond hair swept over   15
one eye.

And his eyes were the problem. He had some fantastically improbable eye cancer. One eye had been cut out when he was a kid, and now he wore the kind of thick glasses that made his eyes (both the real one and the glass one) preternaturally huge, like his whole head was   20
basically just this fake eye and this real eye staring at you. From what I could gather on the rare occasions when Isaac shared with the group, a recurrence had placed his remaining eye in mortal peril.

Isaac and I communicated almost exclusively through sighs. Each time someone discussed anticancer diets or snorting ground-up   25

---

2 **circle jerk of sth.** (sl, derog.): situation where everyone talks about sth. in a group
to make themselves feel better   3 **shrink**: become smaller   7 **competitiveness.**:
feeling that you want to be better than other people   9 **irrational**: not making sense
11 **kick in**: start working   12 **outlast sb.**: live longer than sb.   14 **redeeming
facet of sth.**: aspect of sth. that makes it better   17 **improbable**: (here) rare
20 **preternaturally**: not seeming natural   23 **mortal**: (here) extreme
24 **exclusively**: only; just   25 **snort sth.**: suck sth. into your nose

shark fin or whatever, he'd glance over at me and sigh ever so slightly. I'd shake my head microscopically and exhale in response.

So Support Group blew, and after a few weeks, I grew to be rather kicking-and-screaming about the whole affair. In fact, on the Wednesday I made the acquaintance of Augustus Waters, I tried my level best to get out of Support Group while sitting on the couch with my mom in the third leg of a twelve-hour marathon of the previous season's *America's Next Top Model,* which admittedly I had already seen, but still.

---

1 **shark fin**: *Haifischflosse*   2 **microscopically**: in a subtle way   **exhale**: breathe out   3 **blow** (sl): (here) be boring   5 **make the acquaintance of sb.** (fml): meet sb. for the first time

3. THE FAULT IN OUR STARS: THE ICU

In this excerpt, Hazel wakes up in hospital in the ICU (intensive care unit). Her lungs filled with fluid and she collapsed. She has been sleeping for the past two days.

I woke up in the ICU. I could tell I was in the ICU because I didn't have my own room, and because there was so much beeping, and   5
because I was alone: They don't let your family stay with you 24/7 in the ICU at Children's because it's an infection risk. There was wailing down the hall. Somebody's kid had died. I was alone. I hit the red call button.

A nurse came in seconds later. "Hi," I said.   10

"Hello, Hazel. I'm Alison, your nurse," she said.

"Hi, Alison My Nurse," I said.

Whereupon I started to feel pretty tired again. But I woke up a bit when my parents came in, crying and kissing my face repeatedly, and I reached up for them and tried to squeeze, but my everything   15
hurt when I squeezed, and Mom and Dad told me that I did not have a brain tumor, but that my headache was caused by poor oxygenation, which was caused by my lungs swimming in fluid, a liter and a half (!!!!) of which had been successfully drained from my chest, which was why I might feel a slight discomfort in my side, where there was,   20
hey look at that, a tube that went from my chest into a plastic bladder

2 **fluid**: liquid   5 **beeping**: *Piepsen*   7 **Children's**: (here) children's hospital
wail: shout and cry loudly   15 **my everything** (infml): my whole body
17 **oxygenation**: process of getting oxygen to your organs via your lungs
19 **drain sth.**: make sth. (usu. liquid) flow away   21 **bladder**: (here) bag

half full of liquid that for all the world resembled my dad's favorite amber ale. Mom told me I was going to go home, that I really was, that I would just have to get this drained every now and again and get back on the BiPAP, this nighttime machine that forces air in and
5 out of my crap lungs. But I'd had a total body PET scan on the first night in the hospital, they told me, and the news was good: no tumor growth. No new tumors. My shoulder pain had been lack-of-oxygen pain. Heart-working-too-hard pain.

"Dr. Maria said this morning that she remains optimistic," Dad said.
10 I liked Dr. Maria, and she didn't bullshit you, so that felt good to hear.

"This is just a thing, Hazel," my mom said. "It's a thing we can live with."

I nodded, and then Alison My Nurse kind of politely made them
15 leave. She asked me if I wanted some ice chips, and I nodded, and then she sat at the bed with me and spooned them into my mouth.

"So you've been gone a couple days," Alison said. "Hmm, what'd you miss… A celebrity did drugs. Politicians disagreed. A different celebrity wore a bikini that revealed a bodily imperfection. A team
20 won a sporting event, but another team lost." I smiled. "You can't go disappearing on everybody like this, Hazel. You miss too much."

"More?" I asked, nodding toward the white Styrofoam cup in her hand.

"I shouldn't," she said, "but I'm a rebel." She gave me another plastic
25 spoonful of crushed ice. I mumbled a thank-you. Praise God for good nurses. "Getting tired?" she asked. I nodded. "Sleep for a

---

1 **resemble sth.**: look like sth.   2 **amber ale**: yellow alcohol drink   5 **crap** (sl):
(here) bad   **PET scan**: scan that makes a 3D image of the inside of the body
10 **bullshit sb.** (sl): tell sb. lies   15 **ice chips**: small pieces of ice
19 **imperfection**: fault or weakness   22 **Styrofoam**: polystyrene

while," she said. "I'll try to run interference and give you a couple hours before somebody comes in to check vitals and the like." I said Thanks again. You say thanks a lot in a hospital. I tried to settle into the bed. "You're not gonna ask about your boyfriend?" she asked.

"Don't have one," I told her.   5

"Well, there's a kid who has hardly left the waiting room since you got here," she said.

"He hasn't seen me like this, has he?"

"No. Family only."

I nodded and sank into an aqueous sleep.   10

It would take me six days to get home, six undays of staring at acoustic ceiling tile and watching television and sleeping and pain and wishing for time to pass. I did not see Augustus or anyone other than my parents. My hair looked like a bird's nest; my shuffling gait like a dementia patient's. I felt a little better each day, though: Each   15
sleep ended to reveal a person who seemed a bit more like me. Sleep fights cancer. Regular Dr. Jim said for the thousandth time as he hovered over me one morning surrounded by a coterie of medical students.

"Then I am a cancer-fighting machine," I told him.   20

"That you are. Hazel. Keep resting, and hopefully we'll get you home soon."

---

1 **run interference for sb.**: help sb. by taking care of their problems   2 **check vitals**: check up on a patient with a serious illness/injury   10 **aqueous**: watery
11 **unday** (infml): day that doesn't feel real because you do nothing   14 **gait**: walk
18 **hover over sb.**: (here) stand over sb. who is lying down   **coterie**: small group

On Tuesday, they told me I'd go home on Wednesday. On Wednesday, two minimally supervised medical students removed my chest tube, which felt like getting stabbed in reverse and generally didn't go very well, so they decided I'd have to stay until Thursday. I was beginning
5 to think that I was the subject of some existentialist experiment in permanently delayed gratification when Dr. Maria showed up on Friday morning, sniffed around me for a minute, and told me I was good to go.

So Mom opened her oversize purse to reveal that she'd had my Go
10 Home Clothes with her all along. A nurse came in and took out my IV. I felt untethered even though I still had the oxygen tank to carry around with me. I went into the bathroom, took my first shower in a week, got dressed, and when I got out, I was so tired I had to lie down and get my breath. Mom asked, "Do you want to see
15 Augustus?"

"I guess," I said after a minute. I stood up and shuffled over to one of the molded plastic chairs against the wall, tucking my tank beneath the chair. It wore me out.

Dad came back with Augustus a few minutes later. His hair was
20 messy, sweeping down over his forehead. He lit up …

---

2 **minmally supervised**: with nobody watching you   5 **existentialist**: related to theory of human behaviour and psychology   6 **gratification**: getting what you want
8 **good to go**: able to leave   11 **untethered**: free   18 **wear sb. out**: take sb.'s energy away

4. THE FAULT IN OUR STARS: GUS

In this excerpt, Hazel visits her boyfriend Gus, who also has cancer and has become very sick and weak.

He came home from the hospital a few days later, finally and irrevocably robbed of his ambitions. It took more medication to remove him from the pain. He moved upstairs permanently, into a 5 hospital bed near the living room window.

These were days of pajamas and beard scruff, of mumblings and requests and him endlessly thanking everyone for all they were doing on his behalf. One afternoon, he pointed vaguely toward a laundry basket in a corner of the room and asked me, "What's that?" 10

"That laundry basket?"

"No, next to it."

"I don't see anything next to it."

"It's my last shred of dignity. It's very small."

The next day, I let myself in. They didn't like me to ring the doorbell 15 anymore because it might wake him up. His sisters were there with their banker husbands and three kids, all boys, who ran up to me and chanted who are you who are you who are you, running circles around the entryway like lung capacity was a renewable resource. I'd

---

4 **irrevocably robbed of sth.**: sth. has been taken from you and you will never get it back   7 **beard scruff**: short hair on your face from a period when you don't shave   9 **on your behalf**: for you   14 **shred** (n): small piece   18 **chant sth.**: say sth. again and again   19 **renewable**: *erneubar*

met the sisters before, but never the kids or their dads. "I'm Hazel," I said.

"Gus has *girlfriend*," one of the kids said.

"I am aware that Gus has a girlfriend," I said.

5   "She's got boobies," another said.

"Is that so?"

"Why do you have that?" the first one asked, pointing at my oxygen cart.

"It helps me breathe," I said.

10   "Is Gus awake?"

"No, he's sleeping."

"He's dying," said another.

"He's dying," the third one confirmed, suddenly serious. It was quiet for a moment, and I wondered what I was supposed to say, but then
15   one of them kicked another and they were off to the races again, falling all over each other in a scrum that migrated toward the kitchen.

I made my way to Gus's parents in the living room and met his brothers-in-law, Chris and Dave.

---

5 **boobies** (sl): breasts   16 **scrum**: pile of people   **migrate**: (here) move

I hadn't gotten to know his half-sisters, really, but they both hugged me anyway. Julie was sitting on the edge of the bed, talking to a sleeping Gus in precisely the same voice that one would use to tell an infant he was adorable, saying, "Oh, Gussy Gussy, our little Gussy Gussy." Our Gussy? Had they acquired him?   5

"What's up, Augustus?" I said, trying to model appropriate behavior.

"Our beautiful Gussy," Martha said, leaning in toward him. I began to wonder if he was actually asleep or if he'd just laid a heavy finger on the pain pump to avoid the Attack of the Well-Meaning Sisters.

He woke up after a while and the first thing he said was, "Hazel,"   10
which I have to admit made me kind of happy, like maybe I was part of his family, too. "Outside," he said quietly. "Can we go?"

We went, his mom pushing the wheelchair, sisters and brothers-in-law and dad and nephews and me trailing. It was a cloudy day, still and hot as summer settled in. He wore a long-sleeve navy T-shirt and   15
fleece sweatpants. He was cold all the time for some reason. He wanted some water, so his dad went and got some for him.

Martha tried to engage Gus in conversation, kneeling down next to him and saying, "You've always had such beautiful eyes." He nodded a little.   20

One of the husbands put an arm on Gus's shoulder and said, "How's that fresh air feel?" Gus shrugged.

"Do you want meds?" his mom asked, joining the circle kneeling around him. I took a step back, watching as the nephews tore through a flower bed on their way to the little patch of grass in Gus's   25

3 **precisely**: exactly   5 **acquire sth.**: get sth. for you to keep   6 **model sth.**: do sth. very well in order to show other people how to do it   14 **trail**: walk behind
15 **navy**: dark blue   18 **kneel**: go down on your knees   24 **tear**: (here) run

backyard. They immediately commenced to play a game that involved throwing one another to the ground.

"Kids!" Julie shouted vaguely.

"I can only hope," Julie said, turning back to Gus, "they grow into
5 the kind of thoughtful, intelligent young men you've become."

I resisted the urge to audibly gag. "He's not that smart," I said to Julie.

"She's right. It's just that most really good-looking people are stupid, so I exceed expectations."

10 "Right, it's primarily his hotness," I said.

"It can be sort of blinding," he said.

"It actually did blind our friend Isaac," I said.

"Terrible tragedy, that. But can I help my own deadly beauty?"

"You cannot."

15 "It is my burden, this beautiful face."

"Not to mention your body."

"Seriously, don't even get me started on my hot bod. You don't want to see me naked, Dave. Seeing me naked actually took Hazel Grace's breath away," he said, nodding toward the oxygen tank.

---

1 **commence**: start   3 **vaguely**: without concentrating   6 **audibly**: able to be heard
gag: make a noise as if you are being sick   9 **exceed expectations**: be better than
people expect   10 **primarily**: mostly   **hotness** (infml): (here) good looks
15 **burden**: *Belastung*   17 **bod** (sl): body

"Okay, enough," Gus's dad said, and then out of nowhere, his dad put an arm around me and kissed the side of my head and whispered, "I thank God for you every day, kid."

Anyway, that was the last good day I had with Gus until the Last Good Day.   5

THE AUTHOR

© Jordan Sonnenblick

Jordan Sonnenblick attended amazing schools in New York City. Then he went to an incredible Ivy League university and studied very, very hard. However, due to his careful and well-planned course selection strategies, he emerged in 1991 with a fancy-looking diploma and a breathtaking lack of real-world skills or employability.

Thank goodness for Teach for America, a program that takes new college graduates, puts them through "teacher boot camp," and places them at schools with teacher shortages around the country. Through TFA, Mr. Sonnenblick found his place in the grown-up world, teaching adolescents about the wonders and joys – the truth and beauty – of literature.

Mr. Sonnenblick's first novel, *Drums, Girls & Dangerous Pie*, was published by Scholastic Press in 2005 to great acclaim and was named to several Best of 2005 lists, including the American Library Association's Teens' Top Ten.

In October 2006, Scholastic released Mr. Sonnenblick's second young adult novel, *Notes from the Midnight Driver*. It has received starred reviews from *Publishers Weekly*, *Booklist*, *KLIATT*, and *The Horn Book*.

Mr. Sonnenblick lives in Bethlehem, Pennsylvania, with the most supportive wife and lovable children he could ever imagine. Plus a lot of drums and guitars in the basement.

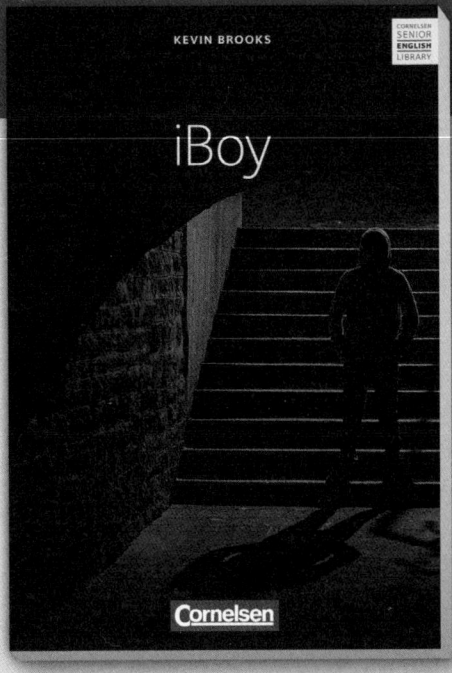